William Holden Hutton

Sir Thomas More

William Holden Hutton

Sir Thomas More

ISBN/EAN: 9783337395865

Printed in Europe, USA, Canada, Australia, Japan

Cover: Foto ©Raphael Reischuk / pixelio.de

More available books at **www.hansebooks.com**

SIR THOMAS MORE

Sir Thomas More.

From the drawing **by Holbein.**

FRONTISPIECE.

SIR THOMAS MORE

BY

WILLIAM HOLDEN HUTTON, B.D.

FELLOW, TUTOR, PRECENTOR, AND LIBRARIAN OF S. JOHN BAPTIST COLLEGE,
OXFORD, AND EXAMINER IN THE HONOUR SCHOOL OF MODERN
HISTORY: BIRKBECK LECTURER IN ECCLESIASTICAL
HISTORY AT TRINITY COLLEGE, CAMBRIDGE

Ars utinam mores animumque effingere possit :
Pulchrior in terris nulla tabella foret.—MARTIAL.

METHUEN & CO.
36 ESSEX STREET, W.C.
LONDON
1895

RICHARD CLAY & SONS, LIMITED,
LONDON & BUNGAY.

PREFACE

Iᴛ is now twelve years since I began to study the life and writings of the great hero of conscience whom this book commemorates. The work has been often laid aside, but never wholly abandoned, and in spite of the demands of a laborious profession I have been able, I think, to become acquainted with most of the literature which describes and illustrates More's beautiful life.

With the exception of Mr. S. L. Lee's admirable, and, for its length, exhaustive, contribution to the *Dictionary of National Biography*, which cannot be obtained in a separate form, and Father Bridgett's valuable biography, which is concerned primarily with the life of More as a defender of the Papal Supremacy, there are no modern works which have made use of all the material that is at the disposal of students of this period.

Much interest attaches to the earlier biographies from the circumstances connected with their composition and publication.

When England, under Mary, had returned to the Roman obedience, William Roper wrote the life of his father-in-law ; Rastell, his nephew, published the great folio of his English Works; his friend, Ellis Heywood, composed his Italian memorial *Il Moro*, and Nicholas Harpsfield the biography, which is still in manuscript in the Library of the Archbishop of Canterbury at Lambeth. In 1555 and 1556 the Latin works were published at Louvain with introductory verses and eulogies.

When Roman projects were most rife under Elizabeth additions were made to the literature of the subject. Stapleton published his *Tres Thomae* when the Armada was about to sail ; and an anonymous life, also in the Lambeth Library, was written in 1599.

After the marriage of Charles I., Roper's biography was published abroad, and Cresacre More's in England. Hoddesdon's compilation appeared in 1662, when secret negotiations were being carried on between the Papacy and the Monarchy of the Restoration ; and Stapleton's life was reprinted under James II.

Roper wrote almost entirely from personal knowledge and from memory. Thus, his work, in spite of its deep interest, is occasionally inaccurate. Stapleton added to the statements of Roper much that he had himself heard from members of More's household, and also collated many of his letters. The anonymous life published by Dr. Wordsworth[1] is apparently based on those of Roper and Harpsfield. It has been attributed to More's nephew, Rastell ; and a chance reference in Lord Herbert of Cherbury's

---

[1] *Ecclesiastical Biography*, vol. ii.

History of Henry VIII.[1] may afford a slight confirmation of the supposition. Cresacre More, the great-grandson of Sir Thomas, had undoubtedly some original information, but his work is mainly founded on those of Roper and Stapleton, and its chief interest lies in the spirit in which it is written. Its authorship was for a long time attributed to his brother Thomas More, a Jesuit; but the mistake was corrected by Mr. Hunter in the edition of 1828.

Among later English biographies the most notable are those by Arthur Cayley (London, 1808), Sir James Mackintosh (1807, republished 1844), and Mr. Walter, a Roman Catholic writer (London, 1839), with Mr. Seebohm's interesting study, *The Oxford Reformers*. Among German lives may be mentioned those of Rudhart (1829) and Baumstark (1879), works of very different character and value.

Some years ago Mr. Cotter Morison undertook to write a life for the series called *English Worthies*, but Mr. Andrew Lang has been kind enough to inform me that he made no progress in the work.

In 1891, following on the Beatification of Sir Thomas More by Leo XIII. in 1886, Father Bridgett published his interesting book.

Those who know the literature of the subject will admit, I think, that there is still room for another biography.

My aim has been to lay most stress on the personal interest of the subject. To this object the introduction of the history of the times, and the

---

[1] Edit. 1682, p. 286.

discussion of critical questions of theology and history, have been subordinated. I have endeavoured not to write as the partisan of any school or opinion, but as a student of the past. I certainly do not claim to be unbiassed; and I must admit that towards such a character as More's I find it very difficult even to fancy myself critical. But I have tried to tell my story simply, briefly, and truthfully, with no extenuation or apology.

That it is impossible to speak rightly of a past age without allowing it to speak for itself is often more true in biography than in history. No apology is therefore needed for the frequent use of the actual words of the early biographers of More, especially of his son and his great-grandson, in whose very language there seems to linger a spirit which modern English could with difficulty preserve. I cannot forbear to add that I have used the copy of More's *English Works* which belonged to William Roper himself, and which by the bequest of Nathaniel Crynes in 1745 came into the possession of the College of which I have the honour to be Librarian.

My references in the early lives are almost invariably to the original authority for the particular statement. Thus, for instance, Cresacre More is not mentioned in the notes when he merely repeats Roper or Stapleton.

Of the mass of English and foreign contemporary books and documents illustrating the life of More it is unnecessary to speak. The references I have given in the notes do not claim to be exhaustive. Erasmus is the most delightful of guides; but the

late Mr. Froude's "abbreviated substitute" for his
writings, charming though it is, is far too untrust-
worthy to be regarded as a serious authority by
any one who has studied the letters and treatises for
himself.

Every student of English History is under almost
immeasurable obligation to the labours of the late
Mr. Brewer, of Mr. James Gairdner, whose authority
on the period is beyond appeal, and of D. Pascual de
Gayangos, through whom the Domestic and Spanish
Papers of the reign of Henry VIII. have been
rendered accessible to the public.

Lastly, I have to thank the Editor and Publishers
of the *English Historical Review* and the *Guardian*
for permission to reprint matter which I have
contributed to their columns.

W. H. HUTTON.

The Great House, Burford.
S. Alphege, 1895.

CONTENTS

SIR THOMAS MORE

CHAPTER I.

EARLY LIFE: INFLUENCES OF RELIGION AND THE RENAISSANCE.

ENGLAND at the end of the fifteenth century was beginning to pass out from the medieval world towards that expanded horizon which stretched ever further as she advanced. The world it seemed was being recreated as the years drew on. The age of English discovery had begun. Piloted by Italians and with as yet no certain knowledge of how widely they were extending the boundaries of European enterprise, and still outstripped by the great feats of the Portuguese and of Columbus, Englishmen had heard of the new world in the Northern Ocean with its riches and its strange peoples. But as yet they looked within rather than without. An Englishman who had been to Italy was more thought of than one who had seen the New found land. Poliziano and

B

Pico della Mirandola were, for years to come, more famous names than Cabot and Vespuce. England's keenest interest lay in learning, in literature, and in art. Foreign painters were finding in England welcome and reward. Foreign scholars were received with enthusiasm which almost reached adoration. And in England every production of the continental Press, Italian, German, French, was awaited with eagerness, and read with avidity. Small though the literary public may have been, it was extremely important. England entered into the literary comity of nations; and her students wherever they wandered in their scholar-pilgrimage still found themselves at home. Whatever were the dark stains on the picture, Europe still stood outwardly undivided. Churchmen were not all ignorant, nor Popes luxurious and worldly. Satire might fix its sharpest darts in the hearts of Monasticism, and indignant reformers might repeat the strange stories that men told of Papal avarice and lust. But society was not yet separated into bitterly hostile sections, Art was not yet corrupt, and the gorgeous pride with which Religion was surrounded still left it power to inform the mind and purify the heart.

In a country of great churches, of rich merchandise and pomp, great ideas were in the air. The men who read and pondered were coming out into the world, and the world was ready to listen to them. And great ideas were represented in great men. Between 1485 and 1535 England had two great cardinals and two greater kings. Fascinating personalities too gave expression to the marvellous richness of the national life. Pico was striving to reconcile the purity of the Christian belief with the beautiful paganism of Greece; Amerigo Vespucci was sailing " to see and know the far countries of the world "; Wolsey was giving England a firm administration and a skilful diplomacy; Erasmus was pleading as a scholar for the liberty of reason while he clung to the faith of the Catholic Church. Of all these and their work More knew well, and with all he sympathized; and so it came about that no one represents more highly or more nobly the greatness and the attraction of the age in which he lived.

The life of More falls within the years in which Europe was passing through a great transition, and England through a great awakening. In his days, as in his person, the Renaissance and the Reformation seemed to meet on British soil. No Englishman was ever more profoundly influenced by the feeling of his age. The delight with which Italian scholars had pored over the precious manuscripts of the classics, and found in them a new completeness in Humanity and a new excellence in Art—the zeal with which German printers had multiplied the opportunities of knowledge and enriched them with every device which labour and ingenuity could suggest—the enthusiasm with which eager priests of every nationality had welcomed the new light that was beginning to shine upon the sacred heritage of the Christian world— appealed to him with an invitation to which he eagerly responded. Not less was he touched by the claims of music, of painting, of the instinct for discovery and distant quest which was coming to be

as the breath of life to the Englishman of the next
age. And with all this his life was passed in the
period of the profoundest religious, political, and social
change that our nation has witnessed. He first saw the
light in an age of civil conflict : he died when religious
strife was at its fiercest. The year of his birth saw
the murder of Clarence; the year of his death found
the English King deposed and excommunicated by
the Pope. As a boy he heard tell of the last
intrigues and the last battles of the War of the Roses
—as a man he took part in the measures by which
England under Wolsey and Henry VIII. was assuming
a position in Europe which the proudest of her
ancient kings might have envied. It was a period
of profound disturbance. Without were fightings,
within were fears. But it was above all a time of
vigorous and exultant vitality. And in all the varied
manifestations of national life, the literary and artistic
interests, and the political and religious struggles, no
man played a more prominent part than the man who
among all changes kept untarnished honour till the
end.

Thomas More was born in Milk Street, Cheapside, in the ward of Cripplegate Within, on February
7, 1478.[1] His father was John More, afterwards to
become Knight and a Justice of the King's Bench.
His mother's name is less easily ascertained. " Matris
nomen nescitur, quippe quae adhuc infante Thoma
Moro mortua est," says one of his earliest bio-

---

[1] See on this point, the appendix to Mr. Seebohm's
Oxford Reformers (2nd edition), where the question is finally
settled ; and *Notes and Queries*, 4th Series, ii. 365.

graphers. His great-grandson, Cresacre More, states that her name was "Handcombe, of Holiewell in the countie of Bedford," but the discovery of Mr. Aldis Wright—a contemporary family register—has generally been accepted as proof that she was really Agnes, daughter of Thomas Granger.[1]

He was of gentle, not noble, blood: "familiâ non celebri sed honestâ natus," says the epitaph he wrote for himself. Little else is known, for the family papers were seized by Henry VIII. and have not been discovered. Cresacre More is anxious to show that "Judge More bare arms from his birth, having his coat quartered, which doth argue that he came to his inheritance by descent"; yet he can say no more of his family than, "as I heard, they either came out of the Mores of Ireland, or they of Ireland came out of us." Mr. Foss, however, has entered into a lengthy examination, the result of which has satisfied him that Sir Thomas More's grandfather was a certain John More, first butler, afterwards steward, and finally reader, of Lincoln's Inn.[2] It seems clear too that the Mores held property in Hertfordshire for several generations. Thomas More had one brother, John, who was his clerk in later days. Of his two sisters, Joan married a certain Richard Stafferton, and Elizabeth became the wife of John Rastell, the poet, and second printer of note in England.

The vision of his mother on her wedding night, recorded by the biographer, differs little from those

---

[1] See note, p. 4.
[2] *Judges of England*, vol. v. pp. 190—203.

told of many mothers of famous men in early times. While he was still an infant he had a narrow escape of being drowned, which is noted with much earnestness by Dr. Stapleton, whose *Tres Thomae* was the earliest printed life, and who delighted to find resemblances in the minutest details between More and S. Thomas of Canterbury. "This escape," says his grandson, "was no doubt a happy presage of his future holiness, and put his parents in mind that he was that shining child, of whom his mother had that former vision; wherefore his father had the greater care to bring him up in learning." He himself tells an anecdote of his childhood which may serve to remind us of the exciting events among which it was passed. When all London was talking of King Edward's death, he heard his father told how, on the very night of the decease, a neighbour had said, "By my troth, man, then will my master, the Duke of Gloucester, be king." Thomas More was then little over five years old;[1] but he never forgot the terror that that grim name evoked.

Before long he was placed under a school-master of fame, one Nicholas Holt, at S. Anthony's in Threadneedle Street. This school, one of the grammar schools founded by Henry VI., had at the time a great reputation, and its master had already taught William Latimer and John Colet, the future Dean.

---

[1] *Latin Works*, p. 46. That he heard the story told to his father is in the Latin, but not in the English version of the *History of Richard III.;* cf. *English Works*, p. 38. Cf. Letters etc. of Richard III. and Henry VII., vol. ii., Preface (by Mr. James Gairdner), p. xxi.

The school maintained its fame down to the days of Stowe, who tells us that in the disputation of the London schools in the churchyard of S. Bartholomew, Smithfield, the boys of S. Anthony's usually carried away the prize. After Thomas More had there "been brought up in the Latin tongue, he was by his father's procurement received into the house of the right reverend, wise, and learned prelate, Cardinal Morton,"[1] probably about 1489.

Morton, then Archbishop and Lord Chancellor, but not to receive the red hat till 1493, was at that time probably the most important man in England; and it may be reasonably inferred from young More's reception into so distinguished a household that his father had then reached a position of some dignity, though he had not yet become a serjeant-at-law. No choice could have been wiser. Morton was a man of learning as well as a sagacious statesman; and the discretion which was his most characteristic quality may well have impressed itself on More. His rise had been due to Cardinal Bourchier, by whom he was originally introduced at Court, and whom he ultimately succeeded in the archiepiscopate, and he was as fortunate in the enmity of Richard III. as he had been in the favour of Edward IV. In his *History of Richard III.*, More says that he "was a man of great natural wit, very well learned, honourable in behaviour, lacking in no wise to win favour;"[2] a character which is improved

---

[1] Roper, *Life of More* (edit. Lumby : Cambridge, 1880), p. 6.

[2] *English Works*, p. 70.

and amplified in the *Utopia*, in a passage so significant of More's position and advantages in his house that it may well be quoted here. "He was of mean stature, and though stricken in age yet bare he his body upright. In his face, did shine such an amiable reverence as was pleasant to behold; gentle in communication, yet earnest and sage. He had great delight many times with rough speech to his suitors to prove, but without harm, what prompt wit and what bold spirit were in every man. In the which, as in a virtue much agreeing with his nature, so that therewith were not joined impudency, he took great delectation. And the same person as apt and meet to have an administration in the weal public he did lovingly embrace. In his speech he was fine, eloquent, and pithy. In the law he had profound knowledge, in wit he was incomparable, and in memory excellent. These qualities which in him were by nature singular, he by learning and use had made perfect."[1]

This is the description which his young *protégé* gives of the great counsellor of Henry VII.—"The King," he makes Master Hythlodaye add, "put much trust in his counsel, and the commonwealth also in a manner leaned unto him when I was there." The whole passage—an imaginary conversation at the Chancellor's house, in which Hythlodaye takes the chief part—may not improbably be a recollection, rather than an invention, of More's, for the social questions of the day undoubtedly received much attention from Morton. He is now remem-

---

[1] *Ralph Robinson's Translation*, Arber's edit. p. 36.

bered chiefly by "Morton's Fork," and the Union of the Roses; and the active good that he did is forgotten. Yet he has left more permanent memorials. Not only did he repair at his own cost the official residence of his See, and carry out various works at Oxford, of which the completion of the Divinity School is the most famous, but he cut the drain from Peterborough to Wisbeach still known as "Morton's Leam," and is credited with the erection of the Tower of Wisbeach and the rebuilding of Rochester Bridge. He was in fact a man from whom More would obtain the training of a philanthropist as well as of a courtier. It is probable also that the very definite views on the position of the English Church for which More afterwards laid down his life had their origin in the archbishop's tuition. Morton was one of the archbishops who followed the example of Chichele and Beaufort, under whom men were taught to forget the claim of the English primate to be *alterius orbis papa*. The very words used by Sir Thomas More on his trial seem an echo of the policy of Morton, a complete abnegation of the ancient national tradition.

Whatever influence his surroundings may have exercised upon him, More seems—child though he was—to have been no unimportant person in the household of the Chancellor. "Though he was young of years," says Roper in a well-known passage,[1] "yet would he at Christmas-tide suddenly step in among the players, and, never studying for the matter, make a part of his own there presently before them, which

---

[1] Page 6.

made the lookers-on more sport than all the players
beside.   In whose wit and learning the Cardinal
much delighting would often say of him unto the
nobles that divers times dined with him, ‘This child
here waiting at the table, whosoever shall live to
see it, will prove a marvellous man.’ ” A happy life it
was in the old world state of the medieval prelates.
Art flourished in all its richness under the shelter
of the Church.   The sharp division of classes which
the Reformation was to accentuate was hardly felt
as yet, and the New Learning from Italy was beginning to brighten the lives of priest and noble alike.
Perhaps it was of this time that Erasmus writes—
“Adolescens comœdiolas et scripsit et egit.” [1]   His
life at any rate was a very happy one, and he looked
back to the archbishop in later years with the reverence and gratitude that belong naturally to the first
who loves and fosters the bright hopes of boyhood.
“I assure you, Master Raphael,” he makes himself
to say in the *Utopia*, “I took great delectation in
hearing you . . . and methought myself to be in
the mean time not only at home in mine own country,
but also through the pleasant remembrance of the
Cardinal, in whose house I was brought up of a
child, to wax a child again.   And, friend Raphael,
though I did bear very great love towards you before,
yet, seeing you do so earnestly favour this man, you
will not believe how much my love towards you is
now increased.”

How long More remained in the Chancellor's
household is uncertain, but the year of his removal

<hr>

[1] *Epp.* x. 30.

to Oxford is now believed to be 1492. That he was sent to the University—no necessary introduction to the profession of the Law, for which his father designed him—was due to the care of his patron, who, says his grandson, " saw that he could not profit so much in his own house as he desired, where there were many distractions of public affairs." [1] Thus, at fourteen, he was introduced to the great centre of culture in England, where already the material prosperity of the time was providing new endowments for scholars, and whence students were crossing to Italy to study Greek at what seemed to be the fountain of all learning. At Morton's table, no doubt, he would have heard talk of the subjects which enchained men's minds in Italy and had begun to touch the colder hearts of Englishmen; but the learning of the ecclesiastics and lawyers of More's childhood belonged to an age that was rapidly passing away, and even in the archbishop's house he could have had little hint of the fulness of that new light to the dawnings of which he was introduced at Oxford. His juvenile performances show the development of his mind very clearly. The string of verses, hardly to be called a poem, entitled " A merry jest how a sergeaunt would learne to playe the frere," in default of any evidence of date, would seem to belong to an earlier period than that to which Sir James Mackintosh assigned it. Its merit hardly deserves the eulogies passed upon it by that author.[2] It is no doubt true that English

---

[1] Cresacre More, p. 9.
[2] *Life of More*, pp. 15—17.

poetry was then at a low ebb, but the fact is hardly to be accepted as proof of genius in all who essayed to write verses. The whole jingle, which fills four pages of the collected edition of More's *English Works*, gives indications of juvenility in the writer as well as of the decadence of English verse, and shows no trace of the higher culture by which More was marked after his Oxford studies had begun. To the view that these lines were written when More was quite a boy some support is also given by the fact that they are printed at the beginning of the collection above-mentioned, in which chrono-logical order is clearly attempted.

An advance is to be traced in the lines which he wrote, probably in some Oxford vacation, under the nine allegorical representations of the ages of man devised by him for his father's house in London. In these a certain elegance of force appears : he was learning at the University that sense of form and style which he never lost. On the first pageant, for instance, was depicted on the "goodly hanging of fine painted cloth" a boy whipping a top, with these lines appended—

> "I am called Chyldhod, in play is all my mind,
> To cast a coyte, a cokstele, and a ball.
> A toppe can I set and drive it in his kynde,
> But would to God these hatefull bookes all
> Were in a fyre brent to pouder small.
> Then myght I lede my lyfe alwayes in play :
> Which life God send me to myne endyng daye."[1]

In the second pageant was shown a "goodly freshe

---

[1] *English Works*, edit. 1537 ; and cf. Warton, *History of English Poetry* (1st edit.), vol. iii. p. 101.

yonge man," riding, with a hawk on his wrist, followed by a brace of greyhounds.   On this the verses were—

> "Manhod I am.   Therefore I me delyght
> To hunt and hawk, to nourish up and fede
> The grayhounde to the course, the hawke to the flyght,
> And to bestride a good and lusty stede.
> These thynges become a very man indede
> Yet thinketh this boy his pevishe game swetter,
> But what no force, his reason is no better."

The third represented the triumph of Cupid, who stood upon the prostrate body of the "freshe yonge man," with Venus at his side—

> "Who so ne knoweth the strength and power and myght
> Of Venus and me her lytle sonne Cupyde
> Thou Manhod shalt a mirrour bene a ryght
> By us subdued for all thy great pryde
> My fyry dart perceth thy tender syde.
> Now thou which erst despiseth children small
> Shall waxe a chylde again and be wythall."

For the fourth there was Old Age—

> "Old Age am I, with lokkes thynne and hore,
> Of our short lyfe the last and best part.
> Wyse and discrete : the publike wele therefore
> I help to rule to my labour and smart.
> Therefore, Cupyde, withdraw thy fyry dart.
> Chargeable matters shall of love oppresse
> The chyldish game and ydle business." [1]

For the others, Death, Fame, Time, Eternity, and the Poet (whose verses are, significantly, in Latin), the treatment is entirely conventional, and the expression much weaker.

Upon these, again, a further advance, with the distinct influence of Italian models, is to be seen in

---

[1] *English Works*, pp. 3, 4.

the *Rufull Lamentation* of 1503; while the English style comes out with ease and freshness in the prose of the life of Pico della Mirandola, in 1504.   We can trace in the beginnings of his literary work the influence of the Oxford of his day. But, to return. More was entered at Canterbury College, one of the foundations which afterwards made way for Christ Church, and seems to have occupied a room also in S. Mary Hall.[1]   There he remained for two years. Of the state of learning in Oxford at that time very different opinions have been expressed. Many, relying on the strong condemnation of Erasmus and More, and forgetting that such language has been used by the more advanced scholars of all ages, would consider that no interest in literature or culture was apparent. This is, surely, a mistake. Though the Universities of England had not the support which was afforded in Italy by the circles of distinguished patrons of learning, the great leaders of the English Renaissance and Reformation, as well as their opponents, had received an academical training. It was already fashionable to patronize learning. Henry VII. was not forgetful of his cultured mother, and Prince Arthur was a constant visitor at Oxford. More significant still, the University had chosen Morton as its Chancellor. When More began to study in Oxford the attempt to transplant Italian culture was being made with energy and success. Grocyn, who had visited Italy

---

[1] *Vide* Ant. Wood, *Athenae Oxonienses* (1st edit.), p. 32, quoting Miles Windsor cf. Cres. More, p. 9, and Hoddesdon, p. 3 ; also Hearne's edition of Roper.

in 1488, was teaching Greek to an eager and increasing audience. Linacre, a younger man, who had also breathed the delicate atmosphere of the Florentine Academy, and studied under Chalcondylas and Poliziano, was More's especial instructor.[1] While these men lectured on the classic literatures, and the hearers began to perceive the dimensions of that vast world of literature and art which it seemed to be within their power to revivify and reconstruct, not only boys like More, but men already working in the world, professed ecclesiastics and parish priests like Colet, gave up active life to enter on the new course of study. For them, as for those who were carrying the English name across the far seas, a new world seemed to be open. Then it was that Colet (the phrase is Mr. Seebohm's) "fell in love with" More. The expression is hardly too strong. He was now only fourteen, but there seems always to have been all through his life a fascination about More which no cultured man could resist. It was the union of simplicity of manner and purity of soul with a swift appreciation of the thoughts, and a true sympathy for the sorrows of others,—of a keen intellect and deep earnestness of purpose, softened by a bright and continual humour. More might well be the "soul" of Colet, as Tommaso Cavalieri was a few years later of the great Florentine sculptor. Colet was then twenty-six. He had already taken the degree of Master of Arts, and was now studying Greek with an intensity which soon induced him,

---

[1] See his *Epistle to Dorpius;* and Stapleton, *de Tribus Thomis (More)*, cap. 1.

not satisfied with what Grocyn and Linacre could
teach, to travel to France and Italy in pursuit of
wider culture. The friendship thus begun was to
last as long as Colet's life. The stern but saintly
priest never forgot his young Oxford friend. Of his
love and prayers he may well have thought when
in old age he bade the children of "Paul's" lift up
their little white hands for him. We have little
information of the actual course of More's studies
at Oxford beyond the bare statement of his letter
to Dorpius already referred to. His life could not
have been an easy one. The accounts we hear of
the hardships of students in Edward VI.'s reign
would probably be as true of forty years earlier.
Many rose between four and five, and after prayer
in the College chapel, studied till ten, when they
dined on very meagre fare—"content with a penny
piece of beef between four, having a pottage made
of the same beef with salt and oatmeal, and nothing
else. After their dinner," continues the description,
"they are reading or learning till five in the evening,
when they have a supper not better than their
dinner, immediately after which they go to reasoning
in problems or to some other study till nine or ten;
and then being without fire are fain to walk or run
up and down for half-an-hour to get a heat in the
feet, when they go to bed."[1]

The path of study was not made smooth to More,
for in spite, or perhaps in consequence, of his diligence, "in his allowance his father kept him very

---

[1] T. Leaver, 1551, in a sermon at S. Paul's Cross, reprinted
by Mr. Arber.

SIR JOHN MORE.

From the drawing by Holbein.

To face page 17.

short, suffering him scarcely to have so much money
in his own custody as would pay for the mending of
his apparel," and demanding a strict account of his
expenses. This treatment, says his grandson, he
would often speak of and praise when he came to
riper years, "affirming that by this means he was
curbed from all vice and withdrawn from many idle
expenses, either of gaming or keeping naughty company, so that he knew neither play nor other riot,
wherein most young men in these our lamentable
days plunge themselves too timely, to the utter over-
throw as well of learning and future virtue as of their
temporal estates."[1] Though the assiduity with which
More pursued his studies must have satisfied his
father, their direction was not so pleasing, for the
worthy Judge believed that Greek literature was not
likely to be of use to a lawyer.[2] Little practical
advantage indeed was to be gained at Oxford by one
destined for the Bar. The Medieval Universities of
the North were as a rule unfavourable to the study
of Jurisprudence and of Medicine. At Oxford a
degree in Law could not be obtained without seven
years' study after the completion of the Arts' course,
and this might well seem a waste of time to the keen
lawyer whose shrewd face we know so well from Holbein's masterly drawing. Harpsfield, who adds a
few touches to Roper's record of these early years,
says that in the short time young More stayed at
Oxford—"being not fully two years, he wonderfully
profited in the Latin and Greek tongues." It was
these on which Colet too was at work : neither of the

---

[1] Cres.More, p. 9.   [2] Stapleton, p. 168.

two fellow-students, it may well be, ran their "full race in the study of the liberal sciences and divinity." It was said of More that he did not learn the meaning of a sentence from the knowledge of the words which composed it, but that rather his swift appreciation of the meaning of a sentence taught him the meaning of the words themselves. He had a genius above grammar, thought Pace. "Est enim Moro ingenium plusque humanum." He learnt to write Latin with great ease, says Erasmus, and to speak it as well as his own tongue.[1] These studies, fruitful as they came to be, were not to the taste of the hardworking lawyer, and so the lad was taken away from Oxford, when he had but learnt to love Colet much and to love true religion and sacred learning more. It was well for poor clerks like Thomas Wolsey to linger on teaching their lads the grammar, or for scholars like Colet and Linacre and Latimer to dally with their books. There was other work for one who would be a lawyer.

Accordingly young More was removed from Oxford, and in 1494 or 1495 entered at New Inn, a House which had not long been made an Inn of Chancery.[2] There he gave his attention to law,

---

[1] See Pace, *De Fructu qui ex Doctrinâ Percipitur;* Basle, 1517 ; and many passages in the Letters of Erasmus.

[2] "The entry under 11 Henry VII. is as follows : 'Thomas More admissus est in Societat. xij die Februar. aº sup. dicto et pardonat. est quatuor vacacões ad instanciam Johis. More patris sui.' Although his name is not to be found on the books of New Inn, a Society then recently established, there is no doubt that he was placed there for some time. . . . He was in due time removed to Lincoln's Inn, and, having passed through the usual course of study, he was admitted as an utter barrister, but the early books of that Society do not

but not even then with an entire devotion. He could not forget the studies of his childhood or the teachings of his good friend Colet; for to this period may probably be attributed the composition of his Latin epigrams, published some years later, and those discursive wanderings among the writings of the Fathers which he afterwards utilized in his theological controversies. On February 12, 1496, he was admitted a student of Lincoln's Inn, where he was to obtain a more severe legal training. Here he continued "with a very small allowance" [1] until his call to the Bar in 1500.

Meanwhile he formed another friendship, which partook, perhaps even more than his affection for Colet, of the nature of love. Erasmus, already famous, came to England with his pupil and friend, William Blount, Lord Mountjoy, and may have met More at the table of Colet's father on his way through London, as Mr. Seebohm suggests.[2] Cresacre More tells us that at their first meeting, and before they were known to each other, an argument arose between them, in which Erasmus, after the scholastic fashion defending the weaker side,

---

give the date of the calls to the Bar. The character he acquired as a lawyer may be judged from his soon after being selected by the governors to deliver lectures on the science at one of the Inns of Chancery dependent on their house. Furnival's Inn was the scene of his readings, which were so highly estimated that this annual appointment was renewed for three successive years."—Foss, *Judges of England*, vol. **v.** p. 206.

[1] Roper, p. 6.

[2] *Oxford Reformers*, p. 113. See too Professor Jebb's delightful Rede Lecture on Erasmus, p. 13.

was so hardly beset by the wit of his antagonist, that, remembering whom Colet declared to be " the one genius of England," he cried out, " Aut tu es Morus, aut nullus." " Aut tu es Erasmus, aut diabolus," was the retort. The acquaintance thus begun became a deep affection ; before a few months had passed Erasmus is found speaking [1] of " my own More," and complaining, in all the glowing phrases of Renaissance friendship, of his delay in writing. Years did not change their feelings ; their affection became famous : twenty years afterwards Tyndale sneeringly spoke of Erasmus as More's "darling," and in 1533 Erasmus himself says, " In Moro mihi videor extinctus adeo μία φυχή juxta Pythagoram duobus erat." It is the phrase of Michaelangelo in the very same year. "I cannot enjoy life without the soul," he wrote to Angelini, and it was Cavalieri that he meant by that endearing title. The Renaissance differed indeed in England and in Italy, but it had the same passionate sense of the value of friendship and fellow-work. Again, wrote Erasmus to Ulrich von Hutten, " More seems to be born for friendship, of which he is a true follower and fast keeper. . . . If any man desires a perfect pattern of friendship, there is none better than More." "When," says he, writing of his first introduction to English society, " when did Nature mould a character more gentle, endearing, and happy, than that of Thomas More ? "

The friends did not often meet during the first two years of their acquaintance, for Erasmus was at

---

[1] *Epp.* vi. 11, p. 354.

Oxford. He left England in 1500, the last week of his stay being enlivened by a practical joke of More's, who, when they were both guests of Lord Mountjoy at Greenwich, induced Erasmus to take a walk, and led him to the royal nursery, where the unfortunate scholar was called upon for Latin verses, and was quite unable to produce them without preparation.[1]

Though Erasmus left England, More had now many friends around him. Grocyn had received the Rectory of S. Lawrence in the Old Jewry; Linacre was also living in London; a new friend, Lilly, also a scholar from Italy, lodged in the Charterhouse; and early in 1505 Colet came into residence at S. Paul's.[2]

Having been called to the Bar, More returned, under the influence perhaps of his old friends, to the study of other than legal subjects. He delivered lectures in Grocyn's church on the *De Civitate Dei*, dwelling on the historical and philosophical lessons of that great work rather than on its theology. That the lectures were intended to advance the cause of the " New Learning " is evident from the manner in which Cresacre More speaks of them. He tells us also, following Stapleton, that Grocyn was deserted : "almost all England left his lecture and flocked to hear More." He was equally successful at the Bar; he obtained a good practice, though he never undertook a case of the justice of which he was not satisfied ;[3] and he was appointed a

---

[1] The letter describing the scene is given by Jortin, vol. iii. p. 105 *sqq.*

[2] Knight's *Life of Colet*, p. 63.

[3] Stapleton, c. ii. ; Roper, p. 6 ; Cres. More, p. 44.

reader at Furnival's Inn, where he delivered lectures
for more than three years.[1]

But he did not therefore relax his study of
theology, or vary his own religious life.   He " applied
his whole mind," says Erasmus, " to exercises of piety,
looking to and pondering over the priesthood in vigils,
fastings and prayers and the like austerities.   In
the which thing he showed himself far more prudent
than most candidates, who thrust themselves rashly
into that arduous profession, without any previous
trial of their powers."   He wore a hair shirt next
his skin, fasted much, and heard mass every day.   He
lived, too, near the Charterhouse, daily attending
its services, but without taking any vow.   In spite
of this devotion, and of his earnest desire for
religious work, which induced him at one time to
think of becoming a Franciscan, secular business
increased upon him.   In January 1504, he was
returned to Parliament; for what constituency there
seems to be no means of discovering.   His return,
probably due to Court influence, may be attributed
—though there is no such hint in any of his
biographies—to his recent poetical lament on the
death of the Queen.   Elizabeth, wife of Henry
VII., died in February 1503, and More celebrated
her virtues and deplored her loss in strains which
may well have reached the royal ear.   The *Rufull
Lamentation* is in itself a work of little merit.
Written on the model of the tragical soliloquies
which had been introduced to English readers by
Lydgate in his adaptation of Boccaccio's *De Casibus*

[1] Life by R. B. : Wordsworth's *Eccl. Biog.* ii. p. 64.

Virorum Illustrium, it is in form much more elegant than in matter. The attempt at such a metre showed that English poetry would not long remain content with the shuffling jingle of its decadence, but the expression rarely rises above the commonplace. Two stanzas, however, may be quoted, the one as a specimen of the style, the other as an illustration of More's own views.

> " If worship might have kept me, I had not gone ;
> If wit might have me saved, I needed not fear :
> If money might have holp I lacked none.
> But, O good God, what vayleth all this gear ?
> When death is come, Thy mighty messenger,
> Obey we must, there is no remedy.
> Me hath he summoned and lo now here I lie."

> " Yet was I late promised otherwise
> This year to live in wealth and delice.
> Lo, where unto cometh thy blandishing promise,
> O false astrology and devinatrice.
> Of God's secret making thyself so wise.
> How true for this year thy prophecy :
> The year yet lasteth and lo now here I lie."

This latter stanza shows that thus early More had repudiated the belief in astrology common even among the educated and eminent men of his time. He repeated his condemnation in several Latin epigrams and in the *Utopia.* For his views on this subject More may have been indebted to the writings of Pico della Mirandola, who, though he had not seen the folly of all magic, had denounced the imposture of judicial astrology. There was, perhaps, less crying cause for the denunciation in England than in Italy, where, in the midst of a laxity of religious and moral life, the pernicious superstition had managed subtly to link itself even with the victorious Humanism of the age; but the manner in which More derided the professors of the "science" at such a moment and in such a poem was not therefore the less daring.

The Parliament of 1504 met in a troublous time. Fears of dynastic war had not yet passed away, and men were feeling under Empson and Dudley, "those two catterpillars of the common wealth," the power of an administration far more tyrannical than that of Morton. For seven years Parliament had not been summoned : money had been obtained from submissive convocations and from the exactions of the King's ministers. Notwithstanding the unpopularity of these men, in which the King shared, the royal influence was strong enough to procure the choice of Dudley for Speaker in the Parliament of 1504.

According to Roper [1] three fifteenths were demanded as aids for the knighting of Prince Arthur, and the marriage of Margaret, the King's eldest daughter, to the King of Scots. Thomas More came into notice by his strong opposition to their request : " at the last debating whereof he made such arguments and reasons there against that the King's demands were thereby overthrown; so that one of the King's Privy Chamber, named Mr. Tyler, brought word to the King out of the Parliament house, that a beardless boy had disappointed all his purposes." The Court, in fact, had to be contented with a grant of £20,000 for each demand, of which £10,000 was remitted. This is the story told by Roper. But there seems reason to suppose that he has made

[1] Roper, p. 7.

a mistake, and has either confused the Parliament
of 1504 with the great Council of 1488 or Parliament
of 1489, or refers to some debate in a Council still
later, not relating to a demand for any feudal aid.
At any rate it is not recorded that three fifteenths
were demanded in 1504, or that there was any
opposition in Parliament on a monetary question.[1]

The opposition—to return to Roper's story—was
not forgotten or forgiven. The King's indignation
could not vent itself on Thomas More, "forasmuch
as he nothing having, nothing could lose"; he
therefore revenged himself on his father, who was
one of the Commissioners for the collection of the
grant, by putting him in the Tower, and making
him pay a fine of £100. Nor was the matter thus
ended. Bishop Fox of Winchester, the Keeper of
the Privy Seal, endeavoured to induce Thomas
More to confess his offence, and thus become amen-
able to punishment, and he was only saved by a
timely warning from the bishop's chaplain.[2]

To this year also belongs a most interesting record
of More's private life, a letter to Colet, printed by

---

[1] The difficulties of the question are considerable, and I
cannot consider any suggestion that has yet been offered as
wholly satisfactory. Perhaps the clearest statement is that
of Bishop Stubbs (*Lectures on Medieval and Modern History*,
p. 365) : "The story that Sir Thomas More in a Parliament in
1502 prevented the Commons from granting an aid for the
marriage of Margaret, though told on good authority, falls to
the ground for the good reason that no Parliament was held in
1502, and that in 1504 the grant was actually made. More
probably was instrumental in limiting the sum." But Roper
is the original authority for the statement, and he does not
mention the year.

[2] Roper, pp. 7, 8.

Stapleton.[1]   We learn from it that the young lawyer was living in seclusion, and under the spiritual direction of his old friend. His mind was disturbed by temptation and anxiety: at one moment he was determined to seek refuge in the cloister : at the next his ambition and his strong social sympathies were predominant.   Of this state of mind the letter, written in October 1504, gives very clear indication. A short extract will suffice : "What is there here in this city which would move any man to live well, and doth not rather by a thousand devices draw him back, and with as many allurements swallow him up in all manner of wickedness who of himself were otherwise well disposed, and doth endeavour accordingly to climb up the painful hill of Virtue?   Whithersoever that any man cometh, what can he find but fained love and the honey-poison of venomous flattery? In one place he shall find cruel hatred, in another hear nothing but quarrels and suits. Whithersoever we cast our eyes, what can we see but victualling-houses, fishmongers, butchers, cooks, pudding-makers, fishers or fowlers, who minister matter to our bellies and set forward the service of the world and the prince thereof and devil? Yea, the houses themselves,[2] I know not how, do deprive us of a great part of our sight of Heaven, so as the height of our buildings and not the circle of our horizon doth limit our prospect." Then after speaking of the simplicity

[1] Stapleton, cap. ii. p. 163.
[2] A significant comparison might be made between this passage and the *Utopia*, pp. 78, 79. (Arber's edition.)

of the country, More turns to the difficulty of finding spiritual instruction skilful enough for the urban population. " There came into the pulpit at S. Paul's divers men that promise to cure the diseases of others; but when they have all done, and made a fair and goodly discourse, their life on the other side doth so jar with their saying that they rather increase than assuage the griefs of their hearers. . . . But if such a man be accounted by learned men most fit to cure in whom the sick man hath greatest hope, who doubteth then but that you alone are the fittest in all London to heal their maladies whom every one is willing to suffer to touch their wounds and in whom what confidence every one hath and how ready every one is to do what you prescribe, both you have heretofore sufficiently tried, and now the desire that everybody hath of your speedy return may manifest the same. . . . In the meanwhile, I pass my time with Grocyn, Linacre, and Lilly; the first, as you know, the director of my life in your absence, the second the master of my studies, and the third my most dear companion. Farewell: and love me as you have ever done." London, October 21.

To the perplexity which this letter suggests More had returned to his old Humanist studies, and his final decision was due probably in equal proportions to the living example of Colet, and to the direction which his literary interests now happily took. It is absurd to assert that More was disgusted with monastic corruption—that he " loathed monks as a disgrace to the Church." He was throughout his life a warm friend of the religious orders, and a devoted admirer of the monastic ideal. He condemned the vices of individuals; he said, as his great-grandson says, "that at that time religious men in England had somewhat degenerated from their ancient strictness and fervour of spirit"; but there is not the slightest sign that his decision to decline the monastic life was due in the smallest degree to a distrust of the system or a distaste for the theology of the Church.

On the other hand, it would be idle to deny that More turned now to what seemed to him a wider sphere, and that he was profoundly influenced in his choice of the New Learning and the Humanism of the day. The cloister, it was unquestionable, did not encourage literary pursuits. No one laughed more loudly than the young lawyer at the *Epistolae Obscurorum Virorum.* He knew something of the miseries Erasmus had endured at Stein. At the same moment he was allured by the extraordinary attraction of the Italian scholar life. It was in fact not the Reformation but the Renaissance which took More from the cloister.[1] More turned then from the life of a professed religious to that of a Christian scholar and man of the world. He read at first in conjunction with Lilly, with whom he translated Greek epigrams. He wrote also "certain meters for the boke of Fortune and caused them to be printed in the

---

[1] Froude, *Life and Letters of Erasmus,* p. 97. Mr. Seebohm asserts, most unwarrantably, so far as I can see—and I believe I have read all the Catholic biographies, certainly all the English ones—that "More's Catholic biographers have acknowledged that he turned in disgust from the impurity of the cloister."

begynnyng of that boke."[1] Of these the following
lines in his description of the fickle divinity may well
be preserved—

> "Fast by her side doth weary Labour stand,
> Pale Fear also and Sorrow all bewept ;
> Disdain and Hatred on that other hand
> Eke restless watch from sleep with travail kept ;
> His eyes drowsy and looking as he slept.
> Before her standeth Danger and Envy,
> Flattery, Deceit, Mischief, and Tyranny."

It is impossible to read the lines attentively
without being reminded of some picture of Botti-
celli's. There is the same quaint beauty and far-
away suggestiveness of an underlying pathos. More
was learning to understand the complexity of life
and struggling to embrace, maybe, all its many and
divergent interests. His "Fortune" is like Botti-
celli's Calumny. It appeals as strangely, and as
widely, at the parting of two ways of life.

It is no affectation to assume that More at this
period was profoundly influenced by the Italian
Renaissance. It is certain that his chief interest
during these years was reserved for the works of Pico
della Mirandola, to which he had been about this time
directed. No attraction could have been more happy.
From the narrowness which might not unnaturally
have arisen from the severe attention which he had
so long paid to the study of the law and from
the self-centred religion which his Carthusian vigils
had fostered, he must be aroused if he were to be of
the real service to his country for which his eminent
abilities and virtues qualified him. But to wean

---

[1] *Eng. Works*, p. v.

More from the purely ascetic and studious life which
possessed such great attraction for his lofty spirit
could be no easy task. That it was attempted by
Colet is very probable, for we know that he advised
More to marry. But the ultimate direction of the
young lawyer's life was very greatly influenced by
the life and writings of Pico. No example could
be more fitting. In that fascinating hero of the
Renaissance there was every beauty to attract, every
virtue to secure, and every talent to confirm the
admiration of such a man as More. In him no
keen eye could detect the subtle flavour of a Pagan
life. Nor was his Christianity cold, unsympathetic,
or unreal. His abilities were remarkable even
among his contemporaries, and his energy and
devotion were as extraordinary. The whole story
of his life, of its fair hopes, bitter disappoint-
ments, and calm peaceful ending, sounds like one
of the poetic legends which the fancy of the age
so freely created and cherished. In him men
might seem to see the Tannhaüser whose fond and
fickle passion for the Pagan goddess had vanished
in the glorious dawn of Christianity. A young man,
" of feature and shape seemly and beauteous, of
stature goodly and high, of flesh tender and soft,
his visage lovely and fair, his colour white inter-
mingled with comely reds, his eyes grey and quick
of look, his teeth white and even, his hair yellow and
not too picked "[1]—so More describes him in his
quaint translation of Gian Francesco's biography.
"Nature," said Poliziano,[2] "seemed to have showered

---

[1] *English Works*, p. 3.
[2] Quoted by Symonds, *Revival of Learning*, p. 329.

on this man, or hero, all her gifts. He was tall and finely moulded; from his face a something of divinity shone forth. Acute, and gifted with prodigious memory, in his studies he was indefatigable, in his style perspicuous and eloquent. You could not say whether his talents or his moral qualities conferred on him the greater lustre."

Pico indeed fills a unique, if not a large, space in the history of the Renaissance. Learned like the ablest of his contemporaries in the classical languages, he was almost alone in making some claim to be an Orientalist, for he studied Hebrew, Arabic, and Chaldee. The favourite of Lorenzo de' Medici, he was also the friend and disciple of Savonarola, and in that age of strong temptations, intellectual and sensual, he had the wisdom to refuse the evil and choose the good. He combined in a remarkable degree the charm and the address of a man of the world with the studious devotion of a man of letters. "I desire you," he wrote to Andrea Corneo, "not so to embrace Martha that you should utterly forsake Mary. Love them and use them both, as well study as worldly occupation." Lorenzo had no courtier more courtly than he, yet he was always a bookworm at heart. His nephew says of him, at the time when he was most earnestly given to religion, that—

"He said once that whatsoever should happen, fell there never so great misadventure, he could never, as him thought, be moved to wrath, but if his chests perished in which his books lay that he had with great travail and watch compiled; but forasmuch as he considered that he laboured only for the love of God and profit of His Church and that he had dedicate unto Him all his works, his studies, and his doings, and sith he saw that sith God is almighty they could not miscarry but if it were either by His commandment or by His sufferance, he verily trusted sith God is all good that He would not suffer him to have that occasion of heaviness."

His curious learning was put to a curious use. He clung passionately to the idea of the unity of knowledge, the unity of truth. Thus he gave himself to an attempt to reconcile Platonic, neo-Platonic, and neo-Pythagorean opinions with Christianity. The difficulty of explaining the extraordinary complications into which Pico's strange jumble of erudition led him is very considerable. Confused he certainly was by his linguistic and cabalistic vagaries; but heretical, so far as he can be understood, he was not. He died at peace with the Church, and was buried in a Dominican habit in Savonarola's own San Marco, where the plain marble tablet that records his virtues and his fame may still be seen. It is rather from the writings of others, and especially from the touching little biography which More translated, little from his own books or the somewhat prim portrait in the Uffizi,[1] that we learn his mental and physical semblance. Almost all those who write about him dwell upon his rare physical beauty. It was the special goodness of God, they say, that kept him pure in his later life. He

---

[1] This picture, long believed to be that of Pico, seems now to be asserted with authority to be that of one of the Medici.

was born, indeed, to be above sensual temptations; his mind was essentially that of a mystic, and, having once tasted the joys of the spiritual life, he could never abandon them. There is much in his sayings and doings that reminds one of Molinos and his followers—

"Of outward observances," says his nephew, Gian Francesco, "he gave no very great force—we speak not of those observances which the Church commandeth to be observed, for in those he was diligent, but we speak of those ceremonies which folk bring up, setting the very service of God aside, which is, as Christ saith, to be worshipped in spirit and in truth. But in the inward affects of the mind he cleaved to God with very fervent love and devotion."

And worthy of Pascal are those famous words of his to Poliziano—

"Love God, while we be in this body, we rather may than either know Him or by speech utter Him: and yet had we rather alway by knowledge never find the thing that we seek than by love possess the thing which also without love were in vain found."

Typical as Pico was of the best side of the Italian Renaissance, no better influence could have touched More at the turning-point of his life, and his translation of the biography, with the letters and poems, marks a definite influence on the life of the English statesman. He was engaged on it, there seems no doubt, at the very time when he abandoned the idea of becoming a Carthusian and decided to live in the world, a student, a lawyer, a man of affairs, but always before all things a Christian. More had

D

assimilated a great deal of the Italian culture of his age without adopting its vices. He was an "Italian- ate Englishman" in a different sense fom that which the expression bore fifty years after his death. He had a genuine love of learning for its own sake and was a strenuous champion of the Greek as well as the Latin classics. He was himself already well acquainted with the chief *savants* and *littérateurs* of Europe, and his introduction of Pico to the English reader was probably undertaken with the intention of making England alive to the importance of the movement in Italian thought, as well as of showing how the progress of learning and inquiry was intimately bound up in the noblest lives with religion.

There is much similarity between Pico and More. Both were keen classical scholars, tinged with the mysticism of Renaissance imaginings, men of wide human interests, bent on bringing the Divine Spirit into every sphere of human thought. What has been said with such fine clearness of Pico's position is almost equally true of More's—

"This high dignity of man"—which was the characteristic belief of both Italian and Englishman in the revival of learning—"thus bringing the dust under his feet into sensible communion with the thoughts and affections of the angels, was supposed to belong to him, not as renewed by a religious system, but by his own natural right; and it was a counterpoise to the increasing tendency of medieval religion to depreciate man's nature, to sacrifice this or that element in it, to keep the degrading or painful accidents of it always in view. It helped man onward to that reassertion of himself, that rehabilitation of human nature, the body, the senses, the heart, the intelligence, which the Renaissance fulfils."

Like the Italian Humanist, More was penetrated with the sense of the beauty and the mystery of life. Rich colours and the strange recesses of occult investigation, the quaintness of old world learning, and the pure human beauty of classic ideals of literature and art, the thrilling chords of music and the simple innocence of animal life, the triumph of self-sacrifice, the joys of friendship and of love, the thoughts of Plato and the divine mysteries of the Christian religion, appealed each in their turn to his sensitive consciousness, and ascetic though he was his inner contemplation never blinded him to the loveliness of human life. Pico was as far removed from the ignorant bigotry satirized in the Letters of obscure men as from the scarce veiled Paganism of many disciples of the New Learning. To him it did not seem that Christianity was less true because Paganism was so beautiful, and the same thought was never absent from the mind of More.

The kinship of soul was natural. Powerfully influenced himself by the story of Pico's life, it was natural that More should desire to share the benefit with others. He accordingly published a translation of the life and Works,[1] which he dedicated as a New

---

[1] " The Life of John Picus, Earl of Mirandula, a great Lorde of Italy, an excellent connyng man in all sciences, and vertuous of liuing: with divers Epistles and other workes of y· sayd John Picus, full of greate science, vertue and

Year's gift to his "right entirely beloved sister in Christ Joyeuce Leigh."

The life begins with mention of the noble ancestry of Pico, and passes on to his extraordinary aptitude for study, reaching its chief interest with the chapter on his famous challenge at Rome. "There nine hundred questions he proposed of diverse and sundry matters, as well in logic and philosophy as in divinity, with great study picked and sought out as well of the Latin authors as of the Greeks; and partly set out of the secret mysteries of the Hebrews, Chaldees, and Arabies, and many things drawn out of the old obscure philosophy of Pythagoras, Trismegistus, and Orpheus, and many other things strange to all folk (except right few special excellent men), before that day not unknown only but also unheard." The story then tells how disappointment and failure attended this hardy challenger, and how he was led to think more especially of the religious life than he had yet done : how he burned five books of love-verses, " with other like fantasies he had made in his vulgar tongue": how he studied the sacred Scriptures and gave himself to prayer and almsgiving, purposing to walk from town to town, crucifix in hand, preaching Christ; how he died, and how the holy friar Savonarola glorified his memory. To this simple story were added two letters to his nephew Gian

------

wisedome : whose life and woorkes bene worthy and digne to be read, and often to be had in memory. Translated out of Latin into Englishe by Maister Thomas More," occupies pp. 1—34 in More's English *Works.* It has also been edited by Mr. J. M. Rigg, London, 1890.

Francesco Pico, and one to his famous merchant friend, Andrea Corneo, marked by a strange spiritual beauty. There is also a meditation on Psalm xvi., and renderings of some of Pico's religious poetry. Quotations from these have been given by Mr. Seebohm in his *Oxford Reformers:* they are interesting rather as illustrating the character of Pico than that of More. It is sufficient to say that the spirit of piety which they breathe was as natural to the Englishman as to the Italian.

To the firm independent tone which marks the whole volume has been attributed, perhaps with truth, the step that More now took. He abandoned the idea of a monastic life, and, in 1505, he married.

The tale of his courtship as told by his son-in-law is peculiar, but characteristic both of the times and of the man.[1] It seems that Master John Colt, of the Essex family of that name,[2] having (as Roper significantly remarks) three daughters, often invited him to his house, New Hall. More thought the second daughter the "fairest and best favoured," and would gladly have made her his wife, but when he thought of the slight that might seem to be thrown upon her elder sister by the choice, he "of a certain pity framed his fancy towards her, and soon afterwards married her." Whatever may be truth of this story, there is no doubt that More was devotedly

---

[1] Roper, p. 6 ; Cres. More, p. 20.

[2] I may be permitted here to refer to the valuable and complete *History and Genealogy of the Colts* (Edinburgh, 1887), by my brother-in-law, the present head of the family.

attached to his wife, and lived most happily with
her. Erasmus, writing some years after her death,
says that she was quite young, and that More had
her taught various kinds of learning, and especially
music. " His affection " — Father Bridgett very
prettily notes in his *Life of More* [1]—" is shown by one
little word in his own epitaph, composed more than
twenty years after her death. He calls her More's
dear little wife (*uxorcula Mori*)." She was not his
first love. As a boy of sixteen he fell in love. He
was but a poor scholar.

> "Then the duenna and the guarded door
>   Baffled the stars and bade us meet no more."

A quarter of a century later they met again, in
1519, and More wrote some pretty verses.

On his marriage he took a house in Bucklersbury,
to be near his father. For the next few years we
have only scattered notices of his life. He was
evidently still studying and practising the Law.
Erasmus seems to have visited him towards the
end of the year 1505,[2] to have found him writing
Latin epigrams, and to have written with him a
declamation in the style of Lucian. The visit, however, was not a long one, and though More was
surrounded by his friends, Colet, Grocyn, Lilly, and
Linacre, he was by no means safe from the King's
resentment. He had even serious thoughts of
flight,[3] and apparently did visit Paris and Louvain.[4]

---

[1] Page 54.   [2] Erasm. *Epp.* x. 30.   [3] Roper, p. 8.
[4] *Ep. ad Dorpium.*

Meanwhile several children were born to him: three daughters, Margaret, Elizabeth, and Cicely: and lastly, in 1509, his son John. In this year the clouds which had overhung More's course dispersed, and on the accession of Henry VIII. he sprang, almost at one bound, into fame.

CHAPTER II.

HOME AND FRIENDS.

"Vidisti ne unquam hoc horto quidquam amoenius? Vix
opinor in insulis Fortunatis esse quidquam jucundius.
Plane mihi videor videre paradisum."—ERASMUS, *Colloq.
Symposium.*

THE accession of Henry VIII. may not unjustly be
considered a decisive epoch. As far as such arbitrary divisions are ever satisfactory, it may seem
to us now to have marked in England the end of
what we call the Middle Ages, and the first distinct
indication of the rise of the modern framework
of society. Whatever be the value we may attach
to modern statements of this kind, we cannot fail
to recognize the fact that to the Englishmen of
that age the year 1509 appeared undoubtedly to
be the beginning of a new era. The country seemed
to cast her nighted colour off, to awake from the
sullen torpor in which she had watched the harsh
avarice of the old King's declining years. All had
been repression, and national policy had spoken
only through the monarch; public feeling finding
no congenial expression had been heard but as a
stifled undercurrent of complaint. Now all was

changed. The King was young and gallant, the representative of all the interests and thoughts of the nation. The daring spirit of adventure and excitement, which was still as much that of the knight-errant as that of the explorer; the delight in luxury, in rich, oriental, imaginative grandeur; the wide social and literary interests of the time,—were all reflected in Henry VIII. He was, in fact, at his accession, as prominent a figure in England's Renaissance as he afterwards became in her Reformation. All that spoke of the past gloom was removed. Empson and Dudley were hastily destroyed by a form of justice, with the spirit of which the new King could hardly have been in harmony. For ecclesiastics and lawyers the new Court substituted gallants and noblemen. And, for the first two years of the reign at least, King and people alike gave themselves up to enjoyment. The fairest hopes surrounded the new King; hopes of which More's congratulatory verses on the accession are the scarcely extravagant expression. The young barrister joined in the chorus of joy which greeted Henry VIII., and commemorated the coronation in several Latin poems. Of these the *carmen gratulatorium* [1] presented to the King himself is the longest and most important. It is introduced by a skilful explanation of the delay which occurred in its presentation. The artist who was to have illustrated it has been ill, More says; but his neglect is after all, perhaps, of no consequence, for so joyful an event must remain ever fresh

---

[1] *Latin Works* (edit. Louvain, 1569), p. 21.

in men's memories. The poem itself contains several characteristic passages, including no obscure reference to the tyranny of Henry VII. The following is More's description of the new King.

> "Tanta tibi est majestatis reverentia sacrae,
>   Virtutes merito quam peperere tuae.
> Quae tibi sunt fuerant patrum quacunque tuorum,
>   Secula prisca quibus nil habuere prius.
> Est tibi namque tui princeps prudentia patris
>   Estque tibi matris dextra benigna tuae.
> Est tibi mens aviae, mens religiosa paterna,
>   Est tibi materni nobile pectus avi.
> Quid mirum ergo novo si gaudeat Anglia more
>   Cum qualis nunquam rexerat ante regat ?"

It has been remarked that prudence is the sole virtue with which Henry VII., in a somewhat emphatic manner, is credited. The Queen Katherine has her full share in the compliments of the ode. She is compared to Cornelia, Tanaquil, Alcestis, and Penelope. The birth of a son is foretold ; but the succession is regarded as already strong, in the presence of a nobility rejoiced at recovering their glory, "nomen inane diu"—and of unshackled trade. The conclusion of the dedication shows the feeling of the whole composition. "Vale, princeps illustrissime, et, qui nobis ac rarus regum titulus est, amantissime."

Other poems of More's describe the splendour of the coronation, when the gorgeous procession was blessed both by Phoebus and "Jovis uxor," and the tournaments passed off without any disaster. Two poems also describe, one the union of the two roses in Henry VIII., the other the beginning of the golden age. The latter gives so characteristic an example of the style of More's Latin poems, that it may well be quoted—

Ad Regem.

"Cuncta Plato cecinit tempus quae proferat ullum,
    Saepe fuisse olim, saepe aliquando fore.
Ver fugit ut celeri, celerique revertitur anno,
    Bruma pari ut spacio quae fuit ante, redit.
Sic, inquit, rapidi post longa volumina cœli
    Cuncta per innumeros sunt reditura vices.
Aurea prima sata est aetas, argentea post hanc.
    Ærea post illam, ferrea nuper erat.
Aurea te, princeps, redierunt principe saecla
    O possit vater hactenus esse Plato."

The exaggeration which some writers consider to be too apparent in the whole series of verses may well be excused by the consideration that the accession of Henry VIII. was a personal relief to More, as well as a national joy. The cloud which had hung over him was removed; and nothing now interfered with his prospects of success. Ere long he began his public career. Before we follow him into his political life it may be well to collect the many notices in the biographies and letters which touch upon his personal appearance, his home, his friends—and, abandoning a strictly chronological progress, to examine the more famous of his literary works. By this arrangement a certain connection of idea is obtained, which would otherwise of necessity be sacrificed.

Cresacre More gives a description of his grandfather's appearance derived from that of Erasmus, but the original is clearer and more precise. With it may well be compared that of Harpsfield, and the whole must be read in the light of Holbein's famous portraits.[1]   He was of middle height and well-proportioned figure, save that through his habit of much writing, his right shoulder became higher than his left.   His limbs were well formed, but his hands were a little clumsy—the pictures generally conceal them. His colour was pale, heightened only by a faint bloom; his hair dark-brown.   His eyes were grey and speckled, "which," says Erasmus, "as a mark of genius are much admired in England."   His expression, as can well be understood from Holbein's masterly representation, was keen and inquiring, but entirely gentle and kind.   "His voice was neither boisterous nor big; nor yet too small and shrill; he spake his words very distinctly, without any manner of hastiness or stuttering; and, albeit he delighted in all kinds of melody, he seemed not of his own nature to be apt to sing himself."[2] He was intensely humorous.   Yet " whatsoever jest he brought forth, he never laughed at any himself, but spoke always so sadly that few could see by his look whether he spoke in earnest or in jest."[3]   He was careless, as men of quick humour often are, about his attire.   He wore his gown awry, a habit which Ascham tells us was imitated by succeeding barristers.[4]   He wore no silk or purple or chains of gold except when he could not avoid it:[5] he left the

---

[1] Cres. More, p. 281 ; Erasm. *Epp.* x. 30 ; Wordsworth's *Eccl. Biog.* ii. p. 229.

[2] Yet like many who have "no vocal talents," he delighted to sing in choir.

[3] Cres. More, p. 179; cf. Pace, *De Fructu Doctrinae* (ed 1517), p. 82.

[4] Walter, *Life of More*, p. 373.   [5] Erasm. *Epp.* x. 30.

direction of his wardrobe entirely in the hands of one of his servants, whom he would call his " tutor." [1] He cared as little about his food as about his dress. He rarely ate of more than one dish, though in the time of his wealth his table was always well provided [2]; and he preferred vegetables, milk, or eggs. He generally drank water; sometimes, to please others, very small beer ; and, when it was necessary to drink a guest's health, a little wine. He was never a strong man, but was able to go through his work well until a short time before his imprisonment. His temperament was calm and equable: of his remarkable presence of mind a curious anecdote has been told. One day as he was meditating on the leads of his gatehouse at Chelsea, a madman who had managed to follow him, seized and attempted to hurl him over the battlements. More, encumbered by his gown, and unable to struggle with the strong man, bethought him of a happy expedient. His little dog was with him—" Stay," he cried, "let us throw the dog down first, and see what sport that will be." The madman left hold of him and tossed the dog over. " This is fine sport," said More, "let us fetch him up and try it again." Then, as the madman went down the stairs, More fastened the door and cried for help.[3]

He was an assiduous student and a fluent talker. His humour was suited to all kinds of society, but especially, says Erasmus, to that of ladies. He was charitable to a remarkable degree: one of his bio-

<hr>

[1] Cres. More, p. 27.   [2] *Ibid.* p. 26.
[3] Seward's *Anecdotes*, vol. iv. p. 111.

graphers calls him "the public patron of the poor." [1]
Not only did he invite his poor neighbours to his
table, and hire a house at Chelsea for use as an
hospital where he maintained many aged, sick, and
indigent people at his own cost, but he would go
privately among the poor and aid them by advice and
liberal alms, "not by the penny or halfpenny, but
sometimes five, ten, twenty, thirty, forty shillings,
according to every one's necessity." He was greatly
interested in natural history, and bought every strange
creature from foreign lands that he could find. There
was hardly any species of bird that he had not, says
Harpsfield. "He kept an Ape, a Fox, a Wesill, a
Feritt, and other beasts more rare. If there had been
anie strange thing brought out of other countries and
worthie to be looked upon, he was desirous to buie
it; and all this was to the contentation and pleasure
of such as came to him; and himself now and then
would make his recreation in beholding them." [2]
The story which Erasmus tells of his animals is
famous. As one reads the passage in the colloquy
de Amicitia one can imagine the grave smile of
the great scholar as he saw the ape save the tame
rabbits from the weasel—"ex quo perspicuum hoc
animantium genus simiis esse carum. Ipsi cuniculi
non intelligebant suum periculum; sed hostem suum
per cancellam osculabantur. Simis opitulatus est
pericli tanti simplicitati." [3]

[1] The Anonym. Life, printed by Wordsworth, *Eccl. Biog.*
ii. 85.

[2] Wordsworth, *Ecclesiastical Biography*, ii. 230.

[3] *Colloq. Amicitia*, p. 529. The ape also appears in Holbein's
picture.

Like many other naturalists, he was very severe in his condemnation of hunting. Several of his epigrams contain stinging reflections on those who find their pleasure in it, and the *Utopia* contains perhaps the strongest indictment of field sport that an Englishman ever wrote. "All this exercise of hunting, as a thing unworthy to be used of free men, the Utopians have rejected to their butchers, to which craft, as we said before, they appoint their bondmen. For they count hunting the lowest, the vilest, and the most abject part of butchery, and the other part of it more profitable and more honest, as bringing much more commodity in that they kill beasts only for necessity. Whereas the hunter seeketh nothing but pleasure of the silly and woful beasts' slaughter and murder. The which pleasure in beholding death they think doth rise in the very beasts, either of a cruel affection, or else to be changed in continuance of time into cruelty, by long use of so cruel a pleasure." [1]

Second only to More's love of animals was his passion for music. Like Erasmus, he is painted by Holbein with a glass of flowers near him; but more especially "Klavikordi und ander seyten Spill uf ein Bretz." [2] He took care that his first wife

---

[1] To More's love of animals a very interesting note has been furnished me by a friend in which the likeness between the Chancellor and one of his descendants—the famous Charles Waterton (by the marriage of Charles Waterton to Anne More, c. 1720, eighth in descent from Sir Thomas)—is suggested.

[2] MS. note of Holbein's on the Basle sketch of the picture of More's family.

should become an accomplished musician, and he induced his second to learn to play on several instruments. For music, as he says in the *Utopia*,[1] though it neither actually gives pleasure to any member of the body nor removes pain, "nevertheless tickleth and moveth our senses with a certain secret efficacy, and with a manifest motion turneth them to it."[2] He cared for few other amusements, hating dice, tennis, and other games.[3] One of the traits which his biographers seem to have passed over is referred to in a letter of Erasmus—his fondness for the sea.[4]

Such was More as his friends saw him in his prosperity. Of his conduct in sorrow, before the days of affliction closed around him, two instances, too touching to be forgotten, are happily preserved. When the terrible sweating sickness had slain thousands in England, and the King and Wolsey were flying from place to place, to keep, if possible, out of the hands of Death, More's daughter, Margaret Roper, whom he loved most of all his children, was stricken with the fearful plague, "so that both physicians and all others despaired of her recovery." More "as he that most entirely tended her, being in no small heaviness for her, by prayer at God His hands sought to get remedy, whereupon after his usual manner going up into his

---

[1] *Utopia*, p. 113, R. Robinson's trans.

[2] Erasm. *Epp.* x. 30.

[3] More was no indifferent musician himself. Pace, *De Fructu Doctrinae*, p. 53.

[4] Erasm. *Epp.* App. 183 (Leyden edition of *Works*, vol. iii. pt. 2).

new Lodging, there in his chapel upon his knees
most devoutly besought Almighty God that it should
like His goodness, unto Whom nothing was impossible, if it were His blessed will, to vouchsafe
graciously to hear his petition." [1] And, as they
believed, his prayer was heard, and she was "miracu-
lously recovered, whom if it had pleased God at that
time to take to His mercy, her father said he would
never have meddled with worldly matters after."

In a lesser grief the same spirit of deep spiritual
trust is evident. The occasion was on More's return
from his second embassy to the Netherlands, in
1529. He had not been able to go home to his
family, but was obliged to go straight to Court,
where he learnt that a severe misfortune had happened to his household at Chelsea, and thereupon
wrote to his wife the most simple and beautiful,
perhaps, of all his letters. "Mistress Alice :—In my
most hearty wise I recommend me to you. And
whereas I am informed by my son Heron of the loss
of our barns and of our neighbours also, with all the
corn that was therein; albeit, saving God's pleasure
it is a great pity of so much good corn lost, yet,
as it hath liked Him to send us such a chance,
we must and are bounden not only to be content
but also to be glad of this visitation. He sent us
all we have lost; and since He hath by such a
chance taken it away again, His pleasure be fulfilled.
Let us never grudge thereat, but take it in good
worth, and heartily thank Him as well for adversity
as for prosperity. And peradventure we have more

[1] Roper, p. 18.

E

cause to thank Him for our loss than for our winning, for His wisdom better seeth what is good for us than we do ourselves. Therefore, I pray you, be of good cheer, and take all the household with you to church and there thank God both for what He hath given us, and for that which He hath taken from us, and for that which He hath left us, which, if it please Him, He can increase when He will; and if it please Him to leave us yet less, as His pleasure be it. I pray you to make good onsearch what my poor neighbours have lost, and bid them take no thought therefor; for if I should not have myself a spoon there shall be no poor neighbours of mine bear less by any chance happened in my house. I pray you be, with my children and your household, merry in God : and devise somewhat with your friends what way were best to take for provision to be made for corn for our household, and for seed this year coming, if we think it good that we keep the land still in our hands. And whether we think it good that we shall do so or not, yet I think it were not best suddenly thus to give it all up, and to put away our folk from our farm till we have somewhat advised us thereon. Howbeit if we have more now than we shall need, and which can get them other masters, ye may then discharge us of them; but I would not that any man were suddenly sent away, he wot not whither. At my coming hither I perceived none other than that I should have to abide the King's grace : but now I shall, I think, because of this chance, get leave to come home and see you; and then we shall

further devise together upon all things, what order
shall be best to take. And thus as heartily fare
you well, with all our children, as ye can wish.—
At Woodstock, the third day of September, by the
hand of Thomas More." [1]

It was natural that the household of such a man
should be a marvel of order and happiness. All who
saw it united in praise, and to their admiration we
owe a more minute knowledge of the daily life of
More's family than can be obtained of any other
household of the time. The two guiding principles of the domestic life were religion and learning.
He rose early, Stapleton says at two in the morning,
and was at prayer and study till seven. Every day
he, after private prayer with his children, said the
Litanies of the Saints and the Seven Penitential
Psalms; and never did he omit to hear mass. Every
evening he had a short service, which all the household attended, in his chapel. He was not satisfied,
however, with this: he always retained his love for
seclusion in religious exercises. After he had lived
a while at Chelsea he built a chapel, library, and
gallery, apart from his house, where he studied and
prayed alone, and where on Fridays he usually
remained the whole day. He undertook no business
of importance without, after confession, receiving the
Holy Sacrament. He enforced the meaning of his
example by constant exhortation. He would often
say to his wife and children, "We may not look at
our pleasure to go to Heaven in feather-beds: it is
not the way. For our Lord Himself went thither

[1] *Eng. Works*, p. 1419.

with great pain and many tribulations, which is the
path wherein He walked there, and the servant
may not look to be in better case than his master," [1]
and that he may well be admitted to Heaven who
is very desirous of seeing God; [2] but that he that
hath no such desire shall never gain admittance.
Roper tells how the Duke of Norfolk coming one
day to see his father-in-law, when he was Lord
Chancellor, found him in church, in a surplice, singing among the choir. And "as they went home
together arm in arm, the Duke said, 'Godbody,
Godbody, my Lord Chancellor, a parish clerk, a
parish clerk, you do dishonour the King and his
office.' 'Nay,' quoth Sir Thomas, smiling upon the
Duke, 'your grace may not think that the King,
your master and mine, will with me for serving
God, his Master, be offended, or thereby count his
office dishonoured.'" [3] He would often also carry
the cross in the customary religious processions, and
when advised during the lengthy progress at Roga-
tion-tide to ride on account of his age and dignity,
he answered that it beseemed not the servant to
follow his Master on horseback when his Master
had gone on foot. [4]

Such humility was natural to him, and he was as
stern to himself in private as he was humble abroad.
He ever wore a hair shirt, which only his confessor
and his wife and daughter Margaret knew of, till
one day his daughter-in-law, a girl of a very different
spirit, discovered the secret. "It pained his flesh,"

<hr>

[1] Roper, p. 17. [2] Cres. More, p. 108.
[3] Roper, p. 30. [4] Stapleton, cap. vi. p. 221.

says his confessor, "till the blood was seen in his clothes."[1] Stern to himself, he was yet of a deeply loving nature—a man certainly very lovable and human, with keen and wide interests, and a gentle, kindly heart. The trifles of Court observance were irksome to him. "It is wonderful how negligent he is," wrote Erasmus in 1519, "as regards all the ceremonious forms in which most men make politeness to consist. He does not require them from others, nor is he anxious to use them himself in conversation or in feastings, though he is not ignorant of their use. But he thinks it unmanly to spend much time in such trifling. Once he was most adverse to attendance at Court, for he hates tyrants,[2] and he loves equality. It was only with much trouble that he was drawn to King Henry's Court, though nothing more gentle and unassuming than that King can be wished for. By nature he is fond of freedom and of leisure; yet though he enjoys leisure, no one is more watchful and patient when business demands."[3]

His first wife, whom there is little doubt— whether we accept the description of a good woman in his Latin poems[4] as applying to her or not— that he devotedly loved, died about six years after her marriage, and in a very short time the needs of his motherless children induced him to marry

---

[1] See the letter discovered in the Public Record Office and published by Mr. James Gairdner in the *English Historical Review*, Oct. 1892: and Wordsworth's *Eccl. Biogr.* ii. **82**.

[2] One thinks of the many epigrams *in tyrannos*.

[3] Erasm. *Epp.* x. **30**.

[4] *To Candidus, Epigrams*, ed. 1520, pp. 59—63.

again.[1] Within a month from her burial he came late on a Sunday night to his confessor, bringing a dispensation to be married next day "without any banns asking."[2] His second wife was a widow named Alice Middleton, whom he jestingly said was "nec bella nec puella."[3] It was reported that he had wooed her at first for a friend, and had married her rather at her suggestion than by his own desire. "No husband," said Erasmus, "ever gained from his wife by authority and severity so much obedience as More won by gentleness and pleasantry."[4] Several of the letters of his friends contain complimentary references to her. Ammonius, Latin secretary to Henry VIII., who was intimate both with More and Erasmus, writes to the latter in 1515, "Morus noster melitissimus cum sua facillima conjuge, quae nunquam tui meminit quin tibi bene precetur, et liberis ac universa familia pulcherime valet."[5]

Two years later More says to Erasmus, "My wife desires a million compliments, especially for your careful wish that she should live many years. She says she is the more anxious for this as she will have the longer to plague me."[6] Again, Erasmus, ridiculing, in 1518, the contemplated war against the Turks, with the Papal ordinances thereon— "prohibet Pontifex ne uxores absentium in bello donii voluptuentur, sed abstineant a cultus elegantia,

---

[1] "Within two or three years," Cres. More, p. 32. "Within a few months," Erasm. *Epp.* x. 30.

[2] *English Historical Review*, vii. 14 (as above).

[3] Erasm. *Epp. Ibid.*   [4] *Ibid.*

[5] *Letters and Papers, Henry VIII.* (Brewer), vol. ii. 477.

[6] 15 Dec. 1517: Erasm. *Epp.* App. 221. (Leyden edit. of *Works*, vol. iii. pt. 2.)

JOHN MORE

(SON OF SIR THOMAS MORE).

From the drawing by Holbein.

To face page 55.

ne utantur **sericis**, auro, aut gemmis aliis, fucum nullum attingant, vinum ne bibant, **jejunent alternis** diebus "—says, jokingly, that More's wife is so good that she would gladly obey these orders. Dame Alice, however, does not seem to have been entirely amiable. There are several stories recorded by Roper and Cresacre More which depict her as a careful but irritable housekeeper, fond of show, slow to appreciate her husband's wit, and too little in harmony with his deep spiritual religion. "Yet she proved a kind and careful stepmother to his children."[1] And with his children it was that More's heart lay.

His only son, John, has been supposed by several writers to have been of somewhat weak mind or character. Their conjecture has the support of a saying of Sir Thomas, that his mother "had prayed so long for a boy that she brought forth one at last that would be a boy as long as he lived." On the other hand, his face in Holbein's portrait is refined and intellectual, and he is represented with a book, as a student. In one of his father's letters there occurs a marked commendation of his diligence and ability.[2] "My son John's letter pleaseth me best, both because it was longer than the others, and because that he seems to me to have taken more pains than the rest: for he not only pointeth at the matter becomingly and speaketh elegantly, but he playeth also pleasantly with me and returneth my jests upon me again very wittily. And this he doth not

---

[1] Cres. More, p. 32.   [2] Stapleton, x. p. 258.

only pleasantly but temperately withal, showing that
he is mindful with whom he jesteth,—his father,
whom he endeavoureth so to delight that he is also
afraid to offend." Erasmus, too, speaks of him in
complimentary terms, and in 1531 dedicated to him
a translation of Aristotle.[1] He was married in 1519
to Anne Cresacre, daughter and heiress of Edward
Cresacre of Barnborough, Yorkshire, a ward of the
King,[2]—by an arrangement usual in those times.
A mistake, however, is said to have occurred in this
selection, and it has been conjectured that the
damsel whom John More should have married was
one of the four co-heiresses of Sir John Dynham, to
whom the other part of Barnborough belonged.[3]

More's eldest daughter, Margaret, was remarkable
both for learning and virtue. References to her
ability are constant in the correspondence of the
happier years of her father's life, and the memory of
her devoted attachment is indissolubly linked with
the sad story of his death. She married, about 1520,
William Roper, son of Sir John Roper, a protho-
notary of the King's Bench, and "a man of good
fortune and blameless morals and with an inclination to learning,"[4] who wrote the singularly beautiful biography which has been frequently referred to.
"Margaret," says Cresacre More, "was likest her
father as well in favour as in wit."[5] Reginald Pole

---

[1] Walter's *Life of More*, p. 56.   [2] Cres. More, p. 31.

[3] *Hunter*, preface to his edit. of Cres. More : *q. v.* also for a
further account of John More. See also the list of his children
in the entries in his book of Hours. Auction catalogue of
Books of Baron v. Druffel, Munster, 1894.

[4] Stapleton, cap. v. p. 118.   [5] Cres. More, p. 139.

was once conversing with Sir Thomas when he received a letter from her. It was shown to the brilliant young scholar, who was astonished at it, and professed himself unable to believe that it had been the unaided composition of a woman.[1] The Bishop of Exeter on a similar occasion was equally delighted.[2] But no one gave her praise more judiciously or more gladly than More himself.[3]

Elizabeth, the second daughter, married a Mr. Dauncey, of whom we hear nothing but that on one occasion he complained of his father-in-law, when Chancellor, showing him no favour, and was justly reproved.[4] A special passage in Elizabeth's praise occurs in one of More's letters—" I take joy to hear that my daughter Elizabeth hath shown as great modesty in her mother's absence as any one could do if she had been present : let her know that that thing pleased me more than all the letters."[5]

Cicely, the youngest daughter, was as carefully taught as the others. She married Giles, son and heir of Sir John Heron, to whom Sir Thomas had been appointed guardian by the King in 1523 and 1524.[6] Giles Heron also seems to have expected countenance in an unjust suit from his father-in-law, but to have been met by a " flat decree against him."[7]

We have a charming illustration of More's affection

---

[1] Stapleton, cap. x. p. 263 ; cap. xi. pp. 266, 267, 268, etc.
[2] Roper, p. 25.   [3] Stapleton, cap. x. p. 253.
[4] Roper, p. 25.   [5] Stapleton, cap. x. p. 253.
[6] See grants dated March 5, 1523, and May 8, 1524, in Brewer, *Letters and Papers, Henry VIII.*, vol. iii. 2900 ; vol. iv. 314.   [7] Roper, p. 25.

for his children in his poetical epistle to them,[1]
written when he was away on an embassy.　We
see from these tender verses how deeply he entered
into all their pleasures, how gladly anticipated their
desires, how sorrowfully reproved their faults.

> "Ah ferus est, dicique pater non ille meretur
> Qui lachrymas nati non fleat ipse sui."

Besides his own children there were his wife's
daughter Alice, "a girl of great beauty and talent," [2]
who married the son of Sir Giles Alington, and who
was devotedly attached to her stepfather, and an
orphan girl named Margaret Giggs, receiving the
same education, and as deeply loved by More.

For instruction there were always learned masters
in the house at Chelsea.　At first there was a little
boy, John Clement, whose marvellous proficiency in
study is noted with delight in the earlier letters
between More and Erasmus,[3] and who afterwards
married Margaret Giggs and became a learned
physician and "reader of the phisicke-lecture at
Oxford."　To him succeeded William Gunnel, a Cambridge scholar of celebrity, and others named Drue,
Nicholas, and Hart.　To the first of these a most
interesting letter of More's has been preserved by
Stapleton,[4] in which his scheme of education is
drawn out, and great stress laid on the care that

---

[1] *Epigrammata* (2nd edit. Basil, 1520), p. 110.　Seebohm,
pp. 421, 422 ; and *Philomorus.*
[2] Erasmus, *Epp.* xvii. 16.
[3] Brewer, ii. 1552 ; Erasm. *Epp.* App. 52. (Leyden edit. of
Works, vol. iii. pt. 2.)　See also *Utopia*, p. 23, and Cres.
More, p. 126.　　　　　　　　　　　　　[4] Cap. x. p. 253.

should be taken lest the children should become proud of their learning or ability. Of Drue and Nicholas the following mention occurs in another letter.[1] "I rejoice that Master Drue is returned safe, of whose safety you know I was careful. If I loved you not exceedingly I should envy this your so great happiness, to have had so many great scholars for your masters. For I think Master Nicholas is with you also, and that you have learned of him much Astronomy; so that I hear that you have proceeded so far in this science that you now know not only the pole-star, the dog, and such like of the common constellations, but also — which argueth an absolute and cunning astronomer—the chief planets themselves; and you are able to discern the sun from the moon."

Besides More's children, who after their marriages still lived with their father and brought up their own children under his roof, at last he had eleven grandchildren to form a new "school." The family included also his father, Sir John More, who, in 1519, married a third wife,[2] and who lived in full possession of his faculties and in active discharge of his judicial duties till 1531. Of the filial reverence paid to him by his son many anecdotes are told, of which the most famous is that preserved by Roper.[3] "Whensoever he passed through Westminster Hall to his place in the Chancery, by the court of the King's Bench, if his father, one of the judges there, had been satte ere he came, he would

---

[1] *More to his whole School*, Stapleton, cap. x. p. 257.
[2] Erasm. *Epp.* x. 30.   [3] Page 26.

go into the same court and there reverently kneeling downe in the sight of them all duely aske his father's blessing."

The fullest contemporary description of this happy household is the famous letter of Erasmus to Ulrich von Hutten. It has formed the groundwork of the pictures of all the biographers. There is another letter of the great Dutch scholar to the learned French humanist, Budaeus, which is not so frequently quoted. A passage may here be given which has an interest of its own as bearing upon the educational movement of the age. "It has been said that learning is unfavourable to common sense. There is no greater reader than More, and yet you will not find a man who is more complete master of all his faculties, on all occasions, and with all persons, more accessible, more ready to oblige, more quick-witted in conversation, or who combines such true prudence with such agreeable manners. His influence has been such that there is scarce a nobleman in the land who considers his children fit for their rank unless they have been well-educated, and learning has become fashionable at Court. I once thought with others that learning was quite useless to the female sex. More has quite changed my opinion. . . . Nor do I see why husbands should fear lest a learned wife should be less obedient, except they would exact from their wives what should not be exacted from honest and virtuous dames." He goes on to talk of the uselessness of sermons to foolish women, and adds — "More's daughters, and such as they, can form an opinion on what they have heard and discriminate the good from the bad." He concluded with an anecdote—that he had once told More that he would grieve with greater sorrow if he lost his daughters upon whom he had bestowed so much care, and was answered—"If they are to die, I would rather they died learned than ignorant." [1]

Among More's household a word must be given to the steward and the fool. John Harris, "a man of good understanding and judgment, and a very trusty servant," [2] was often consulted by More "in his greatest affairs and studies." Henry Pattison, the fool, was deeply attached to his master. An interesting passage in the *Utopia* well illustrates his position in More's household. "They [the Utopians] have singular delight and pleasure in fools: and as it is a great reproach to do any of them hurt or injury, so they prohibit not to take pleasure of foolishness. For that, they think, doth much good to the fools. And if any man be so sad and stern that he cannot laugh neither at their words, nor at their deeds, none of them be committed to his tuition; for fear lest he should not entreat them gently and favourably enough, to whom they should bring no delectation (for other goodness in them is none), much less any profit should they yield him." [3] An anecdote of Pattison, which has been preserved by Ellis Heywood, shows that he was one of those jesters who owed their position as much to infirmity as wit. One day he was standing by the table when More

---

[1] Erasm. *Epp.* xvii. 16; Brewer, iii. 1527.
[2] Cres. More, p. 27.   [3] *Utopia*, p. 126.

was dining, and, noticing that one of the guests had a remarkably large nose, after he had gazed upon it for some time, suddenly exclaimed—"What a terrific nose that gentleman has!" When all pretended not to hear him, Pattison saw that he had made a mistake, and tried to set himself right by saying, "How I lied in my throat when I said that that gentleman's nose was so monstrously large. On the faith of a gentleman, it is in reality rather a small one." At this the company with difficulty restrained their laughter, and More made signs that the fool should be turned out of the room. But Pattison, who had a great opinion of his own powers of bringing everything to a happy conclusion, determined to recover his credit by a great effort, placed himself in More's seat at the head of the table, and called out—"There is one thing I would have you know—that gentleman has not the least atom of a nose."[1]

Erasmus says that so admirable was the management of the household—for no idleness was allowed, but some worked in the garden, others sang or played instruments,[2] but none were allowed cards or dice—so careful the training, "that there was happiness fated for the servants of that house; none lived but in better estate after More's death; none ever was touched with the least aspersion of any evil fame."[3] Such was the happy household which had grown up around More in his home at Chelsea, whither he had removed from Bucklersbury after

---

[1] Ellis Heywood, *Il Moro* (Florence, 1556), pp. 52, 53.
[2] Cres. More, p. 91.   [3] Stapleton, cap. ix. p. 249.

his first wife's death. The house was situated about a hundred yards from the Thames, at the north end of Beaufort Row, and remained standing for more than two centuries after his death, until it was at last pulled down by Sir Hans Sloane.

Ellis Heywood, in introducing a dialogue on the sources of happiness, supposed to take place in More's garden, has given a beautiful description of the scene and of the man.[1]

"Along the banks of the Thames there are many fine houses and castles situated in beautiful spots, in one of which dwelt Sir Thomas More, 'huomo per la sua virtù assai conosciuto.' It was a splendid and comfortable residence, and to this place it was his custom to retire when weary of the city. There, both because of its nearness to London and of the admirable character of its owner, men distinguished for wit and learning who dwelt in the city were accustomed frequently to meet; where when alone and at ease they would enter into some argument or discourse on things pertaining to human life; and, since each used as he could his intellect and knowledge, their arguments were attended with great profit to each other." One day he tells us that six friends, who had dined with More, "retired after dinner into the garden, distant about two stone-throws from the house, and all went together to stand upon a small green mound. . . . From one part almost the whole of the noble city of London was visible, and from another the beautiful Thames, with green meadows and wooded hills all around."

[1] *Il Moro*, p. 9, *et seq.*

The scene too "had a charm of its own. It was crowned with an almost perpetual verdure, and had flowering shrubs and the branches of fruit trees that grew near interwoven in a manner so beautiful that it seemed like a living tapestry worked by Nature herself." There the friends discussed in true Renaissance fashion one of the common topics of humanistic inquiry.

To this house so rare in beauty, external and spiritual, there were naturally many visitors. Never came there to London a poor student from Oxford or Cambridge but he was sure of a welcome at Chelsea. "Quem ille vel mediocriter eruditum ab se dimisit indonatum?" says one of More's friends. "Aut quis fuit tam alienus, de quo non studierit bene mereri? Multi non favent nisi suis, Galli Gallis, Germani Germanis, Scoti Scotis: at ille in Hybernos, in Germanos, in Gallos, in Scythas et Indos amico fuit animo."[1] And besides such stray guests there were the old and tried friends, who, when they could not be at Chelsea, preserved their memory of More by constant letters. Erasmus, who had made so firm a friendship with him in his youth, loved him till his death. He had spent several weeks in the house at Bucklersbury, during the first year of More's married life. There he completed that biting satire, whose punning title was to be a remembrance of the friend who sympathized so warmly with its method, and whose presence was to the author "more sweet than any

---

[1] *Epistola fidelis de morte Thomae Mori.* Cf. also Roper, p. 13 ; Cres. More, p. 59.

thing in life." [1] The *Encomium Moriae* gives a very clear insight into the feelings with which the purer spirits of those eventful years looked upon the confusion of the world in which they lived. As an exposition of the fears and the aspirations of the two friends it may well be regarded as a sportive prologue to the more serious work *Utopia*. Its appearance was naturally not unnoticed or its matter uncondemned : and More came forward to defend it.

It was a happy idea to send Folly abroad with her caps and bells to satirize the grossness and the ignorance that wise men noted and Popes seemed to wink at. It was the first attempt of the new humanism to treat the absurdities of decadent scholasticism and decaying religion in a popular style. In *Moria* Erasmus spoke *ad populum*,[2] as in the *Novum Instrumentum*, four years later,[3] he spoke *ad clerum*. It was the hasty work of a few days' writing, and the iron was red-hot on which it so sharply struck. Folly is the mistress and teacher of the world, he cried ; and most of all she dwells among philosophers and theologians and monks. She is never so much

[1] Preface to *Encomium Moriae*.

[2] The learned writer of an extremely able and valuable article in the *Quarterly Review*, January 1895, states that none "of Erasmus's works" appeal *ad populum*. But I think it is accurate to say that the *Moria* and the *Colloquies* certainly appeal to a wide public.

[3] Mr. Froude states wrongly (*Erasmus*, p. 122) that the *Encomium Moriae* "was brought out almost simultaneously with an edition of the New Testament." Probably he was confusing the former with Erasmus's edition of *S. Jerome*, which appeared in 1516.

F

at home as when she teaches her children to explain
the mysteries of faith and to justify the practices of
superstition. To her is due the belief in the miraculous working of images, in indulgences as bills drawn
upon the spiritual treasury of the Church, in the
automatic efficacy of vain repetitions of sacred offices.
The questions, he says, that belong to "illuminated"
theologians are such as these—"Does the category
of time belong to the Divine generation? Is there
more than one relation of filiation in Christ?
Whether the proposition God the Father hates the
Son can be maintained? Whether God could be
hypostatically united to a woman, the devil, an ass,
a gourd, a flint?"[1] And then he bitterly adds, "no
doubt they devoutly consecrated the Eucharist,"
little as they were competent to define the doctrine.
Nor was he content to deal with generalities—monks
in their ignorant idleness, friars in their dirt and
buffoonery, cardinals in their avarice, even Pope
Julius II. himself in his mad scheming for power, all
come under the lash of Folly. Not only obscurantism
was scourged, but every form of spiritual wickedness
in high places. And who could answer? Might not
Folly speak, and should wise men reply?

It was a masterly book—and its strength lay not a
little in the fact that it was an appeal from a be-
sotted Theology to a Religion that had learnt to keep
its eyes open, and from the false scholasticism to
the true. It was certainly not intended "to turn

---

[1] I venture to use, with a slight alteration, the translation
of this passage given in the article already referred to in the
Quarterly Review, January 1895.

the whole existing system of Theology into ridicule:"[1] it was a protest on behalf of that system against the ignorance of those who professed to interpret it.

Such, very briefly, was the book which Erasmus wrote in More's house. It was the fruit of their talks together, and it came more nearly than anything else that the two friends did to be a piece of fellow-work. Erasmus wrote it; More defended it —and they both spoke as loyal sons of the Catholic Church. And the rulers of the Church spoke no word of condemnation. Julius himself did not protest, and his successor, Leo X., spoke of the book with admiration and delight.

The work of Folly ended, the two friends turned aside to more serious business—More to his *Utopia*, and Erasmus to *S. Jerome* and the New Testament. In the former the great Dutch scholar was to range himself on the side of the Fathers in the questions that were soon to be debated by the world; in the latter he was to appeal to the critical study of the Bible as the one true basis of the Church's doctrine. Erasmus did not give the Bible to an ignorant age. " Popular stories of the Bible being unknown, of the total indifference of the friars to learning, rest like most popular stories on vulgar credulity."[2] He was attacked not because he revealed mysteries to the vulgar, but because of his audacity in attempting to revise the Vulgate, and because it was said he could

---

[1] Froude, *Erasmus*, p. 124.
[2] Brewer, *Reign of Henry VIII.*, i. 287 ; contrast Froude's *Erasmus*, pp. 112, 113.

neither translate nor comment with accuracy upon Holy Writ. Not as an iconoclast, but as the father of modern exegesis, it was that he needed, and found, a defender in the educated orthodoxy of More.

From the time of the completion of the *Encomium Moriae* until July 1514, Erasmus remained in England, and the friends saw each other constantly. Erasmus was principally at Cambridge; and between him and More several interesting letters passed. In December 1510, we find an epistle from the Dutch to the English scholar, detailing the difficulties which he met with in the study of Greek from the ignorant Masters at Cambridge, and urging the English humanist to throw his weight into the scale in favour of the New Learning.[1]

Writing in August 1511, to Ammonius, Erasmus complains of More's negligent correspondence, but says that he would be unreasonable indeed if he did not pardon him, as he is now immersed in grave business.[2] The letters of this year show also the intimate connexion between Ammonius, whose praise of the household at Chelsea has already been mentioned, and the two friends. During the long vacation of 1511, while Erasmus was in London, Ammonius was staying with More, and there was much regret that they chanced to miss each other,[3] but the scholar hoped to meet the diplomatist in January, when he would find London more pleasant than Cambridge.[4] The letters of the same period contain constant references also to the intimacy

---

[1] Erasm. *Epp.* vii. 15.
[2] *Ibid. Epp.* viii. 1.
[3] *Ibid.* viii. 2 ; viii. 23.
[4] *Ibid.* viii. 7.

existing between Warham, Fisher, Colet—who was then busy with his new school—and More. For a time the correspondence almost ceased. More was deep in business: his work at the Bar increased rapidly, and he had been made under-sheriff of London. He was being slowly drawn too into the service of the Court, and what leisure he had was given to the composition of his *History of Richard III.*, and afterwards to the preparation of his *Utopia.* After a while the circle of friends gathered again around him, as after his second marriage he removed to Chelsea. In May 1515, he was sent on a mission to Bruges, which will be mentioned more fully in connexion with his political life. Meanwhile Erasmus had left England, and had been deeply engaged in literary work, having completed—besides many books of very different sorts — his great *Novum Testamentum.*

More, on his return to England, at the successful termination of his embassy, wrote to him in February 1516,[1] complaining that he had only written thrice since he left England. "Were I to lie with most solemn countenance," he continues, "and swear I had replied to you as often, it is ten to one you would not believe me; especially as you know me so well, how idle I am in answering letters, and not so superstitiously veracious as to reckon every white lie as black as murder." More's return to Court is mentioned by Ammonius in a letter to Erasmus on the 17th of the same month,[2] and his devotion to Wolsey noticed. Writing a few

[1] Brewer, ii. 1512.　　　　[2] *Ibid.* ii. 1551.

days later, More sent £20 from Warham, perhaps in answer to the verses which he had addressed to him on the appearance of his friend's New Testament. The archbishop, said More, had made the great work possible for Erasmus.

> " Hanc petit ille sui fructum, Pater alme, laboris,
> Charus ut hoc tu sis omnibus, ille tibi."

In the autumn of the same year Erasmus came to England, and during his visit—he was staying principally with Fisher at Rochester—constant letters of the old mirthful style passed between him and More. The chief part of the *Utopia* had now been finished, and the first or introductory portion was being prepared. On November 12, Gerard Bronchorst, a scholar of Nimeguen, wrote to Erasmus that he had arranged for Thierry, who was bringing out the *Institutio Principis Christiani*, to publish the *Utopia*.

It appeared at the end of 1516, and at once achieved an enormous success. More, known before to a wide circle of friends as possessed of great talents, became a man of European fame. Before three months had passed, a new edition was being thought of. On March 1, 1517, Erasmus wrote to More, sending him Reuchlin's works, and saying that as soon as the MS. had been revised he would send it to Basle or Paris.[1] It was decided that the second edition should be published at Basle; and, on August 25, Erasmus wrote from Louvain to the great printer, Froben, sending him the *Utopia* and *Epigrams*, with a warm eulogy of More. He rejoices,

---

[1] Erasm. *Epp.* vii. 16.

says the letter, to see the high opinion he always held now confirmed by all the learned. What, he adds, might not this great genius, now overwhelmed by political and domestic cares, have accomplished had he been educated in Italy, or devoted himself entirely to letters?[1]

More wrote to Erasmus on September 3, sending a revised copy, and giving suggestions as to the contemplated publication of his *Epigrams*.[2] Meanwhile a second edition of the *Utopia* had been brought out at Paris by Lupset, with an eulogistic epistle from Budaeus; and the Basle edition appeared in November.

On October 7, More wrote again to his friend,[3] having received a picture of Erasmus and Petrus Ægidius, sent him by the latter,[4] and said with great simplicity and feeling, that if there was one thought of ambition in his mind it was the pleasure he felt in knowing that his name would always hereafter be associated with that of Erasmus. The correspondence was now constant; not only did the two friends write on every subject of interest, but More was of great use to Erasmus in business affairs, such as the matter of his pension from Warham, paid through the banker Maruffo.[5]

At the beginning of 1518, Erasmus utters a plaintive regret that More, "though he will serve

---

[1] Brewer, ii. 3627.

[2] Erasm. *Epp.* App. 174. (Leyden edit. of *Works*, vol. iii. pt. 2.)   [3] Erasm. *Epp.* App. 193.

[4] See his verses thereon (*Epigrams*). Brewer suggests that it was by Quintin Matsys.

[5] *E. g.* Brewer, ii. 2004 ; ii. 2367 ; ii. 2409.

the best of kings," is, by his employment at Court, lost to him and to letters.[1] The fame of the discoverer of *Utopia* had now become so great that men were anxious to hear of his private life, and in July 1519, Erasmus had to write to Ulrich von Hutten a description of how perfectly the ideal state was pictured in little in More's household at Chelsea— a letter to which frequent reference has already been made. At the same time More was defending his friend against the attacks of the more bigoted and ignorant of the clergy. A monk had written to him, warning him lest he should be corrupted by associating with the contemner of the Vulgate. More immediately replied.[2] He would be indeed ungrateful, he said, if he did not thank his correspondent who dashes over rocks and precipices at the imminent hazard of his life to save More from stumbling, who is leisurely walking in perfect security on level ground.

That one who had been so candid should become a violent partisan was indeed a wonder to the gentle soul of More.[3] The monk has been his "dearest

---

[1] Erasm. *Epp.* App. 311. (Leyden edit. of *Works*, vol. iii. pt. 2.)

[2] Epistolae aliquot eruditorum virorum. Basil, 1520, pp. 92—138. Jortin's *Erasmus*, iii. 365 *sqq.* See also Froude's *Erasmus*, p. 135 *sqq.*, an extremely inaccurate version, entirely altering the tone of More's letter, which is one of temperate and friendly remonstrance.

[3] It need hardly be said that More's Latin does not contain the words, "Before you were a priest you had candour and charity ; now that you have become a monk some devil has possession of you." The Latin also by no means warrants some of the worst charges that Mr. Froude appears to make More bring against monks.

friend," but no less dear was Erasmus; and the cause of truth, with which his great work seemed to be indissolubly connected, was dearer still. It is clear that More felt both that the question of the study of Greek was vital alike to Christianity and to learning, and also that the enmity of the monastic clergy to the new studies, and in particular to Erasmus, alike in his serious and in his satirical writing, was based only on ignorance, and could be overcome by a temperate and intelligent statement of the case from a learned and Catholic layman. More, throughout his very lengthy letter, argues that it is Erasmus not his opponents who represents the mind of the Church, and points the contrast between the good work he was doing and the wickedness of those who distorted Scripture and those who used the rules of their orders only as the groundwork of debate and faction. A friend of Erasmus and of More himself in his youth, the monk who received this appeal may well have been won over to see the New Learning in a new light. The names of Colet, Fisher, Warham, Mountjoy, Pace and Grocyn — representing in such different stations the wide influence of the movement—may well have brought him to see that Erasmus was the friend, not the enemy, of the Church. And so More leaves him, and it must have been in sadness. His whole tone shows the intensity with which he felt the brute force of the dense ignorance with which the Church Reformers had to contend; and he felt it most when he wrote this letter, for just then his dear friend, the most enthusiastic and impetuous, yet the saintliest, of the new party, had passed away. John Colet died on September 15, 1519. "For centuries," said More, "we have not had among us any man more learned or more holy."

More, Colet, and Erasmus had felt for each other as perhaps none others at the time had felt, and their characters had strengthened each other where they most needed support. Colet's holiness had been an inspiration to Erasmus, his perfect sanity of judgment a wise restraint on More. Now the two friends who were left were drawn more closely together by the loss of him they loved.

In 1520, their correspondence was chiefly concerned with the testy French poet Brixius, and we may leave the mention of it till we treat of the Epigrams which refer to him. But the year also served to turn More's thoughts into another channel. He was forsaking literature for politics, and the change is clearly reflected in his correspondence. Instead of weekly or monthly letters to Erasmus, he wrote almost daily to Wolsey. Political and religious troubles were thickening around him, and he was being forced into practical contact with those great problems which in the *Utopia* he had examined from a distance. In 1525, Erasmus wrote to him to make up some quarrel that had arisen with Polydore Vergil, the historian.[1] At last More broke his silence, and writing on December 18, 1525,[2] acknow-

---

[1] The letter is lost, but that of Erasmus to Polydore Vergil is *Epp.* p. 888.

[2] Erasm. *Epp.* App. 334. (Leyden edit. of *Works*, vol. iii. pt. 2.)　Brewer, iv. 1826.

ledged that he had left several letters **unanswered**. Anxious thoughts—the progress of Lutheran opinions and the King's answer to the heretic's book, **the** terrible *Bauernkrieg*, **and** Erasmus's **own** illness— **weighed** upon him, yet **he did not** forget to promise **his best** help **to** Holbein, whom his friend had recently committed **to his** charge. Then follows another break in the correspondence. At length, in February 1528,[1] Erasmus wrote to More speaking of Henry VIII.'s request to him to return to England, but complaining that **there was** no **hope of peace** but in the grave. The new development **of Ana**-baptist doctrines—more widespread, **he declares, than** any one conjectures—filled him **with horror.** In the next year Erasmus received Holbein's sketch for the picture of More's family, and immediately wrote to Margaret Roper **to** express his delight.[2] "Methought," he said, "I saw shining through this beautiful household a soul even more beautiful"; and he sent **the** warmest messages to **the** kinsfolk **in their** home.

Then another **pause occurs.** More, as Chancellor, was overweighted with work, religious and secular, and the letters to **his** friend, **so** constant in the happy, peaceful portion of **his life, ceased** altogether. But when he resigned the office **which** had become daily more and more irksome to him, he at once resumed the correspondence. On June 5, 1532, More gave **up the** great seal into the hands of the King; **two days later he wrote to** tell the story

---

[1] Erasm. *Epp.* p. 1062. (Leyden edit. of *Works*, **vol. iii. pt. 2.)**
[2] *Ibid. Epp.* **p.** 1232 (*ibid.*).

to Erasmus,[1] rejoicing in being freed from public
affairs, that he might live only to God and himself.
Yet even then he thought most of the religious
troubles, and his letter is almost entirely taken up
with fears of the progress of heresy. Erasmus sent
the letter to John, Bishop of Vienne, with a high
eulogium of the writer. At the beginning of the
next year More wrote again,[2] thanking Erasmus
for two letters, expressing his joy that Cranmer,
the new archbishop, was as favourable to his friend
as Warham had been, and dwelling with pathetic
emphasis on the bitterness of public reports. But
"so long as God approves of my doings I do not
care what men say," was his conclusion, and might
well be the motto of his life. The misery of his
last days was now upon him; and thus in silence
the well-tried friendship ended. "Men can neither
speak nor hold their peace without danger," wrote
Vives to Erasmus, when telling him of More's imprisonment. Letters passed constantly between the
great foreign scholar and his English friends. To
More himself it was dangerous to write, but in his
silence Erasmus thought the more deeply; and when
at length More fell a victim to the King's policy and
passion, his voice was the keenest and most bitter
that was raised in execration of the deed.

The intimate and long - continued friendship
between More and Erasmus is a significant fact in
the history of the Reformation. It shows that in

---

[1] Erasm. *Epp.* p. 1856.

[2] *Ibid. Epp.* p. 1432. (Leyden edit. of *Works*, vol. iii.
pt. 2.) Stapleton, c. vii. p. 231.

the minds of the clearest thinkers of the day there
was no necessary opposition between Religion and
Humanism, between the Catholic Faith and the
internal reforms which the Church's organization
was everywhere felt to need. When it is sought to
paint More as a convinced and constant supporter
of the whole system of the unreformed Church and
the medieval Papacy, it can only be by ignoring his
consistent friendship with the sharpest of its critics.
He knew as well as his friend the stern truth of
many charges against monastic discipline, to which
Popes themselves listened in silence, and the voice
of *Moria* was little less his than that of the man
who actually gave it to the world. It is impossible
to read More's writings with an unbiassed mind
without feeling that he, who laid down his life for
the Church, yet felt to the full the horror and the
danger of her corruptions. His satires against
worldliness and ignorance among the clergy are as
keen as those of Erasmus, if they are less numerous.
Yet he died in persistent opposition to a Lutheran
or an Erastian Revolution. Was he inconsistent?
Erasmus did not think so. Together they had
thought, in mirth and yet half tearfully, of the
wounds the Church was receiving in the house of
her friends, and, when death came to one of them,
in heart they were not divided. "Erasmus, my
darling," said his life-long friend, " is my dear darling
still."

Next to this classic friendship, More owed most to
the companionship of Colet. When they both lived
in London they often met—and thus few traces of

their connexion, which **their letters** might have given, are preserved.   More aided Colet in the founding of his school by advice and inquiry.   Little more do we know of their common work.   Theirs was a peaceful friendship, into which no disturbing element entered, for Colet died before More had been drawn into the troubles of the time.

Among other scholars whose friendship More had first known at Oxford, we find occasional reference in his later life to Grocyn, Lilly, whom Colet sought as master of his school, and Linacre, and a few humorous notices of William Latimer.

Warham was a friend rather of Erasmus than of More, but the latter was constantly a means of communication between the archbishop and the Dutch scholar.   From no man had the earlier efforts of the two friends met with warmer encouragement. The letter which More wrote to him on his resignation of the Chancellorship was friendly as well as respectful.[1]   After compliments on his conduct of the office and expressions of sympathy with his intention in resigning it, he lays before the archbishop, in modest phrase, his own "little book," which had just been published. "Though fully aware how unworthy it is of your dignity, learning, and experience, yet, knowing your candour and indulgence to every endeavour of mine, I have summoned up courage enough to send it to you; and, should the writing be deemed of little worth, the writer is anxious to find favour."

Cuthbert Tunstal, Master of the Rolls, his com-

____
[1] Stapleton, cap. 7.

panion in his first embassy, occupied a place next
to Erasmus in More's heart.[1] The references to
him in the letters are always most affectionate;
and of no man has More left on record a higher
opinion. In the Epitaph which he wrote for himself he refers with pride to his having been joined
in embassy with one "than whom the whole world
hath not a man more learned, wise, or good." The
name of Tunstal also has been immortalized in
the first book of the *Utopia*.[2] But the amplest
memorial of their friendship is contained in two
letters of More's.[3] " Although every letter I receive
from you, dearest friend, is very pleasant to me, yet
that which you wrote last was most welcome, for,
besides the other praises which the rest of your letters
deserve for their eloquence, this last yields a peculiar
grace, for that it contains your own opinion (I would
that it were as true as it is favourable) of my
Utopia. . . . I almost persuade myself that all
those things which you speak of it are true, knowing
you to be far from all dissimulation, and myself too
humble to need flattery and too dear to you to be
mocked. Wherefore, whether you have seen the
truth unfeignedly, I rejoice in your judgment, or
whether your affection to me hath blinded your
judgment, I am no less delighted by your love." Or,
again, "The amber which you sent me—being a
precious sepulchre of flies—was in many respects
most welcome to me; for the matter thereof may

---

[1] Erasm. *Epp.* App. 150. (Leyden edit. of *Works*, vol. iii.
pt. 2.)   [2] Page 27.

[3] Stapleton, C. G., p. 201, *et seq.*

bear comparison in colour and brightness with any precious stone, and the form is more excellent because it represents the figure of a heart, as it were the emblem of our love; from which I take your meaning to be that between us it will never fly away, and yet be always without corruption; because I see the fly —which hath wings like Cupid, and is as fickle—so shut up and enclosed in the amber that it cannot fly away, and so embalmed and preserved that it cannot perish. I am not so much as once troubled that I cannot send you a like gift; for I know you do not expect an interchange of tokens."

That Tunstal fully reciprocated More's affection is seen in his dedication to him of his treatise *De Arte Supputandi.* "When I considered to which of all my friends I should dedicate their collection, I thought you the most fit, because of the tender friendship which of a long time hath been between us, and of the sincerity of your mind."

Another of More's friends was Richard Pace, hardly less famous as a scholar than as a diplomatist. He had been educated in Italy, and there had become acquainted with Erasmus, Tunstal, and William Latimer,[1] through whom he gained the friendship of More. Writing in February 1516,[2] to Erasmus, More says that Pace is away on an embassy: and thus, missing both Pace and Erasmus, he has " lost both parts of himself." How fully he returned this affection Pace showed in his book, *De Fructu qui*

---

[1] Brewer, vol. iv., preface p. liv.
[2] *Ibid.* ii. 1552. Cf. also Erasm. *Epp.* 1097. (Leyden edit. of *Works*, vol. iii.)

ex Doctrinâ Percipitur,[1] which contains one of the earliest public recognitions of More's remarkable genius. "His ability in the rapid understanding of Greek," he says, "may be part, perhaps, of the art of any grammarian; but he has far more than this, —genius; for his ability is something more than human."

More's friendship with Fisher, confirmed and hallowed at the last by suffering, was begun in earlier and happier years, when many a jest passed between them.[2] Among More's younger friends Lupset and Pole claim a word of notice. The former, a pupil of Colet and friend of Erasmus, was a welcome guest at Chelsea.[3] By him the second edition of the *Utopia*, a reprint of the first, was brought out at Paris in 1517.[4] Through him we find More corresponding with Budaeus.[5] On no one do More's talents and virtues seem to have made a greater impression than on Reginald Pole. When More was ill on one occasion, Pole, then at Oxford with John Clement, sent him the opinions of the most learned physicians in the University, and wrote to his mother, the proud Countess of Salisbury, to make up the prescription.[6] Sir Thomas acknowledged the courtesy in a cordial letter.[7]

Pole was deeply impressed by the beauty of More's character, and it was his indignation at his friend's

---

[1] Basil : 1517, p. 82.

[2] Stapleton prints two letters between them; c. v. p. 200. See also Brewer, ii. 3418.   [3] Erasm. *Epp.* viii. 15.

[4] Brewer, ii. 1162.   [5] Bud. *Epp.* 9.   Brewer, ii. 4421.

[6] *Life of Pole* (2nd edit. 1767), p. 67.

[7] Stapleton, cap v. p. 198 ; Cres. More, p. 69.

murder which cut off all hope of his restoration to
the favour of Henry VIII.[1]　To him Ellis Heywood in 1556 dedicated his commemorative study *Il
Moro*.[2]

More's friendships were not confined to English
scholars.　On his first embassy More made the
acquaintance of Jerome Busleiden (Buslidius) and
Peter Giles (Petrus Ægidius).　The former was a
very rich and hospitable scholar of Mechlin, founder
of the college of the Three Languages at Louvain.　Of him More wrote to Erasmus [3]—" Among
other things which delighted me much in my
embassy, not the least is that I made the acquaintance of Busleiden, who entertained me most court-
eously according to his great wealth and exceeding
good nature.　The elegance of his house, his
admirable domestic arrangements, the monuments
of antiquity which he possesses, wherein you know
I take great delight, and lastly his splendid library
and the fund of learning and eloquence which he
possesses in himself, completely astonished me."
To this subject he constantly returned, especially
in his *Epigrams*, where there are several poems
complimenting Buslidius on his coins, his medals,
and his beautiful house, and begging him to publish
his own Latin verses.　With Petrus Ægidius, who
was a magistrate of Antwerp and had been a pupil
of Erasmus,[4] More seems to have been equally

---

[1] See Pole's treatise *De Unitate Ecclesiae*, lib. i. p. 21.
[2] *Il Moro:* especially Dedication, p. 7.
[3] Stapleton, cap. v. p. 208.
[4] Rudhart, *Thomae Morus*, p. 153.

pleased; he was admitted, with Buslidius, as it were behind the scenes of the *Utopia*; the introductory epistle was addressed to him, and the most elaborate scheme of mystification concerning "Raphael Hythlodaye" was concocted between them.[1] The text of the book itself contains a high eulogium upon him, as a politician and as a friend.[2] Guillaume Budé (Budaeus) was another of the foreign scholars with whom the publication of the *Utopia* made More intimate. The French writer contributed a laudatory preface to Lupset's Paris edition of 1518. His works then came into the hand of More. On this a correspondence began which lasted during the next fifteen years, and they met once, when in attendance on Henry VIII. and Francis I. respectively. Writing in September 1518,[3] Budaeus thanks More for the gift of a pair of English greyhounds. He is still more pleased, he declares, with his letter, and says that More's name should be changed to Oxymorus. More replied in equally complimentary style.[4] To Budaeus, Erasmus wrote one of his long descriptions of More's academy, from which extracts have already been given.[5] In it he contrasted with shrewd humour the pains of a student's life as described by the French scholar, with its pleasures as expressed by More. "Budaeus complains that he has brought a scandal upon learning because it has entailed upon him two evils—ill health and ill husbandry. More, on the other hand, produces

---

[1] *Utopia*, pp. 21—26 : 163—66. [2] *Ibid.* p. 28.
[3] Bud. *Epp.* 9. [4] Stapleton, cap. v. p. 204.
[5] Erasm. *Epp.* xvii. 62.

the opposite impression. He says that his health
is the better for study—that he has more influence
with the King—more popularity at home and
abroad—is more pleasant and useful to his friends
and relations—abler for the business of life generally
—and more thankful to Heaven."

Buslidius, Ægidius, and Budaeus knew only by
repute of More's beautiful home life, but there were
many others who had seen it. Polydore Vergil,
Vives, and Antonio Bonvisi[1] may be considered as
naturalized Englishmen; but Hans Holbein from
his first arrival in England was the guest of More.
He came introduced by warm commendations from
Erasmus, and was already known to More not only
by his widespread fame, but by his illustrations to
Froben's exquisite edition of the *Utopia*. The
connexion between the English scholar and the
German painter is too interesting to be passed by
without a word of notice. Holbein had shown by
the skill with which he interpreted and expressed
the ideas of Erasmus in the *Encomium Moriae* that
he had a quick appreciation of literature in addition
to his technical power. He was known already as
the first artist of the age, and his skill was at the
command of Froben. He was obviously the fit man
to illustrate *Utopia*, and his work for the Basle

---

[1] For the connexion of these men with More, see Erasm.
Epp. App. 326 (Leyden edit. of *Works*, vol. iii. pt. 2), p. 888 ;
Vives, *opera*, vii. 180. Roper : **More's** Works, *passim*. Antonio
Bonvisi was godfather to one of his grandsons (Augustine, son
of John More). See *Book of Hours*, formerly in possession of
Baron von Druffel. He was a staunch friend to More till his
death.

edition has undoubtedly great merit. It lacks, however, the appropriateness of his *Encomium Moriae;* and, admirable as are the headpieces and initial letters, it is difficult to see, for instance, the object of a title-page representing Lucretia plunging a dagger into her bosom with Tarquin looking on, in fashion rather humorous than solemn.[1] The chart of the happy island is, however, admirable. Utopia stands in the midst of tempestuous seas, and is itself of a marvellously uneven surface. Three groups of houses are indicated, over each of which hangs a label from the clouds, *Amauroti urbs, Ostium anydri, Fons anydri.* In the foreground, on the main-land, stands Hythlodaye in mariner's boots, "his sea-gown girt about him," conversing with a learned doctor, and enforcing his remarks by much gesticulation. More was much pleased with the illustrations, and from this time frequent mention of Holbein occurs in his correspondence with Erasmus. The edition of the *Epigrams* which Froben brought out in 1520, has an elaborate title-page and tail-piece, as well as some rich initial letters from his hand. Porsenna interrogates Martius Scaevola, and *putti* like the bacchanals of Michelangelo blow trumpets and frisk upon the greensward above.

A few years later the painter was advised to visit England, and in 1525, Erasmus wrote letters to bespeak a welcome for him. More, replying from the royal palace at Greenwich (December 18, 1525), says—"Thy painter is a wonderful artist, but

---

[1] There is no explanation why Tarquin should be there at all.

I fear he will not find England as productive as
he hopes, although I will do the best, as far as I
am concerned, that he should not find it altogether
barren."[1]   Holbein left Basle in the autumn of
1526, and we hear of him in England in 1527.
Whether he was immediately or for the whole of
his sojourn the guest of More is uncertain, but he
undoubtedly spent a long time at Chelsea.[2]   He
was thus at once introduced at Court, and soon
found plenty of work.   One of his first pictures
seems to be the portrait of More, dated MDXXVII.
It is life-size, half-length, and the face and expression are depicted with the intense reality characteristic of Holbein's best work.[3]   Two drawings in the
Windsor collection are, in their way, equally admirable.   They may have been sketches for the known
portrait, or—as is more probable, since they are of the
same size and style as those of his father, his son,
and two of his daughters—studies for the large
picture of the More family which is now known only
through the original sketch and a number of later
copies.   It was probably in the same year (1527)
that Holbein at least began the picture.

The Baroness Burdett Coutts possesses an extremely striking portrait, which is not dated.   It
is probably not Holbein's work, but in details of
pose and costume—the furred cape, hat and collar
of S.S.—it resembles the other portraits.   The face,

---

[1] Erasm. *Epp.* App. 336. (Leyden edit. of *Works*, vol. iii.
pt. 2.)

[2] Vide *North Brit. Review*, vol. xxx. p. 102 *et seq*.

[3] It is now the property of Mr. Edward Huth.

ELIZABETH DANCY.

DAUGHTER OF SIR THOMAS MORE.

From the drawing by Holbein.

To face page 80.

however, is thinner and older than the Windsor drawings, and much darker in tone. It is unquestionably an original portrait, and is worthy of much more attention than it seems to have received from biographers.

A number of small portraits are to be found in English country houses,[1] most of them copies taken when More's martyrdom had made him greatly venerated. The great picture of the More family seems to be irreparably lost; but the authenticity of the sketch preserved in the Musée at Basle is unquestionable. This is undoubtedly the original design for the picture sent by More to Erasmus on Holbein's return to Basle, and acknowledged by him in the letter to Margaret Roper mentioned above. In this sketch More is seated in the middle, having his father on his right hand, and his son on his left. Behind him stands Anne Cresacre, further to his right Margaret Giggs holding an open book, and Elizabeth Dauncey drawing on a glove. Behind young John More stands Harris—or, as some say, Pattison; to More's left Cicely Heron and Margaret Roper, while slightly behind them Dame Alice, a portly woman, kneels before a *prie-dieu*, and is distracted in her devotion by a monkey. How far the sketch was reproduced in the picture is impossible to say; but it is probable from some of the manuscript notes on the drawing that Holbein intended to vary the details; and the known copies present such variations.

[1] One of the most interesting is in the possession of T. H. Cheatle, Esq., of Burford. In this the face is smaller, sharper, and more swarthy than in the better known works.

Two of the pictures demand special notice. Lord St. Oswald at Nostell Priory possesses a large copy, certainly taken in the sixteenth century, which gives probably the truest reproduction of the original that now exists.

In this the family are grouped in a circle. In the middle is Sir Thomas More in a dark furred gown with dog lying at his feet. His face is sad and slim and darkly shadowed, unlike the larger, clearer, and happier countenance of the brighter of the Windsor drawings. To his right sits his father in his red justice's robes—a hale and hearty old man, with a red and shining face. At his feet, too, lies a little dog. Next to Sir John is Sir Thomas's daughter, Elizabeth Dauncey, standing, and drawing on a glove; by her side, at the extreme left of the picture, is Margaret Giggs, the wife of John Clement, holding a book. There are sketches for both of these in the Windsor collection, erroneously entitled Lady Berkeley and Mother Jak. The pose and dress of Mrs. Clement differ in the picture from the drawing. Behind this group is a table with books, and a sideboard with tall grasses in a bowl, and a lute and flowers. Over More's head hangs a clock with long weights. By his right shoulder and behind him and his father stands Anne Cresacre, the betrothed of his son John, who stands also behind him, on his left, a delicate-looking lad reading a book. Sitting next to Sir Thomas is his daughter, Celia Heron, with a book, and by her side her sister Margaret Roper with the *Œdipus* of Seneca open on her lap. At the extreme right is Lady More, a comfortable but rather ugly-looking woman, **seated** in an arm-chair, a monkey plucking at **her gown.** Behind Lady More is a window with flowers and oranges on the sill. John Harris stands behind with papers, and by him Henry Pattison the fool—while in **the** far background a secretary sits writing in an inner room by a window. All the family wear dark clothes, except Sir John, who is in bright red. The servants are in yellow, and have their hats on. It will be seen that there are considerable differences in this picture from the Basle sketch; **but we can-** not tell if these were to be found in Holbein's own picture. The **Nostell work, interesting as it is,** is not a complete guide to its original; and it **has** suffered severely from the attention of restorers.

The second picture referred to is of note because it has received several additions since it was first painted, and because it is in a much better condition than the Nostell picture. It was at one time at Burford Priory, when that house belonged to the Lenthalls.[1] **It** is now at Cokethorpe Park **near** Witney. The general scheme of the picture **is the** same as the Basle drawing and the Nostell copy; but Sir John More is at the extreme left of the picture. He is dressed in his judge's **robes,** and his face is **less** fat and altogether much **more** intelligent and interesting than in the Nostell picture, though the drawing is not nearly so striking as in the Windsor

---

[1] Mr. Hunter, Preface to Cres. More's *Life*, p. xxxviii, *note*, thinks "it probably came from More Place, when the Mores abandoned their estates in Hertfordshire, and returned **to** the north,"

sketch. The face of Sir Thomas, too, is far more characteristic and expressive than in the Nostell picture. It is extremely pale and sad, but full of determination and power. At each side, behind, stand Anne Cresacre in dark green, and John More in black. These closely follow the Nostell picture. Next to her brother sits Cicely Heron, and by her side Margaret Roper, the latter a very pleasing presentment of a kindly and intelligent face. Behind the two seated sisters—a variation from the drawing and from the Nostell picture—stands Elizabeth Dauncey. Her attitude is the same as in the other copy; but her position is changed from the left to the right of the picture. From this point it appears that what originally occupied the right of the picture—probably the figures of Lady More and of the attendants—has been painted out, as the space is now occupied by later representatives of the More family, a man with a high colour wearing a sugar-loaf hat, and an elderly woman, both seated, and behind them a handsome man of middle age, and a boy just growing into manhood. These may probably be identified, by an inscription at the extreme right of the picture, and by the coats of arms that are painted above them, as Thomas More (son of John More and Anne Cresacre), his wife Mary Scrope, and their eldest and youngest sons, John and Christopher Cresacre. On the wall behind hangs the portrait of a lady, who may possibly be Anne More, only daughter of John More and Anne Cresacre, or Anne Cresacre herself. The additional figures appear to have been painted in

1593 "anno regni Elizabethae 35," when Thomas
More was sixty-two and his wife was fifty-nine.
The dates of the original family group imply that
the original picture was being painted in 1530. It
may thus have been an early copy of Holbein's
great picture, or even a replica from the master's
hand. It is in every way superior to the Nostell
picture, and is by no means unworthy of the great
artist.[1] The interest of the added figures is considerable, not least since the dark thoughtful youth
who stands between his father and mother can be
identified as the Cresacre More who wrote the
beautiful biography of his great-grandfather.

Though it is impossible to be satisfied with the
pictures we have, we may at least learn from them
how truly Holbein entered into the beautiful family
life of which he was for a time a sharer. A man
he was worthy to be admitted and to appreciate—"a
grave man," as Mr. Ruskin says, "knowing what steps
of men keep truest time to the chaunting of death,"
and hearing it may be the soft singing which images
the truthfulness of a beautiful life "perhaps ever
low in the room of that family of Sir Thomas More,
or mingling with the hum of bees in the meadows

---

[1] The picture is of great historical and genealogical interest.
The identification of the persons added to the Holbein picture
is rendered practically certain by the discovery of the *Book
of Hours* belonging to the family, which was sold with the
collection of the Baron von Druffel of Munster, Westphalia,
in January 1894. The dates of the ages of the three figures,
Thomas, John and Cresacre, as given on the picture, tally
exactly with the family entries in the book. The writer of
the entries is evidently the Thomas More of the picture. He
refers to his brother-in-law "Mr. Raufe Scrope."

outside the towered wall of Basle, or making the
words of that book more tuneable, which meditative
Erasmus looks upon." A fit man truly to paint
Erasmus and More, the scholar and the saint.

Holbein returned to Basle in 1528, and when he
next visited England in 1531, probably did not
reside at Chelsea.

More's house was not only a home for artists and
scholars. Diplomatists and men of action eagerly
sought his society, among them the Venetian ambassador Giustiniani, and his secretary Nicolo Sagudino.
In 1517, especially, they were constant guests at
Chelsea. Their literary society, says the former—
containing probably, Pace, Tunstal, Ammonius, Linacre, and More—exerted itself strenuously, "ne dies
ullus musis vacuis dilabatur," lest any day should
pass without literature.[1] Sagudino seems to have
been admitted to a close friendship with More,
for he writes, " totum me ei addixi ; in cujus
melitissima consuetudine tanquam in amœnissimo
diversorio saepe acquiescere soleo; ille que qua est
humanitate vir, per benigne amanterque me vidit et
excipit; quo fit ut nunquam eum conveniam quin
me doctiorem suique amantiorem dimittat." [2] Many
more of the distinguished men of the day might
here take their places among More's friends; but
enough has been said to show the deep impression
which the beauty of his family life made upon his
contemporaries.

Yet there is one other figure, most significant and

---

[1] Rawdon Brown, *Giust.* ii. 68.
[2] To Marcus Musurus, April 22, 1517.

most sinister, constantly at one period to be seen
at Chelsea, which must not be forgotten. Of the
familiar intercourse between Henry VIII. and his
faithful servant, the words of Roper give the best
picture. "So from time to time was he by the
Prince advanced, continuing in his singular favour
and trusty service twenty years and above. A good
part whereof used the King upon holidays, when he
had done his own devotions, to send for him into his
travers, and there some time in matters of Astronomy,
Geometry, Divinity, and such other Faculties, and
some time in his worldly affairs, to sit and confer
with him: and otherwise would he in the night
have him up into the leads there to consider with
him the diversities, courses, motions, and operations
of the stars and planets. And because he was of a
pleasant disposition, it pleased the King and Queen
after the council had supped, at the time of their
supper for their pleasure commonly to call for him,
and to be merry with him. When he perceived so
much in his talk to delight that he could not once in a
month get leave to go home to his wife and children
(whose company he most desired), and to be absent
from the Court two days together, but that he should
be thither sent for again, he much misliking this
restraint of liberty, began thereupon somewhat to
dissemble his nature, and so by little and little from
his former mirth to disuse himself, that he was of
them from thenceforth no more so ordinarily sent
for." And, yet later on, "for the pleasure he took
in his company would his grace suddenly sometimes
come home to his house at Chelsea, to be merry

with him, whither on a time unlooked for he came to dinner, and after dinner in a fair garden of his walked with him by the space of an hour, holding his arm about his neck. As soon as his grace was gone, I rejoicing, told Sir Thomas More how happy he was whom the King so familiarly entertained, as I had never seen him do to any before, except Cardinal Wolsey, whom I saw his grace once walk with arm-in-arm. 'I thank our Lord, son,' quoth he, 'I find his grace my very good lord indeed, and I do believe he doth as singularly favour me as any subject within this realm. Howbeit, son Roper, I may tell thee, I have no cause to be proud thereof. For if my head would win him a castle in France—for then there was war between us—it would not fail to go.' "[1] It was this guest, hasty, eager, active, seeking into all the branches of human inquiry, who disturbed the quiet of More's home. He was a king whom men were proud to serve, and on whose praise they seemed almost to live: one who knew how to reward, and better to appreciate, services; but one whose will was relentless and whose heart without pity. More, at least, knew well what was the value set upon his own work, and did not misunderstand the meaning of a Court life.

It was a time, as More well knew, of startling contrasts. As we read of the happy company of scholars and children in the garden at Chelsea, playing soft instruments and singing old songs, we pass

---

[1] Roper, pp. 7, 15 ; cf. Harpsfield.

in thought not unnaturally to that sad scene in the garden at Bridewell, as our great dramatist has shown it to us, when the forsaken Queen would fain for a moment disperse her sorrows with the lute :

> In sweet Music is such art,
> Killing care and grief of heart
> Fall asleep, or, hearing, die.

CHAPTER III.

LITERARY WORK: THE 'UTOPIA.'

"We need some imaginative stimulus, some not impossible
ideal which may shape vague hope, and transform it into
effective desire, to carry us year after year, without
disgust, through the routine-work which is so large a part
of life."—WALTER PATER.

MORE will ever be remembered as a lawyer and
statesman of honour and conscience, and the beauty
of his home life remains a priceless record of family
sanctity: but even more enduring is his fame as a
man of letters. He lived at a turning-point in
English literature, and he did much to guide the
flowing stream into the channel which it has ever
since pursued. English literature with him became
romantic, keenly alive to the sentiment of the past,
imaginative, practical, and pure. The characteristics
of the great age of Elizabeth, which was so soon to
make the little island that had long seemed to live
apart from the culture of Europe to claim rank with
the Italy of the Renaissance, are seen not dimly in
the master touches of his work. More belonged in
spirit to the future—to the England of Elizabeth,
even to the England which centuries later pictures
the art, the beauty, and the happiness that may

come from **fellow-work** and common **life. But he**
belonged to the past as well.   His intense reverence,
his quaintness, his absolute submission **to the one
single Church** of Christ, his reminiscences of **Chau-
cerian** medievalism and of **the literature** of Chivalry,
show that he had been **born** when men still wrote
laborious manuscripts and painted with the minute
devotion of a lifetime. A scholar of the New Learning, to whom Italy had revealed all that the Florentine
Academy had made the heritage of the world, a man
of letters steeped in the literature of past ages and
other tongues, he was yet alert with all the foresight
and inquisitiveness of the seamen **and the free-**
thinkers of **his day.   And thus it is that when life
and** learning have passed on **in** triumphant **march
far beyond the point of** vantage from which **his** eager
gaze pierced into futurity, **men** turn back **with fresh
love** and curiosity to the scholar and the historian
who gave them the *Utopia.*

More lived a busy life, but one which rarely failed
to find time for books. His works were, with **some**
short intervals, the continuous expression of his mind
as thought and work and tribulation shaped it.
Routine-work **indeed** occupied a **large** part of his
days ; from it he sought relief in religion, in scholarship, and in the stimulus of an imaginative ideal.

His literary work then may well precede the record
of his public life ; and we may speak first concerning his *History of Richard III.,* his lesser Latin
compositions, and the *Utopia.*[1]

---

[1] For a complete list of More's Works, see Rudhart, *Th.
Morus,* pp. **430—438.**

Of the lesser Latin works the *Epigrams* and the *Letter to the University of Oxford* alone need mention here. The *Epigrams* are a collection of verses, on every possible variety of subject, composed at different times and in entirely different strains. They are neither much better nor much worse than similar compositions of More's contemporaries. Their merit consists in the easy adaptation to poetic uses of the colloquial Latin of the time, not in style or accuracy of scholarship—for More was by no means always careful of the rules of prosody and metrical composition. They are in fact compositions remarkable neither in their own age nor in ours. In the early part of the sixteenth century every scholar wrote Latin verses, and many gave them to the world. More, at least, showed no anxiety for the publication of his epigrams. A few of them had appeared separately, but the first collected edition was produced under the superintendence of Erasmus from the press of Froben. As the work of More, and as appearing when the *Utopia* had made men aware of his remarkable talents, the *Epigrams* were sure of a cordial reception from the learned world.

" What might have been expected,"wrote Erasmus, " if Italy had given birth to a genius so happy, if he had given himself entirely to the Muses, and if his talent had ripened into autumn's fruit ? For he was but a youth when he amused himself with these epigrams, and no more than a boy when he wrote many others." "Progymnasmata" he called the first part of his book ; and his friend, the scholar Lilly, contributed verses to the volume. It was a fellow-work, " Thomae Mori et Gulielmi Lilii solatium." Dedicated to Bilibald Pirchheimer, who was famous as a statesman and man of letters, it could hardly fail to attract immediate attention.

Stapleton, who is followed by Cresacre More,[1] has collected some of the extravagant commendations which the book received. From these high-pitched laudations a great deal must be subtracted; it must be remembered, for example, that More praises the poems of Budé and Busleiden as warmly as they eulogize his epigrams.

A cursory glance at the volume will suffice. Its wide scope faithfully reflects the wide interests of the age. Politics and literature, the scholar's studies and the exercises of the religious life, loyal eulogies and *vers de société*, all find place.

Among the political epigrams are those on the capture of Norham Castle by the Scots, and its recovery after the battle of Flodden, a sort of condemnatory epitaph on the unhappy James IV., congratulations on the capture of Tournay—in which Henry VIII. is compared to Cæsar—and two which are so important as the expression of views rare indeed at that epoch as to justify their insertion here.

> *Populus consentiens regnum dat et aufert:*
>   Quicunque multis vir viris unus præest
>   Hoc debet his quibus præest,
>   Præsse debet neutiquam diutius
>   Hi quam volent quibus præest.
>   Quid impotentes principes superbiunt?
>   Quod imperant precario?[2]

---

[1] Stapleton, cap. ii. ; Cres. More, p. 12.   [2] Page 53.

De Bono Rege et Populo:
Totum est unus homo regnum, idque cohaeret amore
   Rex caput est, populus caetera membra facit.
Rex quoque habet cives (dolet ergo perdere quemquam),
   Tot munerat partes corporis ipse sui,
Exponit populus sese pro rege putatque
   Qui libet huuc proprii corporis esse caput.[1]

Among the poems on matters of personal interest there are the verses, to which some fame has been given, on More's meeting a lady whom he had loved twenty years before. Their fame has arisen from the conjecture, which it is impossible to verify but which the text of the poem renders exceedingly improbable, that the lady was the younger sister of his first wife;[2] and from the curious coincidence that he expresses his hope of meeting her again after another twenty years have elapsed—in the year, as it turned out, of his own death. In the same division may be placed the exquisite letter to his children,[3] several epigrams addressed to Busleiden, three on the New Testament of Erasmus, one on an escape from drowning, in which he seems to have felt a momentary presentment of the manner of his death, and those relating to his controversy with Brixius.

A word may be permitted on this typical literary squabble. A French scholar named de Brie (Brixius) had written a poem called *Chordigera*, on the fight between the English ship *Regent* and the French *La Cordelière* in 1513. More, fired by the derision heaped on the English, wrote several epigrams, exposing the malevolence, bad faith, and vanity of the French

---

[1] Pages 50, 51.   [2] *Vide* above, p. 38.   [3] *Epigrams*, p. 110.

writer. When these came to the ears of Brixius he revenged himself by an elegy, entitled *Anti-Morus*, pointing out all the faults in the poems of More with which he was acquainted, and commenting especially on the implied slight to Henry VII. in the *Carmen gratulatorium*, on the accession of Henry VIII. This poem remained for some time unpublished, but at last made its appearance at Paris in 1520. More at once wrote indignantly to Erasmus,[1] asking his advice, and also put forth a pasquinade in answer.[2] He detailed the whole occasion of the quarrel, from the burning of the *Regent* to the *Anti-Morus*, and complained of its publication at a time when England and France were in close alliance. His defence, however, of the expressions in the coronation ode on which Brixius had commented is, naturally, somewhat lame. This had hardly been published when More received a letter from Erasmus,[3] urging him to treat the matter with silent contempt and to suppress the version which had given offence. More felt the justice of this advice, and recalled the work from circulation. Brixius, however, did not escape without punishment, for he received a scathing letter from Erasmus,[4] in which the highest praises of More were joined with the most contemptuous reference to his opponent. "I have not seen many of your writings," wrote the scholar, "of More's I have read several and know them well. I think of their writer as all men who know him think;—as a man of incomparable genius, a most happy memory, a most ready elo-

---

[1] Erasm. *Epp.* xv. 16.
[2] *Mori Opera*, p. 319.
[3] Erasm. *Epp.* xv. 15.
[4] *Ibid.* xiii. 33.

quence. When a boy he learnt Latin, when a young man Greek, under the ablest teachers, especially Linacre and Grocyn. In divinity he has made so much progress that he is not to be despised even by the most eminent theologians : the liberal arts too he has touched not unhappily : in philosophy he is beyond mediocrity : to say nothing of his profession of the law in which he yields to no one." [1]

Among the epigrams on subjects of literary and general interest, there are several directed against women, — written indeed more bitterly than we might have imagined More could write. On the other hand, there is the description of a perfect wife, addressed to "Candidus," which in itself would be sufficient to show that More was no woman-hater.

The vices of monks and of particular ecclesiastics are satirized in other epigrams : several painters and poetasters are also derided. A French writer is told that "he is undoubtedly animated by the spirit of the ancients, for he hits upon the self-same lines that have been composed by them." Two smart pieces describe the extravagances of the topers "Fuscus" and "Marcellus." Another tells how More had agreed to write an epitaph on a singer named Henry Abyngdon. His first composition, written in elegiacs, was not "tuneful" enough for the bereaved relations; he then wrote another in the rhyming style of the medieval Latinists, which was much preferred to his first. On this he wrote an epigram

---

[1] For the disputes with Brixius, in addition to the ordinary biographers, see Cayley, *Memorials of Sir Thomas More*, p. 79.

declaring that he who considered the second superior
to the first ought to be buried in the same tomb,
and bear the same epitaph as Abyngdon now had.

His derision of the Frenchified fashions of the day
may be compared with the passage in Shakespeare's
Henry VIII. on the same subject. More ridicules
his friend "Lalus," who has imitated the French in
his outward attire, cloak, hat, belt, sword, gloves,
and—still more—

> "One only man he keeps, and he from France,
>   Who by the French themselves could not, I think,
> Be treated more in fashion of the French.
> He never pays his wages,—that is French.
> Stints him with meagre victuals,—French again ;
> Works him to death,—and this again is French."[1]

Finally, there are several epigrams against astrology
and astrologers, evidently one of More's pet subjects
of aversion. As a specimen of the style of these
compositions one, addressed *In Fabianum Astrologum,*
may be quoted—

> "Uno multa die de rebus fata futuris,
>   Credula quum de te turba frequenter emat.
> Inter multa unum si fors mendacia verum est
>   Illico vis vatem te, Fabiane, patem.
> At tu de rebus semper mentire futuris
>   Si potes hoc, vatem te Fabiane putem."

Not the least striking of his epigrams are those in
which he scourges the vices of the clergy. He shows
certainly no reluctance to expose private vices or to
condemn public errors. "Candidus" is spoken of

---

[1] Archdeacon Wrangham's translation, quoted in *Philomorus*
(1st edit. 1848 ; 2nd, 1879) : *q. v.* for an excellent account of
More's Latin poems.

as endowed with a combination of virtues rare among the fathers of the Church.

> As a faithful mirror view it,
>   Showing what to do,—what shun.
> All he shuns, take care to do it :
>   All he does, take care to shun.[1]

He can see humour in sacred matters too, and objects of satire in lazy friars and worldly priests. Nowhere are More's candour and freedom better seen than in his epigrams.

While his Latin verse represents one side of the interests of this English disciple of the Renaissance —the application of the ancient languages and the classic models to the events of the day—another aspect is illustrated by his famous defence of the study of Greek, a letter addressed to the University of Oxford. This was a composition to which he seems to have attached some value, for we are told by Stapleton that he gave it to his "school," as he called his family, to put into English and then again to translate into Latin. The cause of the letter was the commotion which had been taking place in Oxford ever since Grocyn first lectured, but which had much increased in the year 1518. The study of Greek was regarded by the older men as useless and dangerous; and the students had formed bands of "Trojans" and "Greeks." In Lent a foolish preacher had delivered a violent diatribe against the classics. The Court heard of the commotion. Henry was at the time at Abingdon, whither he had fled from London on account of the sweating sick-

---

[1] *Philomorus*, 2nd edit. p. 126.

ness. More was with him, and wrote an indignant but respectful letter to the "Fathers and Proctors" of the University.[1] He described the struggle, which he had at first regarded as a mere childish freak, and commented severely on the folly of the preacher who had attacked the study of Greek from the University pulpit. "What will be thought of our University abroad?" he exclaimed; and, after an eloquent, if narrow, panegyric of the great poets, historians, and orators of Greece, he insisted on the necessity of a liberal education as the basis for a study of Theology. He contrasted the activity of Cambridge with the apathy of Oxford; brought forward the examples of Warham, Wolsey—"literarum promotor, et ipse literatissimus"—and the King himself, as diligent students; and earnestly exhorted the authorities to put down the ridiculous squabble.

The letter is valuable as an illustration of the liberality of More's views and of his deep interest in his University. It was successful: "the King," says Erasmus, "imposed silence on the rabble." Nor was More's intervention ill received in Oxford, for we find him High Steward of the University in 1524.

To the end of his life he retained his interest in his University. In 1529, Wolsey proposed that he should arbitrate between the University and the Town in one of their perennial quarrels; but the citizens would not agree then to settle the dispute.[2]

---

[1] Jortin's *Erasmus,* iii. **358** : Hearne's edition of Roper, pp. 159—167. The letter was republished, Oxford, 1633.

[2] See Maxwell Lyte, *History of University of Oxford,* p. 429.

In 1530, he joined with Gardiner in pleading for the maintenance of Wolsey's noble foundation of Cardinal College.[1]

But More was not only a satirist and a scholar; he had already begun to write vigorous English prose. In the year 1513, "being at the time under-sheriff of London," he wrote his *History of Richard III*.[2] The work was unfinished, whether from disinclination to the kind of writing or from the increase of business does not appear. Not only was it unfinished, but it was neglected and forgotten, and did not see the light until 1543, when it appeared in Grafton's continuation of Hardyng's *City Chronicle*. It at once took its place as the standard account of the period of which it treated, and was reprinted by Hall, Holinshed, and Stow. In the original publication, however, it had been edited carelessly or garbled intentionally, and in the collected edition of More's *English Works*, in 1557, Rastell gave, for the first time, the true copy from his uncle's manuscript.

Only in title and in intention is the work a history of Richard III., and even without the express declaration of Rastell it would have been evident that it was incomplete. To go no further, the second page of the history shows its aim: "this Duke's (Gloucester) demeanour ministreth in effect all the whole matter whereof this book shall entreat."[3] As printed by Rastell, it stops abruptly

---

[1] Maxwell Lyte, *History of University of Oxford*, p. 482.
[2] *English Works*, p. 35.
[3] *Ibid.* p. 36. Mackintosh, *Life of More*, p. 44, *note*.

just after the murder of the princes. Incomplete as it is, it is a work of the highest value; and this not only as an authority, for in style and method it far surpasses any previous history written in English. A question, however, arises as to the part More took in its composition. May it not have been in reality the work of Cardinal Morton,[1] whether in design or in execution? Or again, was its 'original form the English of Rastell's edition of 1557, or the Latin of the Louvain edition of 1566? Though Morton must almost certainly have been the authority from whom most of the minute information was obtained, there can be little doubt that the history as published by Rastell was written by More. Nor is there any reason to suppose that the Latin version was the composition of Morton. The one, however, is not a translation of the other, and Mr. Gairdner's conclusion is, that while the English history is certainly More's, there is "no very sufficient ground for rejecting the voice of tradition which ascribes the Latin version to More also."[2]

So much for the authenticity of the work: what then is its value? It is undoubtedly written in somewhat of a partisan spirit; there is no pretence of that absolute balance of judgment to which modern historians lay claim.[3] A few statements have been shown not to be severely

[1] Harrington, *Metamorphosis of Ajax*, p. 46. Mr. Clements Markham has also argued for Morton's authorship. *Eng. Hist. Rev.* vol. vi. p. 807.
[2] *Letters of Richard III and Henry VII*. vol. ii. p. xviii.
[3] Gairdner, *Early Chroniclers*, p. 295.

accurate, but the main question depends on the view of Richard, Duke of Gloucester, which is there set forth with so much force, and which has been impressed on the popular imagination ever since. Here More makes no timid utterances: the portrait, whether accurate or not, is distinct and unmistakable. The first mention of the Duke is decisive—" Richard, Duke of Gloucester, by nature their uncle, by office their protector, to their father beholden, to themselves by oath and allegiance bounden, all the bands broken that bind man and man together without any respect of God or of the world, unnaturally contrived to bereave them, not only of their dignity, but also of their lives." [1]

This is hardly the place for an examination of the truth of More's view; all that need be said is that recent investigations tend more and more to confirm it. It must be remembered that the later period of the reign is never reached; and thus there is no opportunity for a judgment on the general policy of Richard as king. As far as facts are concerned, it is the steps by which he reached the throne of which More treats, and it is on Richard as a man that condemnation is passed.

In spite of all that has been said about the intentional misrepresentations of Tudor historians, the considerations of ordinary probability would lead to the conclusion that the history of a time which many of its readers could remember, could not have become so extraordinarily popular if it had not been in sentiment and substance true. Nor had a sufficient

---

[1] *Eng. Works,* p. 36.

period elapsed to allow of the falsification of facts even if false theories would have been accepted. More unquestionably learnt from Morton; and there is no sufficient reason to think that Morton lied.

Of the literary merit of the history there cannot be the shadow of a doubt. The story is unfolded with admirable clearness, and the progress of events is followed by the reader with intense interest. The characters are drawn with remarkable precision and power, and the speeches are not the rhetorical off-spring of the historian's imagination, but might well be the direct utterances of the historical characters themselves. The facts tell their own tale untram-melled by tedious moral commentary. The result is that an extraordinarily vivid picture is presented, the leading features of which are impressed upon the mind with striking and peculiar force. The characters of Richard of Glo'ster and of Jane Shore, the scenes at the deathbed of Edward IV. and in the council chamber of the Tower on the morning of Hastings' execution, are drawn with a vivid power equal to that of Macaulay. From a literary point of view a double interest is attached to this work of More, from the use made of it by Shakespeare, in whose hands its phrases are utilized with wonderful skill. The soliloquies of Richard, the dying speech of Edward IV., and the whole Hastings episode are the most prominent examples; but a minor, though no less insignificant, instance, is the use of chance references to Glo'ster's restless sleep.

The anonymous life in the Lambeth library says that More " wrote also a book of the history of Henry

VII.; but either the book is smothered amongst his kinsmen, or lost by the injury of this time."[1] Of such a work we have only this notice; and inquiry or conjecture on this subject have been at present unfruitful.

It is by the history of Richard III. that More's place as a historian must be estimated. It was he unquestionably who did most to originate the historical sympathy for the Tudor dynasty which has been so striking a feature of English literature. The policy of Henry VII. may have found its gratification in the material prosperity which it fostered, and even may have realized during the first year of Henry VIII. the width of the interests continental and cosmopolitan among which the land had began so freely and powerfully to move. But the last of the Plantagenets died hard: the insecurity of the first Tudor's throne had shown it: and it needed a literary masterpiece to found the security of the new dynasty on the horrors and crimes of the last of the ancient line. More gave to English history an indelible portrait of Richard Crookback, and in giving it, his clear and incisive style taught a new school of historians to write so that all might read. With More history passed from the monastery into the market-place, and where he began, Holinshed, Cavendish, and Stow followed; and Bacon on his lines gave his masterly portrait of Henry VII.

From Richard III. to the *Utopia* is a far cry. We pass from the realism of historic crime to the ideal presentment of a poetic and philanthropic

[1] Wordsworth's *Eccl. Biog.* ii. 49.

vision. If in his *History* More spoke directly to his own day, in his *Utopia* he spoke to the dim future. From the Humanists of the sixteenth century to the Socialists of the Victorian age readers have read and re-read it with unqualified delight.

So much has been written on this beautiful idyll that it may well seem that no aspect of it has remained unstudied; and yet, whether in the clear dignity of the original Latin or in the quaint translation of Ralph Robinson [1]—itself an English classic—it is as fresh to-day as when it was first given to the enthusiastic world of scholars.

The *Utopia* has so generally been accepted as a political ideal of the writer's, or as a dream of the distant future, that its practical importance has been in danger of being forgotten. It is by no means in the first place a philosopher's dream, applicable to all time: it is a scheme of very practical inquiry

---

[1] Of many good editions, perhaps the best are Mr. Robert Roberts' re-issue (1878) of Dibdin's, and Mr. Edward Arber's reprint (1869). Robinson first published his version in 1551. Of the other renderings that have appeared, Bishop Burnet's contains some trifling improvements in accuracy of translation, and Mr. Seebohm in some of the notes to his *Oxford Reformers* has given the exact meaning which in our time we attach to the Latin words of the original; but such alterations are, after all, but half benefits, for it is not so important to translate the sixteenth-century Latin of More with all the refinements of modern scholarship, as to understand what his meaning was as it would be understood by sixteenth-century readers. For this cause Robinson's translation is to be preferred, for its very quaintnesses, even where they do not exactly correspond to the intention of the original, have an intrinsic value which must not be overlooked.

and construction, which receives a thousandfold
more force when read by the light of sixteenth-
century history. It is, in fact, an earnest examination of the phenomena of More's own time,
constructed mainly by the help of Plato.

The groundwork of the *Utopia* is a supposed
conversation between the writer, when a guest of
Petrus Ægidius, at Antwerp, and a mariner named
Raphael Hythlodaye, who had sailed with the navi-
gator Amerigo Vespucci. Hythlodaye, being left
behind his companions, discovered and lived for five
years in an unknown island called Utopia, and it is
his account of his sojourn which More professes to
have written down. The idea was a very natural
one at that date. Within men's memories the
barriers which seemed of old to shut in the world
had all been cast down, and a limitless extent of unknown land lay before the imagination of the age.
The results of the voyages of the great explorers
had been so marvellous that nothing in discovery
could seem too wonderful to be true. At the
very time when the intellectual world was being
rejuvenated by the power of the ancient literatures,
its imagination was aroused and its sympathies
were quickened by the revelation of a New World.
What wonder then if the men who awoke to the
realization of the terrible evils of the social and
political organization in which they lived should
fondly hope to find in the New World a society
purer than their own? This longing created its
own answer. The earnest thinkers of Europe
yearned for the explorers to find an ideal State.

"More sailed over the sea of troubles in which England was set, and discovered Utopia. "

It was indeed the discovery of a new land, a revelation of beauty and righteousness to that hardened age. Instead of empty glitter and show, there was a deep and simple pleasure, so pure and yet so enticing that the most constant courtier might sigh when he thought of its contrast to his own. The great aim of the *Utopia* was to point out the evil of certain conditions of life, and to suggest remedies, by placing a perfectly different state before men's minds. More's book, in fact, was eminently practical: he had no pet theory or philosophic craze to establish. He endeavoured merely to declare the wrongs which the age tolerated; trusting that when they were plainly and unanswerably set forth men would have no difficulty in redressing them.

As has been already stated, the second book of the *Utopia* was written some months before the first, probably about November 1515, while the work was completed in the earlier months of 1516.

The work in the first edition [1] was prefaced by various letters and poems, complimentary and introductory. In these the fiction was maintained with solemn gravity. Apologizing for the delay which had taken place between the publication of the book and the conversation which it recorded, More,

---

[1] "Libellvs vere aurevs nec minvs salvtaris quam festiuus, de optimo reip. statu digne una Insula Vtopia." Louvain, 1516.

blending truth with fable, gave a very interesting account of his daily work.

"Whiles[1] I do daily bestow my time about law matters: some to plead, some to hear, some as arbitrator with mine award to determine, some as an umpire or judge with my sentence finally to discuss. Whiles I go one way to see and visit my friend: another way about mine own private affairs. Whiles I spend almost all the day abroad amongst other and the residue at home among mine own: I leave to myself, I mean to my book, no time. For when I am come home, I must commune with my wife, chat with my children, and talk with my servants. All the which things I reckon and account among business for as much as they must of necessity be done: and done must they needs be unless a man will be stranger in his own house. And in any wise a man must so fashion and order his conditions, and so appoint and dispose himself, that he be merry, jocund, and pleasant among them, whom either nature hath provided, or chance hath made, or he himself hath chosen, to be the fellows and companions of his life: so that with too much gentle behaviour and familiarity he do not mar them, and by too much sufferance of his servants make them his masters. Among these things now rehearsed stealeth away the day, the month, the year. And when do I write then? And all this while have I spoken no word of sleep, neither yet of meat, which among a great number doth waste no less time than doth sleep, wherein

---

[1] *Utopia*, Robinson's translation, p. 21.

almost half the lifetime of man creepeth away.
I therefore do win and get only that time which
I steal from sleep and meat."

After this passage the fiction is continued, and
many little details are thrown in to complete the
deception. More concludes the letter to Petrus
Ægidius by a question whether after all, considering the ignorance, dullness, and perversity of many
men, he is wise in publishing the record.

In the letter of Ægidius to Busleiden, also prefaced to the book itself, Hythlodaye's power of
narration is very highly commended, but More's
work is still more warmly praised. "I promise you,"
says Ægidius, "I can scarce believe that Raphael
himself, by all that five years' space that he was
in Utopia abiding, saw there so much as here in
Master More's description is to be seen and perceived." The whole origin of the fiction is touched
when Ægidius explains the absence of Utopia from
the charts of the ancient geographers; perhaps its
name has been changed, but "now in our time
divers lands be found which to the old geographers
were unknown." Numberless other instances of
similar treatment might be pointed out; and there
can be no wonder that when men were deceived
by the *Epistolae Obscurorum Virorum* they should
be duped by the *Utopia*.

The first book begins by an accurate description of
More's embassy and of his introduction to Ægidius.
To this succeeds a minute description of his meet-
ing with Raphael Hythlodaye in the cathedral of
Antwerp, and of their subsequent converse on a

bench outside More's house. From this point the real importance of the study begins; hitherto in the prefatory letters and the introductory narrative the basis on which the work is to rest has been laid; now we are at once brought face to face with the evils which More deplored and to expose which was his main object in writing.[1]

While in the first book certain political and social questions of the time are discussed, and in the second the commonwealth of Utopia is described, the division between the two books is really an arbitrary one. The object of both is the same, though the end is obtained in one case by the direct reprobation of evils, and in the other generally by inference from the perfect State the constitution of which is described. To all appearance, More, after he had written the second book, saw that the nature of the fiction would prevent it containing much that he wished to declare; he therefore wrote an introductory book in which he expressed his meaning more fully. The first book, then, is so plainly the necessary complement of the second, that the evils of which More complained may be gathered indifferently from each.

We have, firstly, the objections to taking service at any Court, put into the mouth of Hythlodaye.[2] Although More is represented as answering them, there can be no doubt that they were substantially his own views. His political life will show that it was only with great reluctance, and when he

<hr>

[1] Erasm. *Epp.* x. 30.
[2] R. Robinson's translation, p. 35.

had made public these very declarations of its evils,
that he had entered the royal service. Not only,
then, does Hythlodaye desire no riches or honours
for himself, but he has no faith in his being able
to do any good for the State, by taking a position at Court. For most princes delight only in
war and feats of chivalry ("the knowledge whereof I
neither have nor desire"), and seek to increase their
possessions by fair means or foul. Not only is
submission to their will in this matter obligatory
on a courtier; but the great ministers also must be
obeyed and flattered. Nor is there hope of any
reform; for all advice is met by a resolute determination to resist every change: the minister when
asked to ameliorate distress is a consistent "laudator
temporis acti." "These things, say they, pleased our
forefathers and ancestors: would God we could be as
wise as they were." These evils are common to all
European Courts, and every reader of sixteenth-
century history will be able to give instances of their
truth. Hythlodaye then turns to speak especially of
England. He significantly introduces his observa-
tions by saying that they were the substance of a
conversation which took place in the house of
Cardinal Morton, four or five months after the
Cornish insurrection of 1495[1]; and we can perhaps
hardly be wrong in inferring that it was this very
revolt which first drew More's attention to the social
wrongs of his time.

The first of the great evils in England is the wholesale execution of thieves,[2] often "twenty hanged

[1] R. Robinson's translation, p. 36.   [2] Page 37 et seq.

together on one gallows." This severity is useless;
" much rather provision should have been made that
there were some means whereby they might get
their living, so that no man should be driven to this
extreme necessity, first to steal and then to die."
In answer to objections it is asserted that this
infliction of the capital penalty submits God's ordin-
ance to man's judgment. The sanctity of human life
was declared by the Mosaic Law, by which theft
was not punished with death, and we cannot think
" that God in the new law of clemency and mercy "
has given license to greater cruelty. And not only
is the punishment in the highest sense unlawful:
it is also unreasonable. The law which lays the
same penalty on the murderer and the thief is an
encouragement to murder.

The whole history of the English statute book is a
commentary on these noble words of More. As we
pursue the slow record of the gradual restriction of
the extreme sentence of the law, we wonder again
that a truth so clearly expressed in the sixteenth
century should have been so long in winning recognition even from intelligent thinkers. Sad indeed is
the satire on men's slowness to learn the simple
lessons of Christianity, when we remember that a
later generation was aroused not by the arguments
of More, but by those of Beccaria. In the time of
Henry VIII. there seemed a terrible necessity for
the wholesale executions which marked his reign;
and there were not wanting eminent and humane
thinkers to defend them on practical grounds.
England was overrun by " sturdy beggars." In the

towns skilled **labour** was well paid, **but in the**
country the great change in the agricultural system
had led **to** fearful misery ; men, as More **said, were**
forced to be thieves, and **the result,** in the words of
Latimer, was that "two acres of hemp sown up and
down England would **be all too** little to hang the
thieves in it."[1]   More, however, is not without his
own opinion as to what should be the punishment
of thieves.   He refers to the Roman custom of setting the criminals to work in mines, and recommends
the practice of an imaginary people called **the " Poly-**
lerites."   **This** passage, in spite of **a touch of what**
we should call insular narrowness, is an **exquisite**
picture of an ideal society.[2]   "Their **land is both**
large and ample, and also well and wittily governed :
and the people in all conditions free and ruled by
their own laws, saving that they pay a yearly tribute
to the great King of Persia.   But because they be far
from the sea, compassed and enclosed almost round
about with high mountains, and do content themselves with the fruits of their own land, which **is of**
itself very fruitful and fertile : for this cause **neither**
they go to other countries nor other come to them.
And according to old custom of the land they desire
not to enlarge the bounds **of their** dominions : and
those that they have by reason of the high hills
be easily defended : and the tribute which they pay
to their chief lord and king setteth **them free from**
tribute.   Thus their life is commodious rather than
gallant, **and may** better be called happy or wealthy

---

[1] Cf. Erasmus **to** Henry VIII. ; Brewer, *Letters and Papers,*
Henry VIII., iii. 220.   [2] *Utopia*, pp. 47, 48.

than notable or famous." Among these people thieves are compelled to restore what they have stolen, to the rightful owner—" not as they do in other lands, to the king, whom they think to have no more right to it than the thief himself hath "— and then to become bondmen. They are well treated ; but a number of precautions are taken to prevent their running away or conspiring against the State. Death is the punishment of those bondmen who accept alms in money, or give money to any one, or touch alms, or cast off their distinctive badges, or talk with a bondman of another shire. More seems here to forget his own canon of the authority of the Mosaic Law; for, if it is not allowable for the English Government to take life for any crime but murder, why does he, through the mouth of Hythlodaye, praise the wisdom of the Polylerites? Cardinal Morton is at length made to join in the conversation—which had hitherto been carried on by Hythlodaye and a lawyer—and to admit that it might be allowable in England for the King to reprieve those condemned to death in order to see if their plan would succeed. And it would be equally applicable to vagabonds. Of these plans for treating thieves we can only say that they are inconsistent and inadequate. To return ; other evils have been introduced as causing the great number of thieves and vagabonds. The abuse of livery is commented on in justly severe terms, and needs no special notice here. Nor need we dwell on More's condemnation of the enormous luxury of the age.

The agricultural distress which had followed the

change of arable land into pasture, and on the raising of the rents, is pointed out with deep feeling. "Therefore that one covetous and insatiable cormorant may compass about and enclose many thousand acres of ground together within one pale or hedge, the husbandmen be thrust out of their own, or by violent oppression they be put beside it, or by wrongs and injuries they be so wearied that they be compelled to sell all : by one means, therefore, or another, either by hook or crook, they must needs depart away, poor, silly, wretched souls, men, women, husbands, wives, fatherless children, widows, woful mothers with their young babes, and their whole household, small in substance and much in number, as husbandry requireth many hands. Away they trudge, out of their known and accustomed houses, finding no place to rest in. And their household stuff, which is very little worth, though it might well abide the sale ; yet, being suddenly thrust out, they be constrained to sell it for a thing of nought. And when they have wandered abroad till that be spent, what can they then else do but steal, and then, justly, pardy, be hanged or else go about a begging." [1] Then More put before the learned world of Europe the complaint of the poor. On all sides we meet with confirmation of his statements : Brinklow, Latimer, Starkey, deplored what Kett rashly tried to remedy.

Such are some of the evils which England suffers ; and More sadly asks why Hythlodaye, as a philosopher, will not be the King's instructor, since

[1] Page 41.

Plato's ideal of the philosopher king seems far from fulfilment. Then we return to the reasons against Court service,[1] for Hythlodaye replies by a bitter description of the French foreign policy, and demands how his advice would be taken if he were to tell the French King that "it were best for him to content himself with his own kingdom of France as his forefathers and predecessors did before him; to make much of it, to enrich it and to make it as flourishing as he could, to endeavour himself to love his subjects and again to be beloved of them, willing to live with them, peaceably to govern them, and with other kingdoms not to meddle seeing that which he hath already is even enough for him, yea, and more than he can well turn him." Obviously, he would not be heard for a moment. It needs little sagacity to see the bearing of this passage on the politics of England under Henry VIII. /Other grievances from which the people suffer are then brought forward, in a remarkable passage where More, especially glancing at the particular acts of tyranny for which Henry VII. was responsible, seems to foresee the expedients of the whole Tudor dynasty and even of the Stewarts —such as tampering with the coinage, wars feigned for the sake of exacting subsidies, the enforcement of obsolete laws, the use of the dispensing power for the sake of pecuniary profit, the bribing and coercion of the judges. / "If I should rise up," he says, " and boldly affirm that all these counsels be to the king dishonour and reproach, whose honour and safety is more and rather supported and up-

---

[1] Page 55 *et seq.*

holden by the wealth and riches of his people than
by his own treasures : and if I should declare that
the commonalty chooseth the king for their own
sake and not for his own sake : to the intent that by
his labour and study they might all live wealthy,
safe from wrongs and injuries, and that therefore the
king ought to take more care for the wealth of the
people than for his own wealth, even as the office
and duty of a shepherd is in that he is a shepherd to
feed his sheep rather than himself, what heed would
they pay ?" He continues in the same strain, laying
down in terms that seem to belong in turn to the
fourteenth and to the nineteenth century,[1] a theory
of the duties of a king such as was rarely heard in
his time. Then returning again to the main question,
More says that because good advice or the highest
rules of government would be unheeded at Court, a
philosopher ought not to refuse his help to a king :
" you must not forsake the ship in a tempest because
you cannot rule and keep down the winds." Yet
Hythlodaye still holds his opinion, and declares that
there can be no amelioration of existing evils until
the State is constituted on communistic principles.
Here the arguments are marshalled with great skill,
and little space is allotted to the answers to them;
but the question remains, how far were these More's
own opinions ? It is possible that, looking at the
condition of his own time, at the coarse luxury of the
upper and the degradation of the lower classes, he

---

[1] *E. g.* the king is "to live of his own." We may wonder if
More knew the history of this famous phrase, or thought
merely of its recent use : *vide* Rolls of Parlt. 6 Hen. VIII. c. 24.

may have conceived that redress could be obtained
by a restoration of the primitive practice of Christianity, a voluntary and temporary communism. It is
a question impossible to decide; it can only be said
that there is no support whatever in any other of
his works to any socialistic scheme. The passage
referred to runs thus—" Howbeit [1] where the possessions be private, where money beareth all the stroke,
it is hard and almost impossible that there the
commonwealth may justly be governed and prosper-
ously flourish. Unless you think thus—that justice
is there executed where all things come into the
hands of evil men, or that prosperity there flourisheth
where all is divided among a few; which few nevertheless do not lead their lives very wealthily and the
residue live miserably, wretchedly, and beggarly. . .
For where every man under certain titles and pre-
tences draweth and plucketh to himself as much as
he can so that a few divide among themselves all the
whole riches, be there never so much abundance and
store, there to the residue is left lack and poverty.
And for the most part it chanceth that this latter
sort is more worthy to enjoy that state of wealth than
the other be : because the rich be covetous, crafty,
and unprofitable. On the other part the poor be
lowly, simple, and by their labour more profitable to
the commonwealth than to themselves. Thus I do
fully persuade myself that no equal and just distri-
bution of things can be made, nor that perfect
wealth shall ever be among men, unless this private
ownership be exiled and banished. But so long as

[1] Page 67.

it shall continue, so long shall remain among the most and best part of men the heavy and inevitable burden of poverty and wretchedness." The communistic society, says Hythlodaye, is to be seen in the utmost prosperity in the New World.

Here the first book ends. In the second, Utopia, the communistic state, is described. So far the actual evils from which England was then suffering have been plainly set forth: now we see them rather by inference from the perfect constitution of Utopia.

There is no need to linger on the description of the island, of the method by which the inhabitants in turn spend two years in the country, of the "strange fashion in hatching and bringing up pulleyne," or other schemes which are in turn serious suggestions or simply humours to preserve the spirit of the fiction, in which there is so curious a blending of jest and earnest. The description of the typical city, Amaurote, is more tangible; and the marginal note of the translator is not needed to point out that London is always in the writer's mind. The beautiful houses with their gardens and vineyards behind; the streets twenty feet broad, with public halls at equal distances—everything clean, public, and prosperous, because all was common—are a strange contrast to the houses "made of every rude piece of timber that came first to hand, with mud walls, and ridged roofs, thatched over with straw," which "their old chronicler" described as having existed long ago in Utopia, and which the eyes of every reader of More's book saw all around, replenished

" with much uncleanness and filth, with pits, cellars
and vaults lying open and uncovered, to the great
peril and danger of the inhabitants."[1] The work
of every household is brought to the market-places
whence the heads of families take whatever they
need ; there is no sale or barter. There are meat
markets also ; but the slaughter-houses are outside
the city, and the meat is only brought within
the walls when it has been thoroughly cleansed.
" Neither they suffer anything that is filthy, loath-
some, or unclean, to be brought into the city, lest
the air by the stench thereof infected and corrupt
should cause pestilent diseases." With this one cannot but compare the accounts of the terrible sweating sickness with which the histories of the time are
charged. By this fearful scourge Wolsey was several
times stricken down ; and the King but narrowly
escaped.   In More's own household his favourite
daughter was brought to death's door ; and his
friend Ammonius died after a day's illness. Constantly recurring during the reign, it was especially
severe during the years 1516, 1517, and 1518. When
in attendance on the King at Abingdon during the
last year, More himself had to take precautions for
the safety of the Court.[2]

The sickness had broken out at Oxford ; More at
once sent orders to the Mayor " that the inhabitants
of those houses that be and shall be infected shall
keep in, put out wispes, and bear white rods," which

[1] 32 Henry VIII. cap. 18.
[2] Dr. John Clerk to Wolsey, 25 April, 1508 ; Brewer, ii.
4125.

was the precaution that Wolsey had **previously**
directed to be observed in London. **The fearful
ravages of** this plague are **not to be wondered at**
when we recall Erasmus's description of the condition
of the houses and streets in his time, which gives **a**
pathetic force of contrast to More's picture of the
Utopian towns. Erasmus attributed the spreading
of the sickness **to** " bad houses and bad ventilation,
to the clay floors, the unchanged and festering
rushes with which the rooms were strewn, **and** the
putrid offal, bones, and filth which reeked and
rotted together in the unswept and unwashed **dining**
halls and chambers."[1] In Utopia not only was all
precaution **taken** to preserve the public health, but
the most **tender** care was **bestowed on the** sick.
Heights **of** social benevolence **are** here reached
which with all **our** vast and sympathetic organiza-
tions we **can** hardly be said to have yet realized.
" **In the** circuit of the city, a little within the
walls, they have four hospitals, so big, so wide,
so ample and so large, that they may seem **four**
little towns; which were devised **of** that bigness,
partly to the intent the sick, be they never so many
in number, should **not** lie so throng or strait, and
therefore uneasily, and partly that they which were
taken and holden with contagious diseases, such as
be wont by infection to creep from one to another,
might be laid apart, far from the company of the
residue. These hospitals be so well appointed and
with **all things** necessary to health so furnished,
and moreover **so** diligent attendance through **the**

____
[1] Brewer, **pref.** to vol. ii. p. ccix.

continual presence of cunning physicians is given, that though no man be sent thither against his will, yet notwithstanding, there is no sick person in all the city that had not rather lie there than at home in his own house."

The government of Utopia is somewhat complicated; but the distinguishing feature is the responsibility of the Prince, whose office is elective, to the people, by whom he can be deposed for suspicion of tyranny.

The chapter "of sciences, crafts, and occupations" is one of the most interesting in the book, as breathing a spirit of enlightened humanity of which few traces are to be found in the history or legislation of the Tudor sovereigns, and as anticipating the conclusions to which public opinion has but gradually and recently been brought. All the Utopians, men and women, learn husbandry, besides which every one has a trade. "And the chief and almost only office of the Syphograuntes is to see and take heed that no man sit idle; but that every one apply his own craft with earnest diligence. And yet for all that not to be wearied from early in the morning till late in the evening with continual work, like labouring and toiling beasts. For this is worse than the miserable and wretched condition of bondmen, which nevertheless is almost everywhere the life of workmen and artificers saving in Utopia." There the workmen work only for six hours: yet there is no lack of "all things that be requisite either for the necessity or commodity of life." This is possible since all work, whereas in Christendom, women, priests, and rich men are generally idle, besides the many engaged in "vain and superfluous occupations." The Utopians have, however, a few citizens who are set apart and devoted to learning, and perform no handicraft. From these are chosen the 'Philarchs,' and officers of state. Finally "in the institution of that commonwealth this end is only and chiefly pretended and minded, that what time may possibly be spared from the necessary occupations and affairs of the commonwealth, all that the citizens should withdraw from the bodily service to the free liberty of the mind and garnishing of the same. For herein they suppose the felicity of their life to consist."

Over population they avoid by migration and colonization: what one city lacks in goods another supplies. Families live together: all the sons, married or single, under the rule of the eldest of the house. It need hardly be said that in all that relates to the position of women and their relation to the children there is an entire and fundamental divergence from the famous doctrines of the Republic: natural affection is glorified, not abased. All dine in the public halls, except for urgent cause. "They begin every dinner and supper with reading something that pertains to good manners and virtue. But it is short, because no man shall be grieved therewith. Hereof the elders take occasion of honest communication, but neither sad nor unpleasant. Howbeit they do not spend all the whole dinner time themselves with long tedious talks, but they

gladly hear also the young men,—yea, and purposely
provoke them to **talk to** the intent that they **may
have** a proof of every man's wit and towardness,
or disposition to virtue, which commonly by **the**
liberty of feature doth **show and utter** itself."

Such is the common life of the Utopians; cheerful, innocent, happy: and as **More after writing** the
beautiful description **of his ideal would leave the
library in** his " New Lodging " and **walk** across the
soft turf to his house he may well have thought
how nearly it was realized in his own family, and
have forgotten, perhaps, how **very** exceptional were
the causes required to establish such a home.

The Utopians trade in all the things of which
they have a superfluity. **Of** the price they always
give one-seventh to the poor of the country where
they trade. Now, however, they no longer ask
immediate payment for their goods, but leave the
money in charge of the foreign magistrates, of
whom they demand it in **case of** war. Gold and
silver they consider base things, and **use** them for
the meanest **purposes.** "To gold and silver Nature
hath given no use that we may not well lack, **if that**
the folly of men had not set it in higher estimation
for the rareness' sake. But, of the contrary part,
Nature as a most tender and **loving** mother hath
placed the best and most necessary things open
abroad; **as the air, the** water, and the earth
itself; **and hath** removed and put further from us
vain and unprofitable things." Here More abandons
himself to his humour, and gives a picture, ludicrous
enough, of the pains the Utopians **take to show the**

low value they set on gold, silver, and precious
stones; resuming his serious tone in a description of
the evils of a plutocracy.

In Utopia education is carefully considered: the
inhabitants are as well instructed as we are, save
that they have not our refinements of Logic. " In
their place," remarks Robinson in the margin,
"seemeth to be a nipping taunt." Astronomy and
meteorology they have studied with success; but
astrology "they never so much as dreamed of."
They welcomed Hythlodaye's somewhat peculiar
selection of Greek authors with delight; and from
" a certain affinity" easily learned the language.

The Utopian code of ethics is thus expounded,
in a passage which seems to be chiefly based
on Aristotle and Cicero, though the references to
Plato are numerous. The Utopians declare that
" the felicity of man" consists in pleasure: "and,
which is more to be marvelled at, the defence of
this so dainty and delicate an opinion they fetch
even from their grave, sharp, bitter, and rigorous religion." But " they think not," says More
further on, "felicity to consist in all pleasure, but
only in that pleasure that is good and honest,
and that here, as to perfect blessedness, our nature
is allured and drawn even of virtue, whereto only
they that be of the contrary opinion do attribute
felicity. For they define virtue to be life ordered
according to nature, and that we be hereunto
ordained even of God. And that he doth follow the
course of nature, who in desiring and refusing
things is ruled by reason." How far this may be

consistent it is not necessary here to inquire. In the exposition of the Utopian philosophy all is high and ennobling, whether the basis on which it is founded is really capable of sustaining the ideal, or not. Intellectual pleasures are regarded as the highest : virtue is pursued for the sake of a spiritual payment. Examples of the pleasures which the Utopians accepted and rejected are given. In the former passage may be noticed the Platonic idea of pleasure in motion and of the distinction between pure and mixed pleasures. In the latter any delight in fine clothes, jewels, gambling, hunting is condemned. In illustration of the Utopians' position their repro- bation of fasting is referred to. This is a point which serves to remind the reader that More, throughout the book, mingles in a very subtle manner his own opinions with views to which he was entirely opposed. He himself fasted continually, and was as scrupulous in the preservation of the outward forms of religion as he was deeply penetrated by its spirit.

We now return to the social institutions of Utopia. Slavery exists in the ideal State ; but the bondmen are only those who have been guilty of heinous offences, or have been bought when condemned to death in foreign countries. To those who are afflicted with any incurable disease of a very painful nature the priests and magistrates advise suicide, " but they cause none such to die against his will."

The Utopians alone " of the nations in that part of the world be content every man with one wife apiece."

Their rulers have no pomp of office; only the prince has a sheaf of corn borne before him, and the bishop a waxen taper.

Their laws are few and simple, and the whole race of lawyers "they utterly exclude and banish."

The subject of their foreign relations is made the occasion for bitterly ironical reference, both direct and implied, to the politics of the day. They make no leagues, and that "chiefly because that in those parts of the world leagues between princes be wont to be kept and observed very slenderly. For here in Europe, and especially in those parts where the faith and religion of Christ reigneth, the majesty of leagues is everywhere considered holy and inviolable: partly through the justice and goodness of princes, and partly at the reverence and motion of the head bishops. Which, like as they make not promises themselves but they do very religiously perform the same, so they exhort all princes in any wise to abide by their promises, and them that refuse or deny so to do, by their pontifical power and authority they compel thereto. And surely they think well that it might seem a very reproachful thing, if in the leagues of them which by a peculiar name be called faithful, faith should have no place.

"But in that new found part of the world, which is scarcely so far from us beyond the line equinoctial as our life and manners be dissident from theirs, no trust nor confidence is in leagues. But the more and holier ceremonies the league is knit up with, the sooner it is broken by some cavillation found in the words, which many times of purpose be so craftily put in and placed that the bands can never be so sure nor so **strong** but they will find some hole open to creep out at, and **to** break both league and truth. The which crafty dealing, yea the which fraud and deceit, if **they** should know it **to be** practised among private men in their bargains and contracts, they would incontinent cry **out at it** with an open mouth and a sour countenance as an offence most detestable and worthy **to be** punished with a shameful **death,**—yea, even **very they that** avaunce themselves authors of like **counsel given** to princes. Wherefore it **may well be** thought, either that all justice is a base and **low virtue and** which avaleth itself" (*subsidat*, original) "far under the high dignity of **kings; or** at the leastwise that there **be two justices;** the **one** meet for the inferior sort **of the people,** going afoot and creeping **low by the** ground, **and bound down on every side** with many bands **because it shall not run at rovers;** the other **a** princely virtue, which, like **as it is of** much higher **majesty than the other** poor justices, **so** also it is of much more **liberty, as to the** which nothing **is** unlawful that it lusteth after."

There could **be** no clearer reprobation **of any** difference between political and individual morality. The reference to the events of **the European** history of the last twenty years was one which **he who ran** might read. Every line, almost every word contains a sting : and yet there was **nothing** that authority could reprehend. As Mr. Seebohm puts it—" Upon **any** other hypothesis than that the evils against which **its** satire was directed were admitted **to be** *real*, the romance of *Utopia* must also be admitted to be harmless. To pronounce it to be dangerous was to admit its truth."

The Utopians abhor war, and fight only in defence of their own country, or to defend some oppressed nation. They fight also, by preference, with cunning, to avoid bloodshed. They offer large bribes for the assassination of the chiefs of their adversaries, and for treason among their enemies. Here again the inference was obvious. If these actions seemed a detestable contrast to the lofty morality of the Utopians, much more was it a dishonour to a Christian Government to engage in such intrigues as at that very time Henry VIII. was carrying on in Scotland. An equally severe condemnation is implied in the reference to the Utopians' employment of mercenaries. It could have needed no acute intelligence to recognize the Swiss—whom the King was then employing—in the Zapoletes, "dwelling in wild woods and high mountains," who basely hire themselves to the highest bidder, and whom it would be well if war had utterly destroyed.

Lastly we reach the most interesting chapter in the whole book—" Of the religions in Utopia." Of this the barest notice must suffice.

There are several religions in the happy island, but Christianity has been introduced and has made many converts. By an ancient law of King Utopus, who believed that if one religion was absolutely true it must eventually prevail, there is perfect liberty for every man to hold what views he will. This complete toleration excludes only him who does not believe the immortality of the soul; because he lowers the dignity of humanity to the level of the beasts. He is excluded from all public office, but undergoes no punishment, "because," says More, with the great saying of Cassiodorus in his mind, no doubt, "they be persuaded that it is not in any man's power to believe what he list." He is not, however, allowed to propagate his opinions.

The Utopians do not mourn for the dead,—save for those who seem to depart against their will. They honour them by memorials recording their virtues, and believe in their continual, though invisible, presence. Soothsaying and divination they reject, but they are firmly persuaded of the truth of miracles.

There are two kinds of religious orders among them: men who take upon themselves all hard, vile, unpleasant labours, and perform every kind of spiritual and manual work, yet "neither reprove other men's lives, nor glory in their own"; some of whom are vegetarians, ascetic, and celibate, while others marry and enjoy all pleasures which do not hinder their labour. "They have priests of exceeding holiness, and therefore very few." These have power to excommunicate, and are the instructors of children. There are women-priests,—though few, and those widows, and old. The male priests marry. "To no office among the Utopians is more honour and pre-eminence given. Insomuch that if they commit any crime they be under no common judgment, but be left only to God and themselves. For they think it not lawful to touch him with man's hand, be he never so vicious, which after so singular a sort was dedicate and consecrate to God, as a holy offering."

In the churches there is a dim religious light, conducive to concentration of thought and devotion of soul. Though there are many sects, "nothing is seen or heard in the churches but that seemeth to agree indifferently with them all." The sacrifices of the sects are private, but all attend the public services. There is no image of God in the church, "to the intent it may be free for every man to conceive God by their religion after what likeness and similitude they will."

The wives and children always confess at home to the head of the family, before the sacrifice. The offering is not of any living thing, but "they burn frankincense and other sweet savours, and light also a great number of wax candles and tapers, not supposing this to be anything available to the divine nature, as neither the prayers of men; but this unhurtful and harmless kind of worship pleaseth them. And by these sweet savours and lights and other such ceremonies men feel themselves secretly lifted up and encouraged to devotion with more willing and fervent hearts."

The vestments of the priests are embroidered with birds' feathers, and have a solemn signification. At the beginning of the service praises are sung to an exquisitely harmonious accompaniment of various instruments. Afterwards priests and people pray, in words which every one can apply to himself. God is adored as Creator and Governor, and

is implored to show the right way of life, the best
government, and the true religion,—that if the
people do not possess these they may be led to the
knowledge of them—and He is asked to take His
servants to Himself when He will.

When the service is over, the rest of the day is
spent in "play and exercises of chivalry."

No part of the *Utopia* has been more often the
subject of commentary than this; and certain modern
writers have discovered in it many of their own
opinions. This may be more fitly discussed when
More's religious writings are examined. But such
points are of importance in the discussion of the
question which every reader of the *Utopia* must
desire to solve,—how far the views of More are
expressed in his book. In the condemnation of the
political and social evils of the day there can be
no doubt that he was speaking his own opinions
through a safe disguise; but more than this we
can hardly with any certainty declare. It may
be that, eminent lawyer though he was, he felt
deeply the injuries of the law's delay; but his other
writings almost necessarily forbid us to think that
he seriously advocated communism. The arguments
against it which he gives, though slight, are conclusive; and we may infer that he rather looked
for an equality in the future by the influence of
Christianity and the true recognition of its human-
izing spirit.[1] Nor again can the voluntary suicide

---

[1] *Utopia*, p. 144—"Howbeit I think this was no small
help and furtherance in the matter that they heard us say,
that Christ instituted among his all things common : and that

of the incurable be supposed to be sanctioned by More himself. The plain opposition between his own custom and the Utopian opinion of fasting has already been pointed out. A similar divergence is evident on the subject of images or pictures in churches, which he expressly defends in one of his more serious works. Nor can we believe that More would for a moment have tolerated women as priests, or indeed have suffered the marriage of the clergy: of the latter at least there is no sanction in any other of his writings. His own words at the end of the book confirm this view: many things, he says, in the manners and laws of Utopia seemed to him " to be instituted and founded of no good reason."

Was the *Utopia* a lamentation for the Middle Ages which the Renaissance was everywhere burying, not without contempt ? Was it a passionate prophecy of the dim future which More's keen insight foresaw ? No doubt it was in some measure at least a regret for the past. The old system of mutual help, the old relations of society, its feudally patriarchal obligations, and its ties of fraternity and guild, were certainly to him very beautiful, and he witnessed their destruction with something like dismay. But for much of the past he had no reverence and no regret. Wars and the delights of a half-barbarous age had no charm in his eyes. "Hunting and hawking are no longer the choice pleasures of knight

---

the same community doth yet remain among the rightest Christian companies."

and lady, but are jeered at by him as foolish and unreasonable pieces of butchery; his pleasures are in the main the reasonable ones of learning and music." [1]

That his book was a prophecy of the future, or even the full expression of his own idea for England, it would be difficult to show. It has become, we are told, in our own day, " a necessary part of a Socialist's library," [2] but it conflicts with much of the authorized socialist programme. [3] It is rather wide in its scope than definite in its intentions, save only in its direct references to the pressing evils of the day. And its indebtedness to the past is general rather than particular. More " is penetrated with the spirit of Plato, and quotes or adapts many thoughts both from the *Republic* and the *Timaeus.*" [4] But the ideal is still modern, practical, and Christian, and its application is permanent. More looks everywhere to common effort for the redress of wrongs, and to an underlying equality, which yet suffers kings and serfs, priests and officers, to reconcile the wrongs of an age of selfish struggles. He has no toleration for the iniquities of man against man, for luxury and chicanery and oppression, but his remedies are wrapt in an intentional obscurity and exaggeration.

[1] William Morris, Forewords to *Utopia:* Kelmscott Press, 1893.

[2] *Ibid.:* Mr. Morris's beautiful edition which every one would like to possess, but only the very rich can afford to buy.

[3] The instances Mr. Morris gives are those relating to government, the priesthood, and the obligation of the marriage contract, and in the " atmosphere of asceticism, which has a curiously blended savour of Cato the Censor and a mediæval monk." *Ibid.*

[4] Jowett, Introduction to the *Republic, Dialogues of Plato,* 3rd edition, vol. iii. p. ccxxiv.

Erasmus.

*From an engraving by C. Visscher,
after Holbein.*

To face page 141.

It is with an earnest exhortation to common work, to which the continuity of our social order still gives a profound significance, that More ends his picture of "Nowhere." He describes with bitter and indignant remonstrance the glaring inequalities and injustice of the so-called Commonwealths of his day —the "conspiracy of rich men procuring their own ends"; the patient suffering of the poor; the triumph of that "scornful lady," Pride, who "measureth not wealth and prosperity by her own commodities, but by the misery of others." And yet he sorrowfully admits—" As I cannot agree and consent to all things that he (Hythlodaye) said . . . so I must needs confess and grant that many things be in the Utopian Commonwealth which in our cities I may rather wish for than hope after."

Utopia indeed could never be brought down to earth; and More never lost touch of his own practical business, fondly though he might dream of a perfect in his imaginary state. Writing to Erasmus soon after the book was published, he says quaintly that he is in the clouds with the dream of a government offered to him by the Utopians; there he will be too high to think of common acquaintances, yet there will always be a place in his heart for Erasmus and Tunstal—and if they visit him, his subjects shall do them honour as the prince's friends. So he dreams on till morning dawns, and as his royalty vanishes he sinks back into what had now become his familiar mill-round at Court.[1]

In politics and in religion More had to meet the

---

[1] Erasm. *Epp.* App. 250. (Leyden ed. of *Works*, vol iii. pt. 2.)

stern realities of an age of crises; but the longing for brotherhood which illuminates every page of the *Utopia* remained the expression of his deepest thoughts. It was to the union between the Church and the New Learning that he looked for the great hope of the future. "No such cry" as his "of pity for the poor, of protest against the system of agrarian and manufacturing tyranny, had been heard since the days of Piers Ploughman."[1] It was the echo, he thought, of the Church's teaching. For Christ Himself would have all men brothers, and He "instituted among His all things common—and . . . the same community doth yet remain among the rightest Christian companies." It was in this longing for brotherhood that the Utopians with glad minds received the faith of Christ[2]; and it was in the community of the Catholic Church that More believed all wrongs could be redressed and the world pass to its New Birth.

[1] A. W. Hutton, *Sir Thomas More and his Utopia*, p. 17.
[2] Arber's edition of *R. Robinson's Transl.* p. 144.

CHAPTER IV.

POLITICAL LIFE.

"So lieb mir meiner Seele Seligkeit ist, so lieb wird mir
    seyn wenn ich dem allgemeinen Wesen dienen kann."—
    Wallenstein.

MORE's political life may be said to have begun
almost at the same time as the reign of Henry VIII.
His professional income, gradually increasing, had
reached little less than £400 (or about £5000 as the
value of money is now) a year; and work of a more
public character was coming to him. On July 5,
1509, he was named in commission with his father
and another lawyer to take inquisition as to the
possessions in Middlesex of William, Viscount Beau-
mont, deceased. And from February 22, 1510, he
was for many years in the Commission of the Peace
for Hampshire.[1] On September 3, 1510, he was
elected one of the under-sheriffs of the city of
London, and thus acted as judge in the County
Court of London and Middlesex. Erasmus has given
a description of the office and of More's conduct

[1] Feb. 22, 1510: Dec. 15, 1510: July 18, 1511 (Commission
of Array): March 15, 1512: June 3, 1513: Jan. 24, 1514,
etc. etc.

in it, in his letter to Ulrich von Hutten.[1] "This office, though not laborious, for the court sits only on every Thursday till dinner-time, is accounted very honourable. No judge of that court ever went through more causes; none ever decided them more uprightly; often remitting the fees to which he was entitled from the suitors. His deportment in this capacity endeared him extremely to his fellow-citizens." Of his exercise of the judicial duties of this post two amusing anecdotes have been told—one of his restoring a beggar's dog which his wife had found, and another of a trick he played on a conceited old justice, who declared that only fools could have their pockets picked.

In 1509, he became a Bencher of Lincoln's Inn, and he was reader there in 1511 and 1516. On February 1, 1514, we find him in the Commission of Sewers for the district extending along the Thames between East Greenwich and Lambeth.

In such employments the earlier years of the reign were passed, but with the new development of foreign policy into which England gradually drifted, More was forced into a wider sphere of action. For the first four years of the reign the peaceful traditions of Henry VII. had been maintained. Warham and Fox were both peace ministers, and Henry, though eager to enter into the European struggle which it was only a question of time how long England could avoid, perceived the deficiency of trained soldiers, and waited till some organization should have been attempted.

[1] Erasm. *Epp.* x. 30.

When at length war had been made it had been
carried on with wonderful success, and the peace
which concluded it had been in every way honourable. The remarkable development of diplomacy
brought England, now regarded universally as the
great home of money, more and more closely into
connexion with the continental powers. The insincerity of the great States and their distrust of
each other caused constant revolutions in the political
arrangements of Europe; no sooner was one power
victorious, than an ally would immediately make a
treaty with the vanquished. A network of hypocrisy
and tortuous procedure arose, which necessitated
the employment of a large body of professed diplomatists, whether ambassadors, special envoys, or spies.
Into this system More was introduced almost as it
were by chance. The relations of England with
Charles of Castile and the Netherlands had been
much strained, and it was decided to send an
embassy to the Netherlands "for the continuance
of the treaties of intercourse between the late Kings
of England and Castile."[1] On hearing of this, the
London merchants, who had suffered from the sus-
pension of commercial intercourse, desired to be
especially represented. More was already well
known to the merchants of the Steelyard, whose
interests were at stake; and his reputation had
already reached the ears of Wolsey. Thus readily
at their request[2] the King joined More to the
Commission,[3] which consisted of Cuthbert Tunstal,

---

[1] *Letters and Papers, Hen. VIII.* ii. 422.   [2] Roper, p. 8.
[3] *Ibid.* (as above), May 1516.

Master of the Rolls and Archdeacon of Chester; Sir Thomas Spynell, resident at Bruges; Dr. Sampson, vicar-general of Tournay; and John Clifford, "governor of the English merchants."

The next day, May 8, 1514, the Court of Aldermen gave permission for More to appoint a deputy in his office,[1] and he started for Flanders on May 12. Spynell announced his arrival at Bruges with Tunstal[2] on the 18th, and on the 20th Sampson wrote to Wolsey expressing his pleasure at the honour of being named in the King's Commission with Dr. Tunstal and "young More."[3] The business, in which More and Clifford were specially charged with the commercial interests, was a tedious one: French influence was all powerful at the Court of Flanders, and the English envoys met with "taunts and checks, scarce within the bounds of friendly consideration." The Flemish merchants complained of many injuries in their commerce with England, besides the constant grievance of the Staple. Nor were the personal comforts of the ambassadors enviable. More, whose salary was only 13$s.$ 4$d.$ a day,[4] had not been paid; and it was not till Tunstal wrote to Wolsey to tell of his distress—"Master More at this time, as being at a low ebb, desires by your grace to be set on float again"—that a remittance of £20 was sent to him.[5] The Commission moved from Bruges to

---

[1] Extracts from City Records: App. to Mackintosh, *Life of More.*   [2] Brewer, ii. 473.   [3] *Ibid.* ii. 480.

[4] *King's Book of Payments*, Brewer, ii. 1647

[5] July 9, 1515, Brewer, ii. 679. Tunstal and Sampson received £30. See *King's Book of Payments* as above.

Brussels, and eventually to Antwerp, where More made the acquaintance of Petrus Ægidius. At last the negotiations were completed, and soon after the beginning of 1516[1] More was able to return to England. He had not enjoyed his experience of diplomacy. The honour, such as it was, scarcely counterbalanced the inconveniences of the position. Yet More had been able to gain an insight into the evils of the then-existing international relations, which he made abundant use of in his *Utopia*. Writing to Erasmus on his return to Court in February, he gives an amusing picture of its disadvantages. Tunstal, he said, had hardly been ten days in London, "when[2] he was sent off on another embassy; yet such an employment could not be half so inconvenient to him as it was to a layman. We laymen and you priests are not on equal terms on such occasions; for you leave no wives nor children at home, whereas whenever we laymen are away, we are called back by the love of our wives and families. When a priest starts on his mission, he can take his whole family with him, and feed at the king's expense those whom he must otherwise have fed at home. But whenever I am absent, I have two families to keep, one at home, and one

---

[1] Erasm. *Epp.* ii. 16.

[2] Some difficulty arises here about the dates. Roper states that More was sent on two embassies to Flanders, and almost every succeeding writer has accepted his statement—Mr. Seebohm without any comment. It appears, however, that the *second* embassy was that to Calais in August 1577, *after* More's knighthood and employment at Court. Of three embassies there is no record. *Vide* Erasmus to Ammonius, Brewer, ii. 3003, 3634, *et seq.*

abroad. The king provides tolerably well for those whom I must take with me; but no consideration is paid to those whom I leave behind. You know what a kind husband I am, what an indulgent father and lenient master: and yet for all this I cannot prevail on my wife, children and servants, to close their mouths and stop eating till I return." With his conduct of the negotiations the King and Wolsey were much pleased, and he was requested to enter the royal service. He showed his reluctance to obey, even when a pension was pressed upon him, as large as the income he would lose by withdrawal from practice.[1] In the letter above quoted More mentions this to Erasmus, and declares that he believes he shall always decline a pension and office at Court, because it would oblige him either to resign his office in the city, which he preferred to a higher one, or to encourage suspicions of being biassed in favour of the Crown in case of any contest concerning privileges. For a short time the King consented to press no further; but a little later More was induced to accept a pension of £100 for life.[2] But less than a year passed before another occasion brought More into public notice. A Papal vessel at Southampton had been seized probably as a droit of the Admiralty, and claimed as a forfeiture by the King. The Papal envoy, Campeggio, demanded counsel to defend the right of the Pope; and More, who was appointed, argued with such learning and acuteness, that the cause was decided in favour of the Holy See.[3] The

[1] Roper, p. 10.
[2] *Letters and Papers*, ii.   [3] Roper, p. 8.

King, who had **been** present at the hearing of the suit, was **so** delighted with More's **ability, that he could no longer** submit to be **without his service. The appointment of** Master of **Requests was conferred upon him in 1518, and a** month later he **was sworn of the Privy Council.** In March 1517, Erasmus, writing to **Tunstal,**[1] notices that More, hitherto so inflexible, **has been** carried away to Court.

In the interval, **however,** between his rejection and his acceptance of the **royal** offer, More had **published** his *Utopia,* and **thus given** decisively **to the world** his views of **international and domestic policy.** The King accepted his **services under no deception,** and More **fifteen years afterwards was able** to remind him of the " **most godly words that his Highness spake unto him at his first coming into his service, the** most **virtuous lesson that ever** prince **taught his** servant, willing **him first to look unto** God **and after God** to him."[2] Thus, reluctant as he had **been to take** it, More could not **but** regard **his new** position **as an** honour **to** his **opinions** as **well as to** his abilities. **Writing to** Fisher,[3] he said—" **I have** come to court **entirely against my will,** and **as** the king himself often **jestingly reproaches** me for. **And** I am as uncomfortable **as a carpet knight in** the saddle. . . . **Yet** such **is the virtue and learning of** the king, **and his** daily increasing progress **in both, that the more I see him increase** in these kingly **ornaments the less troublesome the** courtier's life **becomes to me."**

<hr>

[1] Brewer, ii. 3003.   [2] Roper, **p. 29.**
[3] Stapleton, cap. vii. p. 229.

In the few months that passed between his summons to Court and his appointment to another foreign mission, More was able to perform some slight service in London, both as a member of the Council, and as still holding the office of under-sheriff, which he did not resign till July 23, 1519.[1] A great tumult took place on April 28, 1517, which was only put down with much difficulty. The jealousy of the London traders against foreigners, who in the last few years had been settling in London in great numbers, had risen to a high pitch. One John Lincolne, having failed to induce the famous Dr. Standish in the Spital Sermon on the Monday in Easter week to introduce the subject, prevailed upon a certain Dr. Bell to do so. From the text, *Coelum coeli Domino, terram autem dedit filiis hominum*, this worthy divine aroused his audience to frenzy by declaring that England was given to its natives, and not to strangers. The Council had due notice of the danger, and sent to enforce precautionary measures, but the very execution of the order caused a riot, which soon assumed alarming proportions. The prisons were broken open and foreigners' houses burnt; and tranquillity was only secured by an armed force, after the heavy ordnance in the Tower had been directed against the city. More had been unremitting in his personal efforts to allay the disturbance, and had only been frustrated by the folly of his companions.[2]

---

[1] Extracts from City Records, *App.* to Mackintosh, *Life of More.*

[2] Stow, *Annals* (ed. 1631,) p. 505 *et seq.* Cres. More, p. 49. Walter's *Life of More*, p. 67.

He was himself appointed when the riots were over
to inquire into their origin. In his *Apology* he
thus described his action.[1] " Even here in London
after the great business that was there on a May
day in the morning, by a rising made against
strangers, for which divers of the prentices and
journeymen suffered execution of treason, by an old
statute made long before, against all such as would
violate the king's safe conduct; I was appointed
among others to search out and enquire by diligent
examination in what wise and by what persons that
privy confederacy began. And in good faith after
great time taken and much diligence used therein,
we perfectly tried out at last that all that business of
any rising to be made for the matter, began only by
the conspiracy of two young lads that were prentices
in Cheapside, which, after the thing devised first and
compared between them twain, perused privily to
journeymen first, and after the prentices, of many of
the mean crafts in the city, bearing the first that they
spake with in hand, that they had secretly spoken
with many other occupations already and that they
were all agreed thereunto, and that besides them
there were two or three hundred serving men of
divers lords' houses and some of the king's too, which
would not be named nor known, that would yet in the
night be at hand, and when they were once up, would
not fail to fall in with them and take their part.
Now this ungracious invention and these words of
those two lewd lads (which yet in the business fled
always themselves and never came again after) did

[1] *Apology,* ed. 1533, pp. 261, 262.

put some other, by their oversight and lightness, in such a courage and boldness that they wende themselves able to avenge their displeasure in the night, and after either never to be known or to be strong enough to bear it out and go farther." From such small causes do great confusions spring, thought More; and he had henceforth a fine contempt for popular demonstrations. He compared the heretics to these misguided prentices, misled by their "pot-headed apostles."

But More was not only useful at home. The tortuous negotiations with France, which Wolsey disguised with so much care even from the keen inquiry of the Venetian Ambassador, were at this time dragging their slow course, and a suitable cloak for deeper projects was obtained in the sending of an embassy to Calais, to settle the disputes between the French and English merchants. On August 27, 1517, a Commission[1] was issued to Sir Richard Wingfield, then deputy of Calais, Dr. William Knight, and Thomas More. They were to meet the French representatives, having full power to receive and adjudicate upon complaints, and make the necessary compensation. It was hoped that the merchants would be thus saved the expenses of the law courts. This negotiation was even more tedious than the former, and from the incomplete records of its progress that are obtainable, we should infer that it lasted for at least six months. The Commissioners' allowance seems to have been higher than on More's previous mission[2]; but Erasmus, writing to Ægidius, declared

---

[1] Brewer, ii. 3634.　[2] *King's Book of Payments*, Aug. 1517,

that More was living at great expense, and engaged in business most odious to him. The French Commissioners did all in their power to delay any result, declaring that their commission was not complete.[1] They appear however to have been reasonable in their demands.[2] More hoped at one time to have seen Erasmus at Calais, but apparently was disappointed.

On his return to England, More was in constant attendance on the Court. In April 1518, Pace, writing from Abingdon to Wolsey, complains of the inconveniences which the Master of Requests was undergoing, his daily allowance of meat not being provided by the Lord Steward, and therefore having to be bought in the town, "which is to him intolerable, and to the king's grace dishonourable."[3] In September we have an amusing admission in the letter of the acute Giustiniani of how difficult it was to extract information from the newly made councillor. On October 4, More was one of the signatories of the treaty between England and France, in which the marriage of the Dauphin with the Princess Mary was arranged.[4] As soon as the negotiations at Calais had been over, there had been others at Bruges, and More's name appears constantly in diplomatic memoranda, and at home, especially during 1519, in correspondence with Wolsey as to politics and international relations.[5] In April 1520, his name occurs among those who signed the treaties between

---

[1] *Letters and Papers*, ii. 3750.
[2] *Ibid.* ii. 3766, 3773, 3803.
[3] *Ibid.* ii. 4055. [4] *Ibid.* ii. 4499.
[5] E. g. *Ibid.* vol. iii. 333, 356.

Henry and Charles V.,[1] and he rode in the gallant train which met the Emperor at Canterbury. In the autumn of that year he was again at Bruges, negotiating with the representatives of the Hanse towns. It was then that he tricked the boastful Fleming who offered to dispute with any man on any thesis, by propounding that fine question of English law—"an averia capta in withernamia sunt irreplegiabilia"—whether cattle seized under writ of distress are irrepleviable.

Abroad he made many friends : but he was most needed at home. The King, so Pace wrote to Wolsey, was earnest to put young men into his affairs, since "old men decay greatly,"[2] and so in 1521 More was knighted, and succeeded Weston as Treasurer of the Exchequer,[3] and from this time was closely attached to the Court. In 1522 he took an important part in the ceremonies attending the second visit of Charles V. At this time he was one of the King's chief secretaries, and through him Henry communicated with Wolsey whenever the Cardinal was not at Court. A number of letters, which passed at this period between Wolsey and More, exist, but the matters with which they are concerned are of no private interest. From chance expressions however various details of More's position at Court may be obtained, which fully confirm Roper's account of the familiarity to which he was admitted.[4] At present the first stirrings of the Reformation had

---

[1] *Letters and Papers*, ii. 739, 740.
[2] *Ibid.* vol. iii. 2900.
[3] Erasm. *Epp.* xvii. 16.
[4] *E. g.* Sept. 21, 1522. *Letters and Papers*, iii. 2555.

served to bring him more closely into connexion
with the King, especially in the matter of Luther's
book. Nor was his service unrewarded: he shared in
the spoil of the unhappy Buckingham, receiving the
manor of South, Kent.[1]

The Parliament which was summoned on account
of the necessities of the great French war, met on
Wednesday, April 15, 1523, in the magnificent hall
at Blackfriars. More was a member, but no inquiries
as to his constituency have as yet been successful.[2]
If we can reason from precedents, however, it was
almost certainly one of the counties. His friend
Tunstal preached the opening sermon, and, probably
by the King's direction, the House of Commons,
on Saturday, April 18, presented as their chosen
Speaker, Sir Thomas More. He made the usual
excuse of disability, comparing himself to Phormio,
and the King to Hannibal, in the tale. Wolsey, as
Chancellor, replied that 'his majesty, by long
experience of his services, was well acquainted with

---

[1] *Letters and Papers*, iii. 2239.

[2] " As the whole of his life passed during the great chasm in
writs for election and returns of members of parliament, from
1477 to 1542, the places for which Sir T. More sat, and the
year of his early opposition to a subsidy, are unascertained;
notwithstanding the obliging exertions of the gentlemen
employed in the repositories at the Tower and in the Rolls'
chapel. We know that he was Speaker of the House of
Commons in 1523 and 1524. Browne Willis owns his in-
ability to fix the place (*Notit. Parliament*, iii. 112); but he
conjectured it to have been 'either Middlesex, where he
resided, or Lancaster, of which he was chancellor.' But that
writer would not have mentioned the latter branch of his
alternative, if he had known that More was not chancellor of
the duchy till two years after his speakership."—Mackintosh,
Life of More, preface. See *Letters and Papers*, iii. 2956.

his wit, learning, and discretion ; and therefore he
thought that the Commons had chosen the fittest
person to be their speaker.' [1]   More again replied
according to usage, accepting the office with reluctance, and demanding the recognition of the privileges
of the Speaker and the House. Roper [2] thinks this
speech worthy of insertion in his work, probably
from his father-in-law's manuscript, but it contains
no point of great interest.

The critical period of More's life now begins.
Wolsey, having obtained a large grant from Convocation, in spite of the opposition of Fisher and Fox,
went down to the House of Commons on April 29,
and, having dilated upon the perfidy of the French
King, and the necessity of giving powerful aid to
the Emperor, demanded £800,000, and proposed
that it should be obtained by a fifth of all goods
for four years. [3] Of the subsequent debates Roper
gives a dramatic account, which has found its way
into most of the biographies of More, but which is
hardly reconcilable with our information from other
sources.

" At this Parliament Cardinal Wolsey found himself
much grieved with the Burgesses thereof, for that
nothing was so soon done or spoken therein, but that
it was immediately blown abroad in every alehouse.
It fortuned at that Parliament a very great subsidy

---

[1] Brewer (pref. to *Letters and Papers*, vol. iii. p. 237)
thinks it probable, Walter (*Life of More*, p. 87) states for
certain, that More was chosen Speaker by the King's command.
The latter writer gives no authority.

[2] Pages 10—12.

[3] Lord Herbert's *Henry VIII.* p. 134.

to be demanded, which the Cardinal fearing it would not pass the common house, determined for the furtherance thereof, to be there present himself; before whose coming after long debating there, whether it were better but with a few of his lords (as the most opinion of the house was), or with a whole train royally to receive him there amongst them, 'Masters,' quoth Sir Thomas More, 'forasmuch as my Lord Cardinal lately, you wot well, laid to our charge the lightness of our tongues for things uttered out of this house, it shall not be amiss in my mind to receive him with all his pomp, with his maces, his pillars, his poleaxes, his crosses, his hat, and great seal too; to the intent that if he find the like fault with us hereafter, we may be the bolder from ourselves to lay the blame upon those that his grace bringeth with him.' Whereunto the house wholly agreeing, he was received accordingly. Where after he had in a solemn oration by many reasons proved how necessary it was the demands there moved to be granted, and further said that less would not serve the king's purpose; he seeing the company still silent, and thereunto nothing answering, and contrary to his expectation shewing in themselves towards his requests no towardness of inclination, said unto them: 'Masters, ye have many wise and learned men among you, and sith I am from the king's own person sent hither unto you, for the preservation of your own selves and all the Realm, I think it meet you give me a reasonable answer.' Whereat every man holding his peace, then began he to speak to one Mr. Marney, who making him no answer neither, he severally asked the same question of divers others accounted the wisest of the company. To whom when none of them all would give so much as one word, being before agreed, as the custom was, by their speaker to make answer; ' Masters,' quoth the Cardinal, ' unless it be the manner of your house, as of likelihood it is, in such causes to utter your minds by the mouth of your speaker, whom ye have chosen for trusty and wise (as indeed he is), here is without doubt a marvellous obstinate silence'; and thereupon required the answer of Mr. Speaker, who reverently upon his knees excusing the silence of the house, abashed at the presence of so noble a personage, able to amaze the wisest and best learned in a Realm, and after by many reasons proving, that for them to make answer was it neither expedient, nor agreeable with the ancient liberty of the house; in conclusion for himself shewed, that though they had all with their voices trusted him, yet except every one of them could put into his own head all their several wits, he alone in so weighty a matter was unmeet to make his Grace answer. Whereupon the Cardinal displeased with Sir Thomas More, that had not in this Parliament in all things satisfied his desire, suddenly rose and departed."[1] Roper then goes on to relate that Wolsey resented the action of his courageous opponent, and cried, "Would God you had been at Rome when I made you Speaker!" and that he wished to have him sent as ambassador to Spain to get rid of him, but that Henry readily accepted More's excuses, saying, "It is not our

[1] Roper, pp. 12—14.

pleasure to do you hurt, but to do you good we should be glad."

Any statement of Roper's, who lived in the closest intimacy with his father-in-law under the same roof for more than sixteen years, must have great weight. In this case, the story is told with remarkable circumstance of detail; and Roper, living at that very time at Chelsea, could hardly be ignorant of the doings of this Parliament and of its Speaker. At the same time there is no support whatever to his statement from any other source, and other information seems directly to point to the improbability of such a scene having occurred; nor must it be forgotten that Roper has made other evident mistakes, though none of such importance as this. It can hardly be conceived that Wolsey would be so ignorant of the privileges and customs of the House of Commons, as he appears in this scene; nor, even on *à priori* grounds, would it be likely that one of the royal secretaries, living in daily intercourse with the King and his great minister as the confidant of most if not of all their plans, would make himself the exponent of direct opposition to a proposal, to which he had previously in all probability agreed. Not only this: but the utmost cordiality seems to have existed between Wolsey and More; and it is certain that in the discussions on the subsidy More constantly supported the royal demands, and at the end of the session received, by Wolsey's express request, a substantial mark of the royal gratitude.

The debates seem in reality to have proceeded quite otherwise than as Roper tells the story. On

Wolsey's departure, after his explanation of the royal demand, there was much discussion. On the next day More supported the Chancellor's plan, and showed that four shillings in the pound could not be considered extravagant on such an occasion. Opposition was raised on the ground that "though some were well monied, in general the fifth part of men's goods was not in plate or money, but in stock or cattle, and that to pay away all their coin would alter the frame and intercourse of all things."[1] Another position was taken in the speech made by Cromwell, who opposed the King's going to the war, and advocated fighting the French on Scots ground. A long speech for the Court is epitomized by Lord Herbert of Cherbury:[2] it is attributed to More, and is certainly much in his style of argument and expression. By this taxation, it was said, the money was not lost to the nation: no more indeed happened than by the ordinary course of markets. Let the rich men go to the war themselves, and show that they deserve their great possessions by the courage with which they can defend them. The objection that the money would be carried out of England was unreasonable, for would it not carry the men also? "Notwithstanding," continued the Speaker, "if you be so obstinate as to believe that making war in a country brings money into it, do but conceive awhile that the French had invaded us. Would the money they brought over, think you, enrich our country, or should any of us be the better for it? Let us

[1] *Henry VIII.* (edit. 1682), p. 134.
[2] *Ibid.*, and Walter's *Life of More*, p. 91.

therefore lay aside those poor scruples and do what may be worthy the dignity and honour of our nation. When you did conceive the worst that can fall out, you should yet eat your beef and mutton here, and wear your country cloth; while others, upon a short allowance, fought only that you might enjoy your families and liberty. But I say confidently, you need not fear this penury or scarceness of money, the intercourse of things being so established throughout the world that there is perpetual derivation of all that can be necessary to mankind. Thus your commodities will ever find out money; while, not to go far, I shall produce our own merchants only, who, let me assure you, will be always as glad of your corn and cattle as you can be of anything they bring you. Let us, therefore, in God's name, do what becomes us; and for the rest, entertain so good an opinion of our soldiers as to believe that, instead of leaving our country bare, they will add new provinces to it, or at least, bring rich spoils and triumphs home."

After debate it was agreed that a subsidy on a graduated scale should be granted; but the sum did not reach what Wolsey had asked. Then the Cardinal came down again to the House to address the members. His speech was heard in silence, but, say Hall and Lord Herbert, More intimated that it could not be discussed in his presence,—"it was the order of the House to hear, and not to reason, save among themselves." Subsequently it was decided that a fifth should be granted by those holding lands to the value of five pounds and upwards. On the

M

reassembling of the House after an adjournment, the knights of the shire agreed to continue their grant to a fourth year, and proposed that it should be paid also by those who had five pounds in gold. After a heated discussion More interfered as a peace-maker, and secured the acceptance of the motion.

It was natural that Wolsey, though all that he had asked had not been obtained, should be grateful to More : and on August 24[1] he wrote to the King, advising the gift of £100 to the Speaker for his household, in addition to the ordinary fee of £100. The reward can never have been better deserved than by the "faithful diligence" of More "in all your causes treated in this your late parliament, as well as for your subsidy." He adds, "I am the rather moved to put your highness in mind thereof, because he is not the most ready to speak and solicit his own cause." So far was Wolsey from feeling any displeasure against More. The latter, writing to the Cardinal two days afterwards, mentions that the King has ordered that he receive the £200 from the exchequer.[2] As the relations between More and Wolsey have here come into prominence, it may be well to notice other references to their connexion. They are to said to have first become acquainted at Oxford,[3] when More was a student at Canterbury College and Wolsey bursar of Magdalen; and the "epigrams" of the former contain a high compliment to the latter. Writing to Erasmus in February 1516, More

---

[1] *Letters and Papers,* iii. 3267.
[2] *Ibid.* iii. 3270. [3] Walter, p. 6.

spoke in the highest terms of the new Chancellor. "He acquits himself," said the young barrister, "so well as to outdo expectation, and, what must be admitted to be very difficult, even after so excellent a predecessor he gives the greatest satisfaction." Ammonius, speaking of More's return to England after his first embassy, describes him as among the earliest in paying salutations to Wolsey. The Cardinal fully appreciated his ability, and was at least as anxious as the King to bring him to Court; nor can his subsequent promotions have taken place without the minister's approbation. At the time of the Parliament of 1523, and for some years afterwards, the two statesmen were in constant correspondence: More was acting, on occasion, as the medium of communication between the King and the Chancellor, explaining, illustrating, enforcing, the views of the latter, with all his energy and skill. The letters that passed between them were always of the most cordial kind. Wolsey commits the most delicate matters to the charge of More, sure of his appreciation and diligence: More repays the confidence with zeal and affection. The biographers of the latter have invariably endeavoured to suggest a hostility between their hero and the great Cardinal, but their case is almost entirely without support. No good minister was ever condemned by his fall to such immediate as well as enduring unpopularity as was Wolsey. Of this feeling Erasmus, probably because he did not consider that he had been sufficiently noticed by the fallen statesman, and quite inconsistently with

the opinions he had expressed during the Cardinal's
exercise of power, made himself one of the ex-
ponents; and—as far as we can see—gratuitously,
informed the world when it was mourning for the
death of More, that the conscientious statesman
"had never been liked by Wolsey." Roper and
succeeding Roman Catholic writers, among whom
Wolsey has never been popular, gave credit to the
same view.

That the relations between the Cardinal and
More continued to be cordial, a glance at some of
the letters that passed between them suffice to
show.

Writing to "my Lord Legate"[1] on September 1,
1523, More described how he had shown his letters
to the King, and how Henry had been delighted
with his skill and wisdom in the difficult business
regarding Scotland, and "perceived what great
labour Wolsey had taken when the reading only of
those papers had held him more than two hours."
"I never saw him like things better," added the
writer, "and, in my poor fantasy, not causelessly;
for it (the letter to the King's sister, the Queen of
Scots) is one of the best made letters for words,
matter, sentence, and couching, that ever I read in
my life." On the 4th,[2] More wrote again—this
time on the directions to be given for the movement of Suffolk's army from Calais—and expressed
his pleasure "that his own services were so well
liked" by Wolsey. The correspondence was constant.

---

[1] *State Papers*, i. 128; Ellis, *Letters*, 1st Series, i. 203.
[2] *State Papers*, i. 130.

More wrote on the 12th,[1] about the preparation for the siege of Boulogne ; on the 13th, about the negotiations with Bourbon ;[2] on the 22nd and on the 24th, concerning the Scotch difficulty ;[3] and on the 30th, in joyful acknowledgment of the success of Suffolk's army.[4] Nor was he solely engaged in attendance on the King; he was on the Commission for Middlesex, to collect the subsidy in the grant of which his own exertions had so greatly aided. He was also on the Commission of the Peace[5] for the same county, and on his own account he seems to have entered into mercantile undertakings.[6]

During the years 1524 and 1525 there is little to notice in the correspondence between More and Wolsey, except the amusing incidents connected with the arrest of one of the servants of the Imperial ambassador by a patrol, and the perusal of the ambassador's reports by More (to whom they were taken when he was still in bed very early one morning) and Wolsey. These are detailed at great length in the indignant correspondence of de Praet, and led to the writing of a great number of State Papers, ending in the publication of an official *Vindication of the English.*[7]

In 1526, More's name occurs among those who took part in the ceremony with which, on June 16,

---

[1] *State Papers*, i. 131.   [2] *Ibid.* 130.   [3] *Ibid.* 140.

[4] Ellis, *Letters*, 1st Series, i. 210.

[5] April and October 1523; *Letters and Papers*, iii. 3195, 2993.

[6] *E. g. Letters and Papers*, iv. 2248 ; License to export 1000 woollen cloths.

[7] See *Spanish State Papers*, 1525-26, especially pp. 50, 62.

the King's natural son Henry, a little boy of six, was created Duke of Richmond. On August 14, he was among the signatories of the truce between England and France, and on the 30th, of the "treaty of the More." He received a further acknowledgment of his services on the death of Sir Richard Wingfield, when he was appointed Chancellor of the Duchy of Lancaster.[1]

In 1526, too, he was made one of a Committee of the Council of but three members, of whom two were every day to see the King,[1] waiting for him "every day in the forenoon by ten of the clock at the furthest, and at afternoon by two of the clock."[2]

Thus almost daily More had long speech with the King, and the talk began more and more to turn upon the religious matters in which he had become keenly interested.

Critical questions began to press on him both in his own thoughts and on behalf of the King in the controversy with Luther. Nor had he been able, much as he wished it, to keep out of the discussions and projects to which the question of the Divorce gave rise. The King early mooted to him his 'secret matter,' and 'sore pressed him' for an answer on it. After excusing himself as long as he could, he at last agreed to confer with the Bishops of Durham and Bath, and taking with him the passages from Scripture with which the King had supported his argument, compared them 'with the exposition of divers of the old holy doctors.' When he returned to

---

[1] Mackintosh, p. 91, *note.*
[2] Brewer, *Henry VIII.* i. 54.

the King, "in talking with his grace of the foresaid matter, he said, 'To be plain with your grace, neither my lord of Durham nor my lord of Bath, though I know them both to be wise, virtuous, and learned, and honourable prelates, nor myself with the rest of your council, being all your grace's own servants, for your manifold benefits daily conferred upon us so most bounden unto you, be in my opinion meet counsellors for your grace herein; but if your grace minds to understand the truth, such counsellors may you have devised, as neither for respect of their own worldly commodity, nor for fear of your princely authority will be inclined to deceive you.' To whom he named 'S. Jerome, S. Augustine, and divers other holy doctors, both Greeks and Latins; and moreover showed him what authority he had gathered out of them, which although the king did not very well like of, yet were they by Sir Thomas More (who in all his communications with the king in that matter had always most wisely behaved himself) so wisely tempered, that he both presently took them in good part and often times had thereof conference with him again." [1]

When Campeggio arrived and was received in London with solemn formality by the religious and secular authorities, to More was committed the task of delivering the Latin oration with which he was greeted. In such ceremonies his position entitled and obliged him to share; but he took no part in advancing the King's great desire. Henry employed him in other matters. It was rumoured at one time

[1] Roper, pp. 20, 21.

that he was to be sent to Ireland;[1] but we hear no
more of it. On May 29, 1529, he was Commissioner[2]
with Stephen Gardiner, then Archdeacon of Taunton,
for the signature of a new engagement with Francis
I., in which Wolsey's visit to France was arranged.
On July 3, the Cardinal arrived at Calais, attended
by a gorgeous train, among whom were the Bishop
of London, the Lord Chamberlain, the Master Con-
troller, and the Chancellor of the Duchy of Lancaster.

It is no part of our task to give any account of
the mission; More has unfortunately left no record
of it, and, indeed, his concern in it seems to have
been purely ceremonial. Wolsey returned to Court
at the end of September, and was followed by a
French embassy, by which 'pensions' were lavishly
distributed, More receiving one hundred and fifty
crowns.[3]

In July, the Chancellor of the Duchy accompanied
Tunstal to Cambray, to mediate, on the part of
England, between Charles V. and Francis I. Their
commission was issued on June 30.[4] After attesting
the treaty of Cambray on August 5,[5] and signing also
a mercantile treaty with the Archduchess Margaret,
they returned to England. On this mission, says
Roper,[6] "Sir Thomas More so worthily handled himself (procuring in our league far more benefits unto
his realm than at that time by the king and council
was possible to be compassed), that for his good service
on that voyage, the king, when he after made him

<hr>

[1] Du Bellay to Montmorency, *Letters and Papers,* iv. 5679.
[2] *Ibid.* iv. 3138.   [3] *Letters and Papers,* iv. 3619.
[4] *Ibid.* iv. 5744.   [5] *Ibid.* iv. 5829.   [6] Pages 22, 23.

Lord Chancellor, caused the Duke of Norfolk openly to declare unto the people, how much all England was bound unto him."

Yet all this while he was sad at heart. "So on a time," says Roper,[1] with the quaint pathos which is the great charm of his work, "walking along the Thames side with me at Chelsea, in talking of other things, he said to me, 'Now would to God, son Roper, upon condition three things were well established in Christendom I were put in a sack and here presently cast into the Thames.' 'What great things be these, sir,' quoth I, 'that would move you so to wish?' 'Wouldst thou know, son Roper, what they be?' quoth he. 'Yea, marry, sir, with a good will if it please you,' quoth I. 'I'faith they be these, son,' quoth he. 'The first is, that whereas the most part of Christian princes be at mortal wars, they were at universal peace. The second, that where the Church of Christ is at this present sore afflicted with many heresies and errors, it were well settled in an uniformity of Religion. The third, that where the king's matter of his marriage is now come into question, it were to the glory of God and quietness of all parties brought to a good conclusion;' whereby, as I could gather, he judged that otherwise it would be a disturbance to a great part of Christendom. Thus did it by his doings throughout the whole course of his life appear that all his travails and pains, without respect of earthly commodities either to himself or any of his, were only upon the service of God, the prince and the realm, wholly bestowed and employed.

---

[1] Pages 16, 17.

Whom in his latter time I heard to say that he never asked of the king the value of one penny."

No sooner had More returned from Cambray than he found the King had by no means given up the hope of winning him over to his views. Henry insisted on his conferring with Stokesley, then Archdeacon of Dorset, who was elevated to the see of London in the next year.[1] Still More remained firm in his opinion, though he made no boast of it, anxious even to see as the King saw, if in honour and conscience he might. The theologian, partisan though he was, admitted " that he found him in his grace's cause very toward, and desirous to find some good matter wherewith he might truly serve his grace to his content." It was a dangerous moment. At the council held, as usual to prepare business for Parliament, the King had treated Wolsey with contempt ; yet, in spite of the disgrace which he had seen preparing for some time, the Cardinal clung to office. It might have seemed that when he fell More would fall with him. Not only, however, was Henry's animosity always personal rather than extensive, but he well knew the value of such a servant. Moreover the Duke of Norfolk, the leader of the party that now had the royal ear, was More's " singular dear friend." [2] Wolsey himself declared, it was said, that More was the only person fit to succeed him.[3] Thus it was, and also, as men

---

[1] Here occurs another of Roper's inaccuracies. He makes Stokesley Bishop of London before More was Chancellor. One must therefore choose at will the date of the conference between them.　　　　　　　　　　　　　[2] Roper, p. 30.

[3] Erasmus to John Faber, Bishop of Vienne.

suspected,[1] from a hope that by such promotion he might be inclined towards the divorce, that when Wolsey had reluctantly yielded up the great seal, it was delivered by the King to Sir Thomas More.

That his greatness was thrust upon him, no one who knows anything of his character can doubt. Long before, he had seen the nature of the King's confidence, and it can hardly be doubted that he foresaw, if not the circumstances, yet certainly the result of his taking office. His onward path was no "blindfold walking"; he well knew that "behind him stalked the headsman." His acceptance of the great seal, rightly estimated, seems one of the noblest and most conscientious acts of a noble and conscientious life.

On Tuesday, October 20, 1529, Sir Thomas More took the oaths in the great hall at Westminster, in the presence of the Dukes of Norfolk and Suffolk and many of the nobility.[2] Not a murmur, open or secret, arose at the appointment; the people "were gathered together with great applause and. joy";[3] even Wolsey, in his misery, declared that no man in England was more worthy.[4] The new Chancellor was installed by the Duke of Norfolk, who delivered a speech, not preserved by Roper, but given in full by Cresacre More.[5] "The king's

---

[1] So said Pole (Stapleton, cap. xiv. p. 294) and Thuanus (*Hist. sui temporis*, lib. ii. cap. 16, "Neutiquam Regis causae aequior").

[2] Rymer, xiv. 349. [3] Cres. More, p. 156.

[4] Stapleton, cap. iii. p. 172.

[5] Pages 166—168. It may seem the language of the seventeenth rather than the sixteenth century.

majesty," he said, "hath raised to the most high dignity of Chancellorship Sir Thomas More, a man for his extraordinary worth and sufficiency well known to himself and the whole realm, for no other cause or earthly respect, but for that he hath plainly perceived all the gifts of nature and grace to be heaped upon him, which either the people could desire or himself wish for, for the discharge of so great an office. For the admirable wisdom, integrity, and innocence, joined with most pleasant facility of wit, that this man is endowed withal, have been sufficiently known to all Englishmen from their youth, and for these many years to the king's majesty himself. . . . He hath perceived no man in his realm to be more wise in deliberating, more sincere in opening to him what he thought, or more eloquent in expressing what he uttered." Then, after declaring that More's virtues were such as made permissible the elevation of a layman to an office which custom of recent times had given to ecclesiastics, he commended the Chancellor to the "joyful acclamations of the people."

It is difficult to regard the speech in the form given by Cresacre More, or, indeed, the reply of the Chancellor, as authentic; both seem to be an expansion, not altogether free from anachronisms, of the simple statement of Roper, who confesses that the speeches "are not now in his memory." Taking, then, the probably more accurate words of Roper, we are told that More, "among many other his humble and wise sayings, answered that though he had good cause to rejoice of his highness' singular favour towards him, that he had far above his deserts so highly commended him, yet nevertheless he must for his own **part needs** confess that in all things by his grace alleged he had done no more than was his duty. And further disabled himself as unmeet for that room, wherein considering how wise and honourable a prelate had lately before taken so great a fall, he had, he said, thereof no cause to rejoice." [1] And so at the moment when all men were reviling Wolsey, the new Chancellor took office with words of praise as honourable to the fallen statesman as to himself.

On the 3rd of November the Parliament assembled at Blackfriars, the King being present. According to the brief account in the Parliament Rolls,[2] Sir Thomas More, as Chancellor, in the opening speech declared the cause of the summons to be, "to reform such things as have been used or permitted in England by inadvertence or by the changes of time have become inexpedient, and to make new statutes and laws, where it is thought fit." "On these errors and abuses he discoursed," continues the Roll, "in a long and elegant speech, declaring with great eloquence what was needful for their reformation : and in the end he ordered the Commons in the king's name to assemble next day in their accustomed house, and choose a Speaker, whom they should present to the king."

Of More's speech Hall [3] gives a more full account, which is scarcely reconcilable with the statement of

---

[1] Roper, p. 24.   [2] *Letters and Papers*, vol. ii. 6043.
[3] Page 764.

the Roll,[1] and still less with More's character. "When the king was seated on his throne, Sir Thomas More, his chancellor, standing on his right hand, made an eloquent oration : ' Like as a good shepherd, which not only keepeth and attendeth well his sheep, but also foreseeth and provideth for all things that may be hurtful or noisome to the flock : so the king, which is the shepherd, ruler, and governor of his realm, vigilantly foreseeing things to come, considering how divers laws by the mutation of things are insufficient and imperfect, and also by the frail condition of man divers new enormities are sprung up among the people, for the which no law is yet made to reform the same—for this cause the king at this time hath summoned his high court of Parliament. And I liken the king to a shepherd . . . and as you see that, amongst a great flock, some are rotten and faulty, which the good shepherd sendeth from the sound sheep, so the great wether, which is of late fallen, as you all know, so craftily, so scabbedly, yea, so untruly, juggled with the king, that all men must needs guess that he thought in himself either the king had no wish to perceive his crafty doings, or else that he would not see nor know them. But he was deceived ; for his grace's sight was so quick and penetrable, that he saw him, yea, and saw through him, both within and without : and according to his desert he hath a gentle correction ; which small punishment the king will not to be an example to other offenders, but openly declareth that whosoever hereafter shall make the like attempts, or counsel

---

[1] *Letters and Papers*, vol. iv.　Preface, p. 538.

the like offences shall not escape with the like punishment.'" This report bears an appearance of exactness, which makes it impossible, in the face of the rather negative than positive evidence of the Parliament Rolls, at once to condemn it as untrue; and it is to some extent corroborated by the long letter which Chapuys wrote to the Emperor detailing the events of the opening of Parliament. More, as Chancellor, was bound to vindicate Henry's action, but there are some considerations tending to throw discredit upon the speech as Roper gives it. If we have been right in inferring that in their account of the Parliament of 1523, the early biographers of More were misled by their feeling against Wolsey into evident inaccuracy, there is no reason why a similar error should not have been committed by a writer who is well known as extremely hostile both to Wolsey and More. The speech is inconsistent with Roper's account of his father-in-law's words in the Chancery, and even more so with the tone of bis long correspondence with the Cardinal. Nor was More a man to turn on a fallen minister in such a manner, or join in a popular cry of resentment.[1] It must not be forgotten that Hall is the only authority for the speech in this form.

It must be added, however, that the name of the Chancellor appears at the head of the signatures to the articles against Wolsey presented by the House

---

[1] I speak not without temerity, for Bishop Creighton, whom it is rash indeed to oppose, accepts the speech without demur, and writes of " unworthy taunts at his defeated adversary " (*Wolsey*, p. 190). But Wolsey was not More's adversary.

of Lords to the King, on December 1. And Chapuys shows that More did vindicate the King's action, and speak severely of Wolsey's policy.[1]

During the short session of this Parliament much important business was done, but we have no record of More's share in it. There can be no doubt that when the prorogation came, the release from his parliamentary duties would be felt as a great relief; for he had little sympathy with the work that was now in hand. The legal work of his office, especially during the prevalence of heresy, was sufficient to tax the energies of any man. Of the Chancellor's duties, apart from those connected with religion, a few words will suffice. It may be noticed in passing that for salary More received £142 15s., and 'for his attendance in the Star Chamber,' £200 a year. 'Also the chief butler was to allow him £64 a year for the price of 12 tuns of wine, and the keeper of the great state robe £16 a year for wax.'[2]

The occupation of the Court of Chancery was, of course, trifling, according to more modern ideas. In the century after More's time—when it seems to have decided on an average a hundred and sixty suits a year—its business had increased tenfold. "At the utmost," says Sir James Mackintosh,[3] "More did not hear more than two hundred cases and arguments yearly, including those of every description. No authentic account of any case tried before him,

---

[1] *Spanish State Papers*, 1529-30, pp. 322-323.
[2] *Letters and Papers*, iv. 6079.
[3] *Life of More*, p. 125.

if any such be extant, has yet been brought to light.
No law book alludes to any part of his judgments
or reasonings. Nothing of this higher part of his
judicial life is preserved which can justify us in
believing more than that it must have displayed
his never - failing integrity, reason, learning, and
eloquence."

He sat every afternoon in "his open hall, to the
intent that if any person had any suit unto him they
might the more boldly come into his presence, and
there open complaints before him." [1]

So indefatigable was he in the exercise of his
office that on one occasion when he called for the
next case, he was answered that the list was
exhausted.[2] He ordered the fact to be put upon
record, "and deservedly so," says one of his modern
biographers, "as it is probably the only miracle of
the kind mankind will ever witness." [3] Though his
strict justice was remarkable in that age, his 'injunctions' did not pass without complaint from the
common lawyers. This was brought to his notice
by Roper, and he thereupon so satisfactorily explained
all the injunctions that he had issued that the
judges were forced to confess that they in similar
cases would have done the same.

When they declined themselves to attempt any
humane interpretation of the law, More said—"Forasmuch as yourselves, my lords, drive me to that
necessity for awarding out injunctions to relieve the
people's injury, you cannot hereafter any more justly

---

[1] Roper, p. 25. [2] Stapleton, cap. iii. p. 179.
[3] Walter, *Life of More*, p. 171.

blame me." To Roper he added—"I perceive, sir, why they like not so to do: for they see that they may, by the verdict of the jury, cast off all quarrels from themselves upon them, which they account their chief defence, and therefore am I compelled to abide the adventure of all such reports."[1]

Parliament was repeatedly prorogued "on account of the pestilence in London and its suburbs," and did not reassemble until January 6, 1531. During the recess More had as far as possible confined himself to his legal duties, for he was gradually more and more estranged from the Court in the matter which the King had most at heart. To the famous address to Clement VII. his name was not appended.[2] Yet while he never yielded unconscientious compliance, he shunned unnecessary disobedience. Indeed, the great difference between More and Henry VIII., even were we to accept Mr. Froude's apologies for the King, can never be obliterated. The former never thought it right to do for the sake of public policy what in private life would have been a wrong act.[3]

On March 31, More, as Chancellor, went down

---

[1] Roper, p. 27.

[2] The date of the address has been the subject of discussion: Lord Herbert puts it, probably correctly, under the year 1530. Mr. Froude assigned it to 1531, giving arguments for the date, in which he quite forgot that the signature of Wolsey, who died Nov. 29, 1530, is appended to it.

[3] Cf. Froude, *Hist. Eng.* vol. i. p. 417—"Let us compensate the poor queen's sorrows with unstinted sympathy, but let us not trifle with history by confusing a political necessity with a moral crime."

to the House of Commons to declare the favourable answers of the Universities on the Divorce, 'and to exhibit above an hundred books of several doctors, confirming the same opinion.'[1]   Yet his views on this question, as well as on that of the supremacy, were perfectly well known.   The letters of Chapuys to Charles V. contain very interesting references to the Chancellor's position.   Of the assumption of the supremacy the ambassador wrote—"There is none that do not blame this usurpation, except those who have promoted it.   The Chancellor is so mortified at it that he is anxious above all things to resign his office.[2]   And again, of his feeling towards Queen Katherine and the Emperor[3]—"The Chancellor, as I have formerly written, has conducted himself most virtuously in this matter of the Queen, and certainly showed himself as well inclined towards your majesty as could be.   He is the true father and protector of your majesty's subjects. Whenever any man of my suite has been at court, he has broken off his conversation with everybody else to attend to our business, and every one whom I have recommended to him he has despatched with a favourable answer."   There are many other passages which show that More was in constant communication with the imperial agents and a most loyal supporter of the cause of the unhappy Katherine.

More retained his office for two years and a half. Amid ceaseless anxiety on account of the pro-

---

[1] Lord Herbert, p. 352.
[2] *Letters and Papers*, v. 112, from Vienna Archives.
[3] *Ibid.* v. 120.

gress of heresy, and domestic grief—the death of
his father whom he loved with such devotion and
reverence—in spite, too, of the beginnings of a
painful disease, he endeavoured manfully to do his
duty according to his conscience. But the legislation of 1531 and 1532 was carried against all his
sympathies, and the King still pressed him "to
weigh and consider his great matter."[1] During
the session of 1532 he continued to support the
political and financial projects of the Court;[2] but
he opposed the King's wishes in religious matters.[3]
The passing of the Annates Act confirmed the
resolution he had already formed, and he begged
the Duke of Norfolk to submit his resignation to
the King. After some trouble it was accepted; and
on May 16, "about three o'clock in the afternoon,
in the garden of York Place, by Westminster," he
delivered the great seal into the King's hands.
Henry seemed for the moment to feel a return of
his old affection. "So pleased it his highness to
say unto him, that for the good service he before
had done him, in any suit which he should after
have unto him, that either should concern his
honour (for that word it liked his highness to use
unto him) or that should appertain to his profit, he
would find his highness a good and gracious lord
unto him."[4] More himself gave as his reason for
resigning, "a sharp and constant pain in the chest";[5]

[1] Roper, p. 29.
[2] See Chapuys to Charles V., April 10, 1532: *Letters and Papers*, v. 941.
[3] *Ibid.* v. 1013, 1046. [4] Roper, p. 30.
[5] Erasm. *Ep.* 1857. (Leyden edit. of *Works*, vol. iii.)

but public opinion took another view. " The Chancellor," wrote Chapuys to his master, "has resigned, seeing that affairs are going on badly, and likely to be worse, and that if he retained his office he would be obliged to act against his conscience or incur the King's displeasure—as he had already begun to do, for refusing to take his part against the clergy. His excuse is that his entertainment was too small, and that he was not equal to the work. Every one is concerned : for there never was a better man in the office." [1]

The morning after his resignation of the Chancellorship, More took a strange means of telling his wife what he had done. It was the custom for one of his attendants to go to Dame Alice's pew in Chelsea Church, on Festival Days when Mass was over, and tell her that "'my lord had gone before.' So on this morning More himself came, and, opening the door for her, said, 'Madam, my lord is gone.'" Then, as she imagined it to be but "one of his jests, as he used many unto her," he told her his meaning.[2]

After the resignation of his office,—receiving now no income from his profession or from the city as he had done when he entered the royal service,— he had only £50 a year, independent of grants from the Crown.[3] It was thus impossible for him to maintain his former household. For his gentlemen and servants, though with tears in their eyes they declared that they would rather serve

---

[1] *Letters and Papers*, v. 1046 : from Vienna Archives.
[2] Roper, p. 32, and Cres. More, in further detail, p. 186.
[3] *English Works*, p. 867.

him for nothing than others for high salaries,
he found good positions.[1] His barge and eight
watermen he gave to his successor, Sir Thomas
Audley; his fool to the Lord Mayor. Then he
called all his children together and told them how
poor he had become: much as he wished that they
should continue to live together, he could no longer
pay for them all. "When he saw us all silent, and
in that case not ready to show our opinions unto
him"—so Roper describes the scene [2]—"'Then will
I,' said he, 'show my poor mind unto you. I have
been brought up at Oxford, at an Inn of Chancery,
at Lincoln's Inn, and in the King's Court, so forth
from the lowest degree to the highest; and yet have
I in yearly revenues little more than one hundred
pounds at this present left me. So that we must
be hereafter contributors together, if we look to
live together. But by my counsel it shall not be
best for us to fall to the lowest fare first. We
will not therefore descend to Oxford fare, nor to
the fare of New Inn, but we will begin with Lincoln's
Inn diet, where many right worshipful and of good
years do live full well, which if we find not ourselves
able the first year to maintain, then will we the
next year after go one step down to New Inn fare,
wherewith many an honest man is well contented.
If that exceed our ability too, then will we the
next year after descend to Oxford fare, where many
grave, ancient, and learned fathers be conversant
continually; which if our ability stretch not to
maintain neither, then may we yet with bags and

[1] Cres. More, p. 187.　　　　　[2] Roper, p. 31.

wallets go a begging together, and, hoping for pity
some good folk will give their charity, at every
man's door to sing *Salve Regina*, and so keep company merrily together.'" And Roper adds that when
Sir Thomas's debts were paid he had not in his
possession gold and silver, excepting his chain, to
the amount of £100. There is a pathetic touch to
be found in Harpsfield's Life,[1] which shows that
this poverty, so cheerfully borne, was full of real
hardships. "He was not able for the maintenance
of himself and such as necessarily belonged to him,
sufficiently to find meat, drink, fuel, apparel and
such other necessary things; but was enforced and
compelled, for lack of other fuel, every night before
he went to bed, to cause a great burden of ferns to
be brought into his own chamber, and with the blaze
thereof to warm himself, his wife and his children;
and so, without any other fire, to go to their beds."
There could, indeed, be no better proof than his own
life of the truth of his saying, "Good deeds the world,
being ungrateful, is wont never to recompense;
neither can it, were it grateful."

[1] Harpsfield, *Life of More*. Lambeth MS. No. 827, quoted
in a note, pp. 98-99 of Wordsworth's *Ecclesiastical Biography*,
vol. ii.

CHAPTER V.

"Philosophia veritatem quaerit, theologia invenit, religio
possidet."—PICO DELLA MIRANDOLA.

THE early theological studies of More have already
been mentioned, and his connexion with the awakening of religious inquiry in England has been referred
to. A few words may recall his position, before his
writings are specifically examined.

That his views were throughout his life in substantial accordance with those of Erasmus there can be
little reason to doubt. In so far as humanism "consisted in a new and vital perception of the essential
dignity of man apart from theological determinations"
the whole tone of More's writings proves him to
have been a humanist. But this consciousness of
man's own dignity and power was combined in him
with no under-estimation of the value of Christian
doctrine. Rather was the ideal of his humanism
distinctly the product of Christian thought. He was
thus able to combine intense devotion to the Church
with the strongest reprobation of ecclesiastical
scandals and the most acute perception of the follies
of a stagnant theology. He wrote some of his most

stinging epigrams against ignorant and immoral priests and incompetent bishops. Before the publication of the *Utopia*, his antagonism to the tyranny of the Scotist theologians was well known, and he was looked upon with suspicion by those who thought that knowledge of Greek fostered heresy. In 1517 Pace could say of him (it was after telling an amusing story of one of his wit-combats with dull theologians)—

"This one piece of ill-luck, I grieve to tell you, follows More: whenever he speaks most skilfully and acutely among your white-mitred fathers with reference to their special science, they always condemn him and call all he says childish folly, not because they really think him worthy of condemnation, but because they are envious of his remarkable genius and his knowledge of other sciences whereof they are ignorant—in a word, because a mere boy (so they call him) a long way excels his elders in wisdom."[1]

When Erasmus published his New Testament, More warmly commended it to the great men of the time, exclaiming in his verses to the reader (printed among his epigrams)—

"Nova Christi lex nova luce nitet."

In 1519, he gave a most clear exposition of his dissent from the extravagances of popular belief and practice in a letter to a monk who had warned him against associating with the contemner of the Vulgate.[2]

[1] *De Fructu qui ex Doctrinâ Praecipitur*, pp. 83, 84. Basil. 1517.

[2] *Epistolae aliquot eruditorum virorum*, pp. 92—138. Basil, 1520. See above, pp. 72 *sqq.*

In spite, however, of his sense of the vices of the clergy, More had abandoned few, if any, of the doctrines of the Church, in whose name it was that he rebuked sin and defended learning. This is most clearly seen in his controversial works, but even the *Utopia* is not without traces of the same attitude. No portion of More's ideal republic has been more often the subject of commentary than the chapter *De Religionibus Utopiensium.* On the beautiful picture of a benign and rational toleration which it presents Mr. Seebohm [1] has rightly laid much stress, but he has surely gone beyond his text when he finds in the Utopians a " fearless faith in the consistency of Christianity with science " and a " significant denial of any sacerdotal sense " to their priesthood. Is there any less slender foundation for a statement of the Utopians' faith in the consistency of Christianity with science than the words *gratum Deo cultum putant naturæ contemplationem laudemque ab ea ?* [2] The "significant denial" of sacerdotalism Mr. Seebohm supports by a quotation which is scarcely correct; and he does not observe the prostration of the people on the priest's entrance, or the distinctly mentioned eucharistic significance of his vestments. The question is of interest only as showing how far the *Utopia* represents More's own opinions, for few who have read any of his writings would imagine that any question of the " consistency

---

[1] *Oxford Reformers*, pp. 355 *sqq.*

[2] *Latin Works*, Louvain, 1555, p. 17*a*. Translated by Ralph Robinson, " They think that the contemplation of nature and the praise thereof coming is to God a very acceptable honour " (Arber's reprint, p. 149).

of Christianity with science" ever occurred to him;
nor can there be the least doubt that More attributed
a "sacerdotal sense" to the Christian priesthood.
In so thinking he may of course have been bigoted
and ignorant, but he can hardly be said to deserve
an undenominationalist's eulogy. Indeed, all such
arguments, both on the religion and on the philosophy of the Utopians, are based on an inference
which, whether just or not, More himself never
draws. For instance, it has been said that the
Utopians "recognized, as Mr. Mill urges that Christians ought to do now, ' in the golden rule of Jesus
of Nazareth the complete spirit of the ethics of
utility.' "[1] Now the passage which is alluded to
refers unquestionably to the views of the Utopians
before their conversion to Christianity, and therefore
cannot prove any connexion between their philosophy
and the revelation of Christ. It is, of course, open
to any one to say that their conversion would have
made no change in their philosophic opinions, but
it is hardly permissible to take the point for granted.
It must indeed be admitted that throughout his
book Mr. Seebohm, while he rightly lays stress on
the agreement between the views of Colet, Erasmus,
and More, seems to exaggerate the freedom of their
opinions. One instance of their cordial acceptance
of views which we are accustomed to regard as
especially medieval will suffice. The question of
ecclesiastical privilege may be regarded as a typical
one. In England at least the claim to exemption
from civil jurisdiction had always been warmly

[1] *The Oxford Reformers*, 1st edition, p. 286.

contested, and the progress of the Reformation pronounced more and more decisively against it. But More, even in his *Utopia*, uses the strongest arguments in its favour, while Colet, in his famous sermon before the Convocation of 1512,[1] expressly declared it to be just. The " Oxford reformers " were indeed liberal, tolerant, and pious beyond the standard of their time, but in doctrine they firmly maintained the principles of the Catholic Church. Colet did not live to express an opinion on the great movements of the foreign reformers; Erasmus, after hesitating for a while, opposed them ; More strongly and decisively condemned their whole position.

Before he was forced into the arena of theological controversy More had begun to write a short devotional treatise of great value on the text *Memorare novissima, et in aeternum non peccabis.*[2] The book, which is almost unknown, is well worthy to be reprinted : it is exceedingly interesting, not only as an illustration of the sincerity and beauty of More's character, but also as an example of the highest standard of Catholic devotion immediately before the Reformation. The title names it a " treatysse (unfynysshed) upon these wordes of Holye Scrypture, *Memorare nouissima, et in eternum non peccabis*, ' Remember the last thynges, and thou shalt neuer synne,' " and adds that it was " made about the yere of our Lorde 1522." The interest which attaches to the few pages lies not only in the quaint and

<hr>

[1] Given in *The Oxford Reformers.*
[2] *English Works*, 1557, pp. 72—102. The treatise is unfinished.

peculiar style in which the deepest thoughts are
with all sincerity expressed, but also in the period
at which they were written. In 1522 More was on
the point of making that choice between politics and
literature which has come to so many great men at
the crisis of their lives. He was already famous in
Europe as a scholar, as a writer of brilliant epigrams,
as the author of a book of which every one was still
speaking, which had run through three editions in
a year, and which had put forth such keen criticism
of the age and such bold schemes for reformation.
"What might not this great genius have accomplished," said Erasmus, "had he been educated in
Italy, or were he not being overwhelmed by political
and domestic cares?" More had already performed
several important diplomatic missions, and was
gradually more and more sought after by the King,
whose offers he had at first steadily refused. He
had assisted him in his book against Luther; he
was probably already preparing his own reply to
that heretic, which was published in the next year.
He was in almost daily correspondence with Wolsey.
A great political career seemed open to him.

It was at such a time that More deliberately turned
his thoughts to the most solemn of all matters,
Memorare novissima, et in aeternum non peccabis.
The little meditation, as we should call it, which he
wrote on this text, evidently came freely and sin-
cerely from his heart. It is the ready humour,
playing even round subjects the most tremendous
that man can contemplate, that gives it distinction
and freshness. Not seldom does the treatment, and

sometimes even the style, remind us of Jeremy Taylor, for the quaint incongruity which admits "the Ephesian woman that the soldier told of in Petronius" to a share in our thoughts at the very moment when we are preparing the bodies of our friends for the grave, has its parallel again and again in the thirty pages of More's little work. In other ways the writing recalls the dignity of Hooker and the tenderness of George Herbert. It is a model of clear and expressive English. The subject itself may have been suggested by the *Cordiall de Quatuor Novissimis*, attributed to Henricus de Hassia, of which an English version by Anthony Wydville, Earl Rivers, had been printed by Caxton; but the matter is entirely original.

The scheme was not completed—we have indeed not finished the consideration of the least terrible of the **Four Last Things**—when the meditation suddenly breaks off. Yet there is enough to show on what practical lines the religion of the great lawyer and humanist ran, and how much there was in the devotion of the Catholic Church in our land on the eve of the Reformation which, in modern phrase, was thoroughly Anglican in temper. The book, indeed, might have been written by an English writer, not of the Puritanical school, either before or after the Reformation, and is a striking instance of how little our devotional standards are modelled upon foreign examples, and how distinct a style the mental attitude of our own race has contributed to the devotional treasury of the universal Church. This is well illustrated also by a comparison with that earlier religious work of More's own—his translation of Gian Francesco's biography of Pico della Mirandola, with its devotional letters and verses, which contain such a touching picture of the deep religious earnestness of the fascinating hero.

More, it is plain to see, had been profoundly influenced by the Renaissance spirit in general and by the beautiful soul of Pico in particular. Yet his meditation on the Four Last Things, which might bear for a motto the last words of the dying humanist to his nephew, is in literary tone and style utterly unlike anything that the Italian mystic left behind. The treatise indeed is as thoroughly English in its manner as it is in its matter; it is truly a work of English literature as well as of English religion.

The thought of death, so he begins, is a sovereign medicine for the soul's diseases—

"The phisicion sendeth his bill to the poticary, and therin writeth sommetime a costlye receite of many straunge herbes and rootes, set out of far countreis, long lien drugges, al the strength worn out, and some none such to be goten. But thys phisicion sendeth his bill to thyselfe, no strange thing therein, nothing costly to bie, nothing farre to set, but to be gathered at times of the yere in the gardein of thyne owne soule."

It is no doubt a bitter and painful medicine, yet this should in no way dissuade us from its use—

"Nowe yf a manne bee so dayntye stomaked, that, goyng where contagion is, he would grudge to take a lyttle tryacle, yet were he very nycely wanton if he might not at the lestwise take a little vynegre and rose water in his handkercher."

Pleasure, indeed, stands in the way of solemn thoughts; yet how much superior is spiritual to worldly delight! And a joy in spiritual exercises is of all things the best preventive of sin. But here the chief end of the Christian life, it will be argued, is not attained—

"Thou wilt happely say, that it is not ynough that a man do none euyl, but he must also do good. This is verye truth that ye say. But first if ther be but these two steppes to heaven, he that getteth him on the one is halfe up. And over it, who so doeth none euil, it will be very hard but he must nedes do good, syth man's mind is neuer ydle, but occupyed commonly either with good or euil."

Let the mind ever be occupied with good thoughts or with good speech, and yet not ever babbling. There is a

"Time to speke and time to keep thy tong. Whansoever ye communicacion is nought and ungodly, it is better to holde thy tong and think on some better thing the while, than to giue ear therto and underpinne the tale. And yet better were it then holdynge of thy tong properly to speake, and with som good grace and pleasant fashion to break into some better matter. By which thy speache and talking thou shalt not onely profite thyselfe as thou sholdest have done by thy well-minded sylence, but also amend the whole audience, which is a thynge farre better and of much more merite. Howbeit, if thou can find no proper meane to break the tale, than excepte **thy** bare authoritie suffice **to com-maunde silence,** it were paradventure good rather **to keep a good** silence thyself, than blunt forth **rudely** and yrryte **them** to anger, which shall happely therefore not let to talk **on, but speake much the more,** lest thei should seme **to lene at thy** commandement. And **better were it for** ye while **to let one wanton worde** pass **uncontrolled** than geue occasyon of twain."

But **to join** in good conversation is far **better than silence, for** to sit in meditation till folk suddenly say, "A penny for your thought," is neither wisdom nor good manners.

So far **More has spoken by way of introduction.** He then **turns to the remembrance** of death. He begins **by drawing** the awful moment in all its terrors. **"Never were we so** greatly moved," he says, **"by the** beholding **of the daunce of** death pictured in **Poules," as** by imagining of the hour itself. Imagination **can** with readiness call up the pains of the **very** easiest death in bed—

"Thy hed shooting, thy **backe** akyng, **thy vaynes** beating, **thine heart panting, thy** throte ratelyng, thy fleshe trembling, **thy mouthe** gaping, **thy** nose sharping, thy legges coling, **thy fingers** fimbling, **thy** breath shorting, all thy strength fainting, thy lyfe vanishing, and thy death drawyng **on."**

There are few more vividly realistic descriptions in the **English** language **than that** which follows **on this passage.** As the dying man **lies** helpless in bed, friends **and executors flock** round **him troubling him** with questions he has no strength to answer; children lament; and the wife (it is a sudden touch of almost coarse irony), who before spoke not one sweet word in six weeks, now weeps, not without an eye to the future. And all the while the devil is never absent from him that draws towards the end; for at death the final destiny is fixed, and afterwards no change can touch the salvation or the loss of the soul. Temptations throng around, be it through a false hope of life or a false security of salvation "as a thing well won by our own works." So instead of sorrow for sin the enemy of the soul

"putteth us in mind of provision for some honourable burying, so many torches, so many tapers, so many black gownes, so many merry mourners laughing under black hodes, and a gay hers, withe delite of goodly and honorable funeralles, in which the folish sicke man is sometyme occupied, as though he thought that he should stand in a window and see how woorshipfullye he shall be broughte to church."

There is a false feeling of security which buoys up both old and young for a while. There is no man so old, "as Tully saith," but he expects to live a year longer. The young think not upon those dead younger than themselves, but measure their own prospects of life by the age of the oldest man they know. Sickness is a preparation for death, but it is not a preparation that all obtain. And in a sense all life is a sickness, and so all life should be a preparation.

The thought of death is then taken as a medicine for many diseases of the soul. Pride, the " mother of all vice," stands first, and next ambition, which tricks out a man in borrowed robes like those of the actor who, after playing a great lord on the stage, goes out again "a knave in his red coat." Envy and wrath, too, are vices for which the contemplation of death is a meet cure. At the root of all these sins lies our self-exaltation—

"By which, though we marke it not, yet indeede we recken our selfe worthye more reuerence than we do God Himselfe. . . . Loke not whether we be not more angry with our seruantes for the brech of one commaundement of our owne than for the breche of God's al tenne, and whether we be not more wroth with one contumelious worde spoken against ourself than with many blasphemous wordes unreuerently spoken of God."

Behind the wrath which blazes out on trivial occasion lies the cardinal vice of pride—

"Now shal ye see men fall at varyance for kissyng of the pax, or goyng before in procession, or setting of their wives' powes in the church. Doubt ye whether this wrath be pride? I dout not but wise men will agree that it is either foolyshe pride or proud foly."

And so in the same strain he speaks of "covetise" and "glotony." Of the vice of intemperance he says much that is forcible and pointed, and there is ever in his keenest sayings a deep spiritual earnestness and a true sympathy with tempted souls. Enough is quoted to show the style of his work, but yet it reads far better as it was written than in fragmentary extracts. Standing alone, it might only deserve notice for its quaintnesses, but when it is considered in connexion with the other religious writings of the author—such as the *Treatise on the Passion*, the *Book of Comfort in Tribulation*, and the private prayers—it will be seen to be worthy of remembrance as a touching and characteristic work of one of the purest and most single-hearted of England's worthies. Unfortunately More's theological studies could not be confined to such devotional exercises; he was led into religious controversy, as he was led into politics, by the King.

As early as 1518, Henry VIII. had been preparing a book against the heretics, which, if the conjecture of Mr. Brewer be correct,[1] was the original draft of the attack upon Luther published in 1521. It was natural that Pace and More should be frequently consulted during the progress of this work, but it does not appear that they took any actual part in the authorship,[2] their aid at most extending to the composition and the correction of the Latin style. Of a conversation which he had with the King at this time More has left a curious record.[3]

" I was myself" [he says] " sometime not of the mind that the primacy of the [Roman] see should be begun by the institution of God, until I read in the matter those things that the king's highness had written in his most famous book against the heresies of Martin Luther. At the first reading whereof I

---

[1] *Calendar of State Papers*, vol. ii. **Preface**, p. **202**.

[2] More stated that he was only "a sorter out and placer of the principal matters therein contained."—Roper, *Life of More* (Pitt Press ed. p. 37).

[3] Letter to Cromwell, *English Works*, the two pages both numbered by mistake 1427. Cf. Roper, pp. 37, 38.

moved the king's highness either to **leave out** that point or else to touch it more slenderly, for **doubt** of such thing **as** after might hap to fall in question between his highness and some **pope, as** between princes and popes divers times **have done.** Whereunto his highness answered me that he would in no **wise** anything minish of that matter, of which thing his highness showed **me** a secret cause, whereof **I never had** anything **heard** before. But surely after **I had** read his grace's book thereon, and so many other things as I have seen in that **point of the** controversy of this ten[1] years since **and more, I** have found a general consent of **fathers and councils** agreeing **in that point."**

It **is evident, then,** that the opinion for which **More died was first** instilled into him **by** the **King by whose orders he** was executed. **A very important** question arises **from** this statement of his as to what **may have** been **the** "secret matter" which induced **Henry VIII.** in his book against Luther so strongly **to** support the Papal supremacy, and which, when declared to More, who **was** before incredulous of **the** Papal claim, **convinced him of its** importance **and** finally made a "**Romanist**" **of him.** Mr. Seebohm has suggested[2] that the secret was **that** the marriage **between** Arthur and Katherine **had been** consummated. Thus **in** view of the succession of **the Princess Mary or of** any child that the King **might have by Katherine, and of the** social position **of** others married in **the same way,** More would feel

---

[1] "Seven" in More's *Works*, but "ten" in the original.
[2] *Fortnightly Review*, ix. 508, **599.**

with overpowering force the necessity of maintaining
the Papal authority in granting dispensations and
the other powers of the holy see which required a
similar belief in the supremacy for their basis. The
conjecture is ingenious, but is open to obvious objections. As, however, it is quite impossible to
discover with certainty what the "secret matter"
may have been, the subject need be no further
alluded to here.

Henry's book won him the title of "defender of
the faith," and exposed him to an answer from
Luther which no one denies to be violent and in-
decent to the last degree. Seeing the King thus
attacked, More was moved to take up the cudgels
in his defence, writing, says his great-grandson,[1] in
accordance with the precept *Responde stulto secundum
stultitiam ejus*, and with such effect that his worthy
descendant considers that " to see how he handleth
Luther would do any man good."[2] His *Vindicatio
Henrici VIII a calumniis Lutheri*, published under
the name of "Gulielmus Rosseus," appeared in
1523.[3] Though there has been some question,
there can be no real doubt, of the authorship. The
style in all its good points is eminently characteristic of More, but it is unfortunately quite foreign
in tone to what we should have expected from his
mild and beautiful nature. It is sad that he should
have descended to coarse and scurrilous jesting, and
have made no attempt to raise the tone of the

---

[1] Cresacre More, *Life of Sir Thomas More*, ed. 1726, p. 311.
[2] *Ibid.* p. 110.
[3] It is published in the *Latin Works*, ed. 1565, pp. 57—117.

controversy into which he had flung himself. With
all Luther's horror of monastic degradation and
longing for reform he could fully sympathize; but
he was aroused by the same feelings to amend
rather than to destroy. It was the coarseness of
the attacks upon all which he held dear that moved
him to write; Savonarola he could have followed,
but not Luther. The whole attitude, indeed, of
More towards the Reformation may be very largely,
though not entirely, explained by his mental constitution. A disposition such as his, in which the
feelings of charity and veneration were so prominent, could not easily lend itself to the iconoclastic
vehemence in which the energy of Luther took
refuge, and which demanded of necessity a harsh
rending of old ties and a cruel treatment of even
honest opponents. When More answered the reformers in their own strain he was simply using the
weapon which they had proved to be effective, but
his conduct is none the less to be regretted. It
may, however, be said that his controversial works
show that he put some restraint upon himself, while
there is no sign that Luther ever did so. Nor
should the spirit in which More wrote be forgotten.
He says with much feeling at the end of this work—

"Imo nihil mihi magis in votis est quam ut illam
aliquando diem videam, qua et has nugas meas et
illius omnes insanas haereses mortales omnes abjici-
ant; ut obruto pessimarum rerum studio, sepultis
jurgiorum stimulis et contentionum obliterata me-
moria, illucescat animis serenum fidei lumen: redeat
syncera pietas et vere christiana concordia: quam

aliquando precor, ut reddat, ac restituat terræ, Qui
in terram venit pacem daturus e coelo."[1]

It is not surprising that More, like so many other
opponents of the reformers, blamed Luther and his
followers for the excesses of the *Bauernkrieg* of
1525. In that year Bugenhagen, then newly con-
verted to the Lutheran opinions, addressed his
letter "to the saints in England," and More, who
heard all the most terrible stories of the peasants'
excesses from Goclenius, thought it necessary to
reply to it. Here, however, he had no desire to
enter into public controversy ; his letter was entirely
private,[2] and was written in a most conciliatory tone.
He took pains to refute the Antinomian opinions
of the Anabaptists, which he attributed to Luther,
and called attention to much in the writings of the
Wittenberg doctor which it seemed impossible to
reconcile with any reasonable standard of theology.
From such violence of opinion and expression he
thought that the revolts and massacres were legiti-
mate deductions. He was at pains also to point out
that the true Catholic doctrines were misrepresented
by the reformers, and instanced the famous point of
justification by faith.

"The Church both believes and teaches that
man's works cannot be well done without the grace
of God, or be of any merit without faith in Christ.
Nor are they, even in that case, in their nature fit

---

[1] *Latin Works*, p. 118a.

[2] *Mori epistola in qua non minus facete quam pie respondet
litteris Johannis Pomerani.* Louvain. It was not published
till 1568.

for heaven. When we have done all, we are unprofitable servants, we have done no more than we ought to have done. We do not fight against grace or deny Christ, or confide, like the Pharisees, in works; for we know well that they are worth nothing without faith, that they have no value except from the pure bounty of God. But they fight against faith and deny Christ, who, while they extol only grace and faith, deny the value of faith and make men callous to living well." [1]

Nothing, surely, could be more sound than this statement, and a comparison with the thirteenth article of the Church of England is immediately suggested. From such passages we are encouraged to inquire what More's position would have been if he had lived a little later. Mr. Froude assures us that "his mind was too clear and genuine to allow him to deceive himself with the delusive mirage of Anglicanism." Rather, in one sense More *was* Anglican, while in another sense 'Anglicanism' was never placed before him. And, in spite of the vehemence with which he defended some of the more especially medieval doctrines, it is interesting to notice several occasions on which he clearly held and expressed the views of primitive Christianity as they have been expounded by Anglican theologians since the Reformation.

[1] I use the translation of this passage given in an article in the *North British Review*, vol. xxx. pp. 102 *sqq.*, to which I am much indebted. I believe that Mr. Seebohm has somewhere admitted the authorship of this article. If so, our regret must be the greater that he has not given us a complete life of More.

The progress of events soon brought More forward again as a controversialist, and in 1528 he assumed the position, which he maintained almost until his death, of the most prominent defender of the Church against the attacks of the English reformers. The writings of the heretics had been largely disseminated in England, and it was felt that some stronger weapon than the law afforded was necessary for general use. More, as a layman whose tolerant views were well known and whose literary fame was European, was admirably fitted to meet the pamphleteers on their own ground. Accordingly, in March 1528, Tunstal entreated him to come forward as the defender of the Church, and sent him a formal license "to read and keep certain books of Luther and certain other heretical publications," in order that he might write an answer to them in the vernacular tongue.[1] More at once applied himself to the study of the volumes, and was not long in discovering that side by side with Luther as a powerful antagonist of the Church he must place William Tyndale, the translator of the New Testament and author of *The Wicked Mammon*, and *The Obedience of a Christian Man*. The result of his reading was the publication of 'A Dialogue of Sir Thomas More, Knighte; one of the Counsaill of our Sovereign Lorde the Kinge, and Chancellour of his duchy of Lancaster. Wherein be treated divers maters, as of the veneracion and worship of ymages and relyques, praing to Saintes, and goying on pylgrimage. With many other thinges touchyng

---

[1] *Letters and Papers,* iv. 4028.

the pestilente secte of Luther and Tyndale, by the tone bygone in Saxony and by the tother labored to be brought into England.'[1] This was a work of remarkable skill, and has always been considered by Roman writers to be More's greatest achievement. It must in justice be admitted that the questions discussed are treated with ability and tact, and in a much more moderate tone than was usual in the controversies of the time. The method of the book was admirably chosen. It professes to be a dialogue on the great questions of the day between More and a messenger from one of his friends who was imbued with many of the opinions of the reformers. The objections of the heretics are brought forward with some force and are met with every artifice of ridicule and illustration as well as of sober argument. Thus the simplicity of the reformer who considers "logic but babbling, music to serve for singers, arithmetic meet for merchants, geometry for masons, astronomy good for no man, and as for philosophy, the most vain of all,"[2] and knows nothing but a little Latin and the Bible, is sketched with delightful humour. Turning to argument, More cites a number of examples to prove that images were not forbidden to Christians. In attempting a dilemma as to the reverence to be paid to the name of Jesus, More seems as oblivious of logic as his opponent, but with regard to the veneration of saints he is more straightforward.

"Well they [the heretics] wot that the Church

---

[1] First edition, 1529. *English Works*, ed. 1557, pp. 104—228.   [2] "Dialogue," *English Works*, p. 111.

worshippeth not saints as God, but as God's good servants, and therefore the honour that is done to them redoundeth principally to the honour of their Master, like as in common custom of people we do reverence sometimes, and make great cheer to some men for their master's sake whom else would we not haply bid once good-morrow." [1]

Speaking of pilgrimages he denies that they are maintained because they are a source of revenue to the clergy, and defends the consecration of special places for God's service.

" Where ye say that in resorting to this place and that place, this image and that image, we seem to reckon as though God were not in every place alike mighty or not alike present, this reason [he says] proceedeth no more against pilgrimages than against all the churches in Christendom; for God is as mighty in the stable as in the temple." [2]

He thus narrows down the question to a point, the decision of which does not affect the question that he is supposed to answer. Because God had set apart certain places to be hallowed to Him, and ordered men to assemble together to worship Him, it did not follow that prayers " should be better heard of our Lord in Kent than at Cambridge."

For the proof that special localities are more pleasing to God than others, More relies on the evidence of miracles. This introduces several very interesting chapters in which he meets the argu- ments against the possibility of miraculous mani- festations. Into this subject he enters at great

<hr>

[1] *English Works*, p. 118.   [2] *Ibid.* p. 121.

length and with much skill, distinguishing between
a belief in miracles in general and the evidence for
particular cases. While admitting that the devil can
work miracles, he declares that if the Church had
acknowledged such the Holy Spirit would have
deserted her. The rest of the first book explains
and defends at great length the doctrine of the
Church and of her interpretation of the Holy Scripture. On this latter point More maintains that the
Church cannot err on any necessary article of the
faith, and arrives at the following conclusion—

"Whoso will not unto the study of Scripture take
the points of the Catholic faith as a rule of interpretation, but of diffidence and mistrust study to
seek in Scripture whether the faith of the Church
be true or not, he cannot fail to fall in worse
errors and far more jeopardous than any man can
do by philosophy, whereof the reasons and arguments in matters of our faith have nothing in like
authority."[1]

In the second book the subject of the Church is
continued. What, asks the objector, is the Visible
Church? More replies that it must be open and
obvious, a city set on an hill that cannot be hid;
no sect can be the Church, for the Church existed
before them all, the tree from which they, as
withered branches, dropped. The Church also must
contain good and bad men together, and is, in fact,
"the common known multitude of Christian nations
not cut off nor fallen off by heresies."[2] The subject
of the views of the reformers is then again intro-

---

[1] *English Works*, p. 163.　　　　[2] *Ibid.* p. 185.

duced; for the objector asks why, if the good and bad be together in the Church, the good may not be those who believe the worship of images to be idolatry. More then defends in turn the invocation of saints, the reverence paid to relics, and pilgrimages. The canonized saints must be saints indeed, or the Church would have erred in a matter nearly touching God's honour, which cannot be. To the objector's complaints about relics it is answered that the Church could not have received pig's bones, or the bones of the damned, as worthy of reverence, for she is guided by the same Spirit through whom the Canon of Scripture was chosen. And, even if God permitted a mistake to be undiscovered for a while, no harm would happen, for the intention of those that pay reverence is good, as though there could be no harm in paying reverence to an unconsecrated host. Nor do the bad customs that disgrace some shrines prove that the shrines themselves should be destroyed any more than that holy days should be abolished because in some places foolish or wicked deeds are done on them. "In some countries they go a-hunting on Good Friday in the morning: will ye break that evil custom, or cast away Good Friday?"[1]

More begins the third book of his dialogue by deciding the question whether belief is to be accorded first to the Scripture or to the Church. He declares that faith is before Scripture, as well chronologically as logically. The trial and abjuration of Bilney are then described, and the burning

[1] *English Works*, p. 198.

of Tyndale's New Testament is praised. More's criticism of the reformer's translation is extremely bitter. He distrusts the spirit in which it was undertaken, and points out many instances in which new renderings of words have been adopted for the purpose of concealing the meaning of the original. His deepest anger is reserved for the change by which "priest" becomes "senior," "the Church," "the congregation," and "charity," "love." Nor was this all, "for he changeth," cries More, "grace into this word 'favour,' whereas every favour is not grace in English, for in some favour there is little grace. 'Confession' he translateth into 'knowledging,' 'penance' into 'repentance.' 'A contrite heart' he changeth into 'a troubled heart,' and many more things like and many texts untruly translated for the maintenance of heresy."[1] Of Tyndale's other works More also speaks in strong condemnation. "Tyndale," he says, "hath put out in his own name another book entitled *Mammona*, which book is very *mammona iniquitatis*, a very treasury and well-spring of wickedness. And yet hath he sithence put forth a worse also named *The Obedience of a Christian Man*, a book able to make a Christian man that would believe it leave off all good Christian virtues, and lose the merits of his Christendom."[2] Turning then to the attacks made upon the priesthood, More says much in answer that is fair and just. He could not deny that many of the clergy lived scandalous lives, but he attributed that to episcopal neglect of the canon that none

[1] *English Works*, p. 222.   [2] *Ibid*. p. 223.

should be ordained for whom provision was not made.   He also reminded the objector how eagerly every one caught up tales against any particular priest, and straightway condemned the order.   If priests were bad, how much worse were laymen! And he quoted a sermon of Colet to the same effect.[1]

On the marriage of the clergy he has an important chapter, in which his argument is that the Church binds no man to chastity against his will, for men only take sacred orders by their own desire.   "And as touching whether the order of the Church therein is better than the contrary, good men and wise men both had the proof of both before the law was made, and it was well allowed through Christendom long time since.   Which ere I would assent to change I would see a better author thereof than such an heretic as Luther and Tyndale, and a better sample than the seditious and schismatic priests of Saxony."[2]   This position, it will be observed, though not extreme, is quite incompatible with a belief that the *Utopia* was intended to advise the marriage of priests.

More recognizes the wisdom of having the Bible translated, though he says much of the danger of an unauthorized translation.   Yet how narrow was the liberty that he would concede may be seen by the following passage—

"It might be with diligence well and truly translated by some good Catholic and well-learned man, or by divers dividing the labour among them, and

[1] *English Works*, p. 226.   [2] *Ibid.* p. 233.

after conferring their several parts together, each with other. And after that might the work be allowed and approved by the ordinaries, and by their authorities so put into print as all the copies should come whole into the bishop's hand. Which he may after his discretion and wisdom deliver to such as he perceiveth honest, sad, and virtuous, with a good monition and fatherly counsel to use it reverently with humble heart and lowly mind, rather seeking therein occasion of devotion than of despicion. And providing as much as may be that the book be after the decease of the party brought again and reverently restored under the ordinary."[1]

The fourth book contains a violent attack upon Luther and his followers, a repetition, with all the force of More's ability, of the charges to which they had long been exposed. Speaking of the burning of heretics, More lays great stress on the fact that it is the work of the secular power, and declares that just as princes are bound to resist the Turks, so are they bound to destroy heretics who reject all the offers of the long-suffering Church. With this, the conversion of the objector being complete, More departs to the Court.

Such is a most imperfect sketch of the contents of the *Dialogue*. From a perusal of it, it becomes evident that any attempt to represent the author as satisfied with a latitudinarian or even a purely spiritual creed must break down. There is no reason to assume that More's views had changed since he wrote the *Utopia*, and the distinct declar-

---

[1] *English Works*, p. 245.

P

ation of them in his controversial works seems to prove that no importance is to be attached to the ideal picture of religion in the happy island. It is equally plain that More was well aware of the strength of the reformers, that he had clearly grasped many of their arguments and decisively rejected their whole teaching. It is at least possible also that he saw much of the weakness of his own cause; the significant changes of style and the absence of even casual allusion to points of extreme importance seem to suggest this conclusion. From this work also an opinion may be formed as to the extent of More's theological knowledge. The *Dialogue* is most evidently the work of a layman, who had a taste for but had made no special study of divinity. It owes all to its skill, nothing to its learning. The reading of its author appears to be confined to some of the works of S. Augustine, to Peter Lombard, and to the canon law. The strength of More's books lay in the popular ground which they took up; they were almost the only works which attempted to answer the reformers after their own fashion. Fresh, unforced humour is visible on nearly every page. Surely it is a special touch of English religious writers that they blend delightful humour with their serious thought. What is true of Hooker and Jeremy Taylor and George Herbert is doubly true of Sir Thomas More. Some extracts we cannot refrain from quoting. The following has additional interest from its autobiographical reference—

"If he mean to read his riddle on this fashion,

then he soyleth his strange riddle as bluntly **as an**
old wife of Culnaw (? Cumnor) did once among the
scholars **of** Oxenford that sojourned with **her for**
death [in the time of the plague]. Which, **while**
they were on a time for their sport purposing riddles
among them, she began **to** put forth one of her's
too, and said, 'A **read** my riddle, what is that? I
knew one that shot at a hart and killed a haddock.'
And when we **had** everybody much mused how
that might be and then prayed her to declare her
riddle herself, after long request, **she said at the**
last that there were once a fisher that **came a land**
in a place where he saw a hart **and shot thereat,**
but he **hit it not;** and afterwards he went again to
the sea **and caught** a haddock and killed it."

No less quaint **is** the story of Davy the Dutchman,
who was about **to** marry a second time, when it was
discovered that his first wife was still alive—

"'Marry, master,' quoth he, 'that letter saith, me-
think, that my wife is alive.' 'Yea, beast,' quoth I,
'that she is.' 'Marry,' quoth he, 'then I am well apaid,
for she is a good woman.' 'Yea,' quoth I, 'but **why**
art thou such a naughty, wretched man, that thou
wouldest here wed another? Didst thou not say
she was dead?' 'Yes, marry,' quoth he, 'men of
Worcester told me so.' 'Why,' quoth I, 'thou false
beast, did'st thou not tell me and all my house
that **thou** wert at her grave thyself?' 'Yea, marry,
master,' quoth he, 'so I was, but I could not look
in, **ye wot well.'"**

Such passages abound in **his** writings, as do quaint
saws and old proverbs, many **of** which are still in

use. Nor are passages of genuine eloquence and deep solemnity wanting. More's style was indeed the mirror of the man; he wrote as he lived, absolutely without ostentation, simply, merrily, honourably and in the true faith and fear of Christ. In such a passage as this he touches the true note of genuine devotion—

"When we feel us too bold, remember our own feebleness. When we feel us too faint, remember Christ's strength. In our fear, let us remember Christ's painful agony that Himself would (for our comfort) suffer before His passion, to the intent that no fear should make us despair. And ever call for His help, such as Himself list to send us, and then need we never to doubt but that either He shall keep us from the painful death, or shall not fail so to strength us in it that He shall joyfully bring us to heaven by it. And then does He much more for us than if He kept us from it. For as God did more for poor Lazar in helping him patiently to die for hunger at the rich man's door, than if He had brought him to the door all the rich glutton's dinner; so, though He be gracious to a man whom He delivereth out of painful trouble, yet doth He much more for a man if through right painful death He deliver him from this wretched world into eternal bliss."

Passages such as these—and More's works are full of them—show how close to him always was the divine beauty of the spiritual life.

It was evident that the controversy would not cease with the publication of the *Dialogue*. Tyndale, then in safety in the Netherlands, was anxious to meet it, but while he was preparing to do so More entered into a new contest. On May 24, 1530, the Council, by the King's command, issued a declaration against Luther's writings, and a list of the errors contained in certain heretical books, English and Latin, among others Tyndale's translation of the Scriptures, for the benefit of preachers, to be published by them in their sermons. It had been drawn up by Warham, Tunstal, More, Gardiner, Hugh Latimer, and others. Meanwhile a tract had been published, probably at the same time as the *Dialogue*, which took up with considerable force a peculiar mode of attack. The *Supplication for the Beggars* struck at the Church through the clergy. In language of extreme violence "the foul, unhappy sort of lepers and other sore people, needy, impotent, blind, lame, and sick, that live only on alms," petition the King to grant them succour. They declare that they are dying of hunger because of the multitude of stout and strong beggars, the clergy, who possess more than a third part of the kingdom, and obtain by their numberless exactions more than £40,000 a year in addition to the tithes. They demand that "these sturdy lobies" and "holy idle thieves" be driven abroad into the world, "to get them wives of their own, to get their living with their labour in the sweat of their faces, according to the commandment of God," and that they should be "tied to the carts to be whipped naked about every market town till they will fall to labour."[1]

---

[1] *A Supplication for the Beggars*, by **Simon Fish**, reprinted by Mr. Arber, 1878.

Mr. Dixon speaks of More as "condescending" to answer the "atrocities" of Simon Fish.[1] The expression is scarcely too strong; the work was indeed far below the level of those which he had previously attacked, and it was only the knowledge that its very vehemence would win it credit among a certain class that induced him to notice it. His answer was written in a very different tone. It took the form of a pathetic appeal from "the poor prisoners of God," the souls in purgatory, "to all good Christian people."[2] The *Supplication of Souls* is in every way more interesting than the *Dialogue*. In exposing the extravagant follies of such a work as that of Fish, More is at his best, clear, trenchant, and exhaustive, and not only does he completely defeat his adversary—which he can hardly be said to have done in the *Dialogue*—but it is possible to feel a certain satisfaction in his victory. The exquisite humour of the first part will scarce admit of detached quotation, since it owes its success to the accuracy with which, while following closely the steps of its original, it ridicules and exposes its statements. The elaborate calculations of the "beggars" are entirely upset. More points out the inconsistency of declaring in one place that the clergy are so many as to check the growth of population and prevent a proper supply of merchants and soldiers, and in another that they are not one in every four hundred of the population, that they are the cause of the increase of beggary, and yet that they should be turned

---

[1] *History of the Church of England*, i. 142.
[2] "A Supplication of Souls," *English Works*, pp. 288—339.

adrift to diminish the number of beggars. There are several other features of interest in the book, such as the remarks on Peter's pence and King John's gift of the kingdom to the Pope, and the prophecy that any robbing of the Church would be followed by a great increase of pauperism. The doctrine of purgatory is introduced by the consideration that the majority of religious establishments were endowed for the express purpose of insuring supplication for the souls of the founders. Thus More declares that the confiscation of the endowments would be not only an injury to the living, but a most grievous cruelty to the dead. Into his arguments in defence of the doctrine it is unnecessary to enter. He fights, not without effect, by confusing the intermediate state with a state of torment, by lavish reference to the Church's authority, and by incorrect accounts of the belief of early Christianity. Yet there is a pathos worthy of the writer in the passage where the suffering souls plead their membership in the Catholic Church, their claim on the prayers of the faithful, and their right to the compassion which by their benefactions they had shown to those on earth.

At this point in More's life he was brought into active personal relation to heretics by his duties as Lord Chancellor.

That he had frequently attended the examination of heretics is proved by several passages in the *Dialogue*: it was not, however, until his appointment as Lord Chancellor that his official duties obliged him to do so. As Chancellor he took the oath " to

use all his power to destroy all manner of heresies."[1]
It was one of his duties to the discharge of which
he could give himself with much sympathy; but we
should be surprised to discover that he used with
harshness or violence the power committed to him.
His conduct, however, in all that relates to heresy
has been the subject of such vehement attacks from
Protestant writers, that an impression has arisen
that he at this period belied the promise of his past
life and became a relentless persecutor. Wolsey's
mildness has almost universally been contrasted with
More's severity; and, while it has been commonly
supposed that the latter exercised the duties of his
office with stern rigour, Mr. Froude has gone so far
as to accuse him of distinctly illegal acts. A closer
examination, however, seems to show that not only did
he keep strictly within the limits of his duty, and
do no more than he was legally bound to do, but
that he took especial pains—and for some time
successfully—to avoid the infliction of the extreme
penalty. Mr. Froude, after dwelling on the illegal
imprisonments which followed Wolsey's resignation,
declares that " no sooner had the seals changed
hands than the Smithfield fires recommenced."[2] It
appears, rather, that not only were the imprisonments
to which the Protestants were subjected the strictly
legal acts of the bishops rather than of the Chancellor, but that for nearly two years after More's
appointment—and he did not hold his office three

---

[1] 2 Henry V. stat. 1 : see also Proclamation of 1527, Foxe,
ed. 1597, p. 930.

[2] *Hist. England*, vol. ii. p. 83.

years—there was no infliction of the extreme penalty.

The law provided that if a heretic, arrested and examined by the bishops, refused to recant, he should be burnt. The decision once made, and sentence passed, the end could not be avoided. But by the proclamation of 1529 power was given to the bishops to imprison, at their discretion, both before and after conviction. Thus to More in the execution of his office the only escape from his clear legal obligation to destroy the heretics was by advising the bishops to use the power committed to them. By the exercise of this power many were saved who must otherwise have been burned; and there can be little doubt that those whose petitions to the Crown after More's resignation have caused much of the blame that has been attached to him, would, but for his intervention, have suffered death.

It may be well to notice the cases of those who were burned during More's Chancellorship and of those who were, according to Mr. Froude, illegally imprisoned, and the accusations of personal cruelty alleged by Foxe against the Chancellor.

It was not till within the last nine months of his tenure of the seals that any execution took place. Bilney, Bayfield, Tewkesbury, and Bainham, who had previously abjured, relapsed into heresy. In such cases the law was explicit. The Chancellor had no power to save. He was forced to issue the writ ordered by the statute *De Haeretico Comburendo;* and he can with no more justice be considered responsible for the law he carried out

than the many judges who in this century condemned men to death for forgery and theft. He is
thus without doubt legally absolved. The stories of
his cruelty to these prisoners rest only on the
unreliable assertions of Foxe; and there can be no
higher testimony to his personal conduct than that
afforded by the martyrs themselves, who died with
such prayers on their lips as "May the Lord open
the eyes of Sir Thomas More!"

The two cases of the Chancellor's illegal action
quoted by Mr. Froude are those of Thomas Philips
and John Field.[1] The only evidence for the first is
the petition of the sufferer, and even there Sir
Thomas is not mentioned except as issuing the
warrant for his arrest, and as examining him from
time to time, in conjunction with the Bishop of
London. The whole responsibility lies upon the
Bishop; and the proclamation of 1529 gave him his
authority. Mr. Froude has not thought it necessary
to notice More's own account of the matter, which
bears the strongest marks of truth. "When," wrote
Sir Thomas,[2] "I had spoken with Philips [on first
sending for him] and honestly entreated him one
day or twain in mine house, and laboured about his
amendment in as hearty, loving wise as I could:
when I perceived finally the person such that I
could find no truth, neither in his word nor in his
oath, and saw the likelihood that he was in the
setting forth of such heresies a man meet to do
many folk much harm, I by indenture delivered

---

[1] *Hist. England*, vol. ii. pp. 70—83.
[2] *Apology : Eng. Works*, p. 905.

him to his ordinary." After explaining how the prisoner was transferred to the Tower, he adds, "and yet after that he complained thereof, not against me but against the ordinary."

"If, however," says Mr. Froude, "it be thought unjust to charge a good man's memory with an offence in which his part was only secondary, the following iniquity was wholly and exclusively his own." He then quotes, "without comment," the petition of the sufferer. In this case it has been well argued [1] that the petition itself [2] proves that the offence of Field was not heresy at all. It is to be noticed that the bishops were not concerned in it; that after Field had been set free for a time he was re-arrested by the Duke of Norfolk who had no connexion whatever with ecclesiastical jurisdiction; that he was examined before the Star Chamber, and imprisoned in the Fleet; and that the books taken from him were not heretical writings, but "a Greek Vocabulary, S. Cyprian's *Works*, with a book of the same Sir Thomas More's making, *The Supplication of Souls*." Finally, not only is there no allusion in the petition to heresy; but Foxe, who would hardly have neglected so remarkable a case, makes no mention of it whatever, and More, in his *Apology*, where he defends himself specifically concerning his treatment of heretics, is equally silent.

As to the minor cases of cruelty we shall find them most clearly stated in More's own answer.

---

[1] *North Brit. Rev.* vol. xxx. p. 162 *et seq.*
[2] *Letters and Papers, Hen. VIII.*, vol. v. 1059.

"Divers of them have said that of such as were in my house when I was chancellor I used to examine them with torments, causing them to be bound to a tree in my garden and there piteously beaten. . . . What cannot these brethren say that can be so shameless to say thus? . . . I never did cause any such thing to be done to any at all in all my life, except only twain. One was a child and a servant of mine in mine own house, whom his father, ere he came to me, had nursed up in such matters, and set him to attend upon George Joy. This Joy did teach the child his heresy against the Blessed Sacrament of the altar: which heresy this child in my house began to teach another child. And upon that point I charged a servant of mine to strip him like a child before mine household, for amendment of himself and ensample of such other. The other was one which after that he had fallen into these frantic heresies fell soon after into plain open frenzy." More then declares that he had the man beaten, as the common method of recovering lunatics, the result being that the man came to himself. "And verily, God be thanked, I hear no harm of him now. And of all that ever came into my hand for heresy, else had never any of them any stripe or stroke given them, so much as a fillip on the forehead. And some have said that when Constantine (a heretic who had been put in the stocks at Chelsea) was gotten away, I was fallen for anger into a wonderful rage. But surely, though I would not have suffered him to go if it would have pleased him to have tarried still in the stocks . . .

never will I be so unreasonable as to be angry with any man that riseth if he can, when he findeth himself that he sitteth not at his ease." There can be no reason to doubt this statement. It was made at a time when More was known to have lost the King's favour and to be in imminent danger, and it was never contradicted, though many must have been aware of its truth or falsehood. It may be added that a humorous instance of his leniency is given by Strype—"Examining a Protestant, whose name was Silver, he told him, after his jesting way, that 'Silver must be tried in the fire.' 'Ay,' said Silver, 'but quick-silver will not abide it'—with which ready answer being delighted, he dismissed him."

The case of Bainham has been brought also as conclusive evidence of More's cruelty, but the evidence of Foxe is certainly not conclusive. It has been shown that the martyrologist, after making in one edition the cases of Tewkesbury and Bainham present an extraordinary parallel, in another transferred the statements concerning the former entirely to the latter. And Foxe, it must be remembered, was neither a contemporary writer nor a man of balanced or critical judgment.

That he searched for heretical books—that he chastised offenders in his own garden, that he imprisoned prisoners in his own house—an act of lenity rather than harshness—is admitted; but it may fairly be said that, although the scarcity of record makes it difficult to speak with certainty, as far as has appeared, on evidence at present known, the charges against More made by Foxe, and repeated, among others, by Burnet, Strype, and Mr. Froude, have not been substantiated. We are therefore justified in forming a conclusion in harmony with all that we know of More's character.

It only remains to notice More's religious writings subsequent to his acceptance of the seals. These are a confutation of Tyndale's answer to his *Dialogue,* a letter impugning the erroneous writing of John Frith against the Blessed Sacrament, the *Apology,* the *Debellation of Salem and Bizance,* an answer to the book of a "nameless heretic"[1] on the Lord's Supper, and several lesser books written in prison.

Tyndale's answer to More's *Dialogue* was published in the spring or early summer of 1531. In it he explained his view of the Church, defended his translation of the New Testament, and scornfully disposed of his antagonist's book. He did not adopt the comparatively moderate tone of More, but, moved apparently by personal animosity, wrote in a coarse and violent manner. He believed More to have been actuated by the basest motives in his opposition to the reformers. Speaking of the Council which had taken place in London in May 1530, at which his own works had been condemned, he declared that "More was the special orator of the bishops, to feign lies for their purpose."[2] Not only this, but he specifically charged the Chancellor with

---

[1] Tyndale (Demaus, *Life of Tyndale,* p. 281), or George Joy (Lumby, Notes to Roper, *Utopia,* Pitt Press ed. p. 180).

[2] Tyndale's *Answer to More,* p. 168, quoted by Demaus, p. 272.

having accepted bribes from the bishops, and with writing against his convictions. Little as More was inclined to heed personal accusations, it was impossible for him, for the sake of the Church as well as of his own reputation, to leave this book unanswered. The charges against himself he barely referred to, but the whole system of Tyndale he once more denounced in the voluminous *Confutation* which he published in 1532, and revised and continued up to within a short time of his death. The first three books appeared in 1532, the second part, containing the next five, in 1533, and the ninth book was first published in the collected edition of his English works. The enormous length of this *Confutation* prevents any reasonable analysis, nor does its interest demand one. It is concerned chiefly with a recapitulation of the writer's previous arguments, especially on the character of the visible Church, and does not possess the vivacity and clearness of the *Dialogue*. To say that it is a keen and powerful work is only to say that it is More's ; but it must be admitted that, in spite of the success with which the Chancellor treated particular points— such as the relation of the early Church to the gospel and the degrading views of his opponents concerning marriage—the victory on the whole remained with Tyndale. One passage, however, for its autobiographical interest, may find a place here.

"He asketh me why I have not contended with Erasmus, whom he calleth my derling, of all this long while, for translating this word *ecclesia* into this word *congregatio*. And then he cometh forth with his fit proper taunt that I favour him of likelihood for making of his book *Moria* in my house. There had he hit me, save for lack of a little salt. I have not contended with Erasmus, my derling, because I find no such malicious intent with Erasmus, my derling, as I find with Tyndale. For had I found with Erasmus, my derling, the shrewd intent and purpose that I find with Tyndale, Erasmus, my derling, should be no more my derling. But I find in Erasmus, my derling, that he detesteth and abhorreth the errors and heresies that Tyndale plainly teacheth and abideth by; and therefore Erasmus, my derling, shall be my dear derling still. . . . As touching *Moria* in which Erasmus doth merely touch and reprove such faults and follies as he found in any kind of people, perusing every state and condition, spiritual and temporal, leaving almost none untouched, . . . in these days in which men by their own default misconster and take harm of the very scripture of God, if any man would now translate *Moria* into English, or some works either that I have myself written ere this,[1] albeit there be none harm therein, folk yet being (as they be) given to take harm of that is good, I would not only my derling's books but mine own also help to burn them both with mine own hands, rather than folk should (though through their own fault) take any harm of them, seeing that I see them likely in these days so to do." [2]

In the eighth book of his *Confutation*, which he

---

[1] Is this an allusion to the *Utopia*?
[2] *English Works*, pp. 421—423.

styled a *Confutation of Frere Barne's Church*, More gained a partial victory. He exposed the error in defining the Church as merely the invisible company of the elect, but his claim for it of absolute freedom from all error is not, perhaps, equally successful. It is interesting to notice that in the course of his argument More enunciates the dogma of the infallibility of the **Pope**.

He had now other antagonists besides Tyndale. He wrote a letter on the Blessed Sacrament, impugning the treatise which John Frith had written in prison.[1] It is pleasant to find him here writing in a tone of tender remonstrance rather than of indignant denunciation. From this short letter and from the larger work, " The Answer to the Poisoned Book which a Nameless Heretic hath named the *Supper of the Lord*," [2] More's views on the doctrine of the Eucharist may be seen to have not departed from those of the medieval Church.

After his resignation of the Chancellorship More wrote also his *Apology* [3] and the *Debellation of Salem and Bizance*.[4] In addition to its personal interest the former of these books is to be noticed as an answer to a treatise called *The Pacifier*, written by a lawyer named Saintgerman. More's main thesis was that heresy, being a great crime against God, deserved a severe punishment from the secular power. The latter was an answer to Saintgerman's rejoinder, *Salem and Bizance*. Its

---

[1] *English Works*, pp. 833—844.
[2] *Ibid.* pp. 1035—1138.
[3] *Ibid.* pp. 845—929.   [4] *Ibid.* pp. 929—1025.

plan is that which More had adopted in all his later works, a minute quotation and answer of his opponent, point by point, but there is nothing in the substance that had not been suggested in his earlier writings. The *Answer on the Blessed Sacrament* was the last of More's controversial works. During his imprisonment he wrote several devotional studies, but the spirit of strife and contention he laid for ever aside.

His services were not unappreciated by the clergy. The bishops were so delighted by his support of the Church that they offered him a large sum of money, to which the clergy liberally subscribed. When their deputation appeared to present it, More told them "that like as it were no small comfort to him that so wise and learned men so well accepted his simple doing, for which he intended never to receive reward but at the hands of God only, to whom alone was thanks thereof chiefly to be ascribed, so gave he most humble thanks unto them for all their bountiful consideration."

"When they [continues Roper, who tells the story], for all their importunate pressing upon him, could by no means make him take it, then they besought him to be content yet that they might bestow it upon his wife and children. 'Not so, my lords,' quoth he; 'I had liever see it all cast into the Thames than I or any of mine should have thereof the worth of one penny. For though your offer, my lords, be indeed very friendly and honourable, yet set I so much by my pleasure and so little by my profit that I would not, in good faith, for as much more have lost the rest of so many a night's sleep as was spent upon the same. And yet wish I would, for all that, upon conditions that all heresies were suppressed, that all my books were burned and my labour utterly suppressed.' Thus departing, they were fain to restore to every man his own again." [1]

The value of More's controversial works has, indeed, always been recognized by the Roman Church, and, as one of its writers confesses, they "have often been resorted to by later divines as arsenals stored with materials for the defence of the faith." [2]

Vehement as had been More's partisanship, he had not carried it into his private life. Miles Coverdale, while working at his translation of the Bible, was a guest at Chelsea.[3] Protestant servants were not excluded from the Chancellor's household.[4] Even Roper was at one time "weary of auricular confession, fasting, and vigils, and vehement in the new opinions," yet lost none of his father-in-law's affection. Sir Thomas argued with him in vain; then at length "in sober sadness said, 'I see, son, no disputations will do thee any good: henceforth therefore I will dispute with thee no more, only will I pray for thee that God will be so favourable as to touch thy heart.'" It was not long before this gentle silence succeeded.[5] Such facts as these must always be remembered when the violence of

---

[1] Roper, pp. 27, 28. Cf. More's *English Works*, p. 867.
[2] Walter, *Life of More*, p. 204.
[3] *State Papers*, i. 383.   [4] *English Works*, p. 901.
[5] Cres. More, *Life of More*, pp. 120, 121.

More's controversial writings seems to invite a stern condemnation on the man. It is easy for one who is not moved to preserve a calm balance of language; but to More the religious questions of the day were matters of life and death, and he could not restrain his fears for the result of the struggle.

"If any of the new learned,"[1] he wrote—and the passage contains the only excuse that can be made for his language—

"If any of the new learned use their words at their own pleasure, as evil and villanous as they list, against myself, I am content to forbear the requiting thereof and give them no worse words again than if they had spoken me fair. . . . But railing as they do against all holy things, I purpose not to bear that so patiently as to forbear to let them hear some parts of their language, though not with the grace that they use it. But to match them herein I neither can, though I would not if I could; thinking it much worth rebuke therein to strive for mastery."

Again—

"If these gospellers will not cease to be heretics, let them at least be reasonable heretics and honest men: let them write, if not reason, at least after a reasonable manner, and leave railing. Then hardly let these evangelical brethren find fault with me if I use them not in words as fair as the matter may bear, but assure them, if they write as they do, I will handle them no otherwise than I have done."

[1] *English Works*, pp. 865, 866.

CHAPTER VI.

TROUBLES, IMPRISONMENT, AND DEATH.

"Virtue is like precious odours, most fragrant when they are
incensed or crushed : for prosperity doth best discover
vice, but adversity doth best discover virtue."—BACON.

WHATEVER may be the differences of opinion on
More's religious life, there can be no feeling but
admiration for his conduct in adversity. His resignation of the Seals was made, as has been said,
without apparent loss of the King's favour. For
some time afterwards Henry gave no sign of his
displeasure. In November 1532, he pricked More
as Sheriff for Somerset and Dorset; but he did not
recall him to Court. He remained in comparative
seclusion at Chelsea, writing his theological works
and avoiding as far as possible all conversation on
politics. But the sinister figure of Cromwell had
already risen into prominence. Roper mentions that
when the new minister came one day to see him,
More gave him some advice which showed how
thoroughly he understood his master. "Master
Cromwell," quoth he, "you are now entered into the
service of a most noble, wise, and liberal prince : if
you will follow my poor advice, you shall in counsel

giving unto his grace ever tell him what he ought
to do, but never tell him what he is able to do, so
shall you show yourself a true faithful servant and
a right worthy counsellor. For if the Lion knew
his own strength, hard were it for any man to rule
him." [1]   More soon suffered from Cromwell's neglect
of this advice. The Lion at last knew his own
strength, and rejoiced in the declaration of it. Sir
Thomas foresaw the result: when the King's marriage to Anne Bullen was announced, he said to
Roper, " God give us grace, son, that these matters
within a while be not confirmed with oaths." [2]

While preparations were being made for the
coronation of the new Queen, More received a letter
from Tunstal and the Bishops of Winchester and
Bath asking him to join in the pageant. The King
had ordered also that they should send him £20
to buy a fitting robe. But More, though he saw
his danger, would not be led into apparent consent
to Henry's marriage or take part in the joyful
celebration of what was to him a sorrowful event.
His refusal was the signal for the crowd of courtiers
to fall upon him. As early as July 1533, he complained to Sir William Fitzwilliam that a gentleman
had used him very ill, and requested the intervention
of Cromwell.[3]   He had congratulated himself that
not one voice had been raised against the justice of
his conduct as Chancellor; but no sooner was it
known that he had lost the King's favour than several
accusations of corruption were brought against him.

<hr>

[1] Roper, p. 32.   [2] *Ibid.* p. 33.
[3] Ellis, *Letters*, 3rd Series, ii. 244.

A man named Parnell charged him with accepting a "great gilt cup" as a bribe. More, when examined before the Council, admitted having received it, whereon Queen Anne's father, now Earl of Wiltshire, broke out into unseemly rejoicing. More with calm humour continued the story, when it appeared that he had only accepted the cup to restore it immediately as a new year's gift. Two other accusations failed as signally.[1] His enemies then tried another plan. They charged him with writing a book published by his nephew William Rastell against the Articles on the Marriage and Divorce which had been officially issued at Christmas 1532. It was an accusation which he was able easily to rebut, for his last book, *The Answer on the Sacrament*, had been printed before the issue of the Articles, and had no reference whatever to them.[2]

He was soon, however, in much greater danger. The visions and prophecies of the Nun of Kent had become too evidently the instruments of others in attacking the King's proceedings to be suffered by the Government to continue. Cromwell had received intelligence of all that she said, and of the intrigues in which her supporters were engaged. Among the eminent men who had been led by curiosity or credulity to encourage her, More had taken some slight part. All that passed between them was at once made known to Cromwell,[3] and More's name

[1] Roper, pp. 34, 38.
[2] *English Works*, p. 1422.
[3] See the letter (*Letters and Papers, Henry VIII.*, vol. vi. 1467) in which information is given exactly corresponding to More's subsequent explanation.

began to occur ominously in the Minister's "remembrances." [1] When the imposture was exposed, and the offenders brought to trial, the utmost eagerness was shown to implicate the Bishop of Rochester, and More. In March 1534,[2] More wrote a long letter to Cromwell at his request conveyed through Roper, explaining his whole connexion with the Nun.

Eight or nine years before, he said, Warham had given to the King "a roll with certain words spoken in trances," and Henry had asked More his opinion of it. He had replied that "there was nothing in it that he could at all regard or esteem, for except that some was in rhyme, and that full rude, there was nothing that a right simple woman might not speak of her own wit"; but he added that as men talked of a miracle, he must not be bold to judge. Henry it seemed thought the matter, said More, "as light as it afterwards proved lewd."

From that time till Christmas 1532, More heard no more of the Nun. Then Father Resbye spoke of her one day as one in whom God wrought most wonderful works, and began to speak of her political revelations. More refused to speak of "the king's matter"—and so Resbye left him with a last eulogy of the Nun as having saved Wolsey's soul by her mediation. A few months later Father Rich questioned him, but he still avoided all talk of politics, for he thought some of her 'revelations' were very strange and some very childish. Finally the Fathers of Sion House told of things they misliked

---

[1] See *Letters and Papers*, vi. 49, 108, etc.
[2] *Ibid.* vol. vii. 287.

in her, and thereupon begged him to see her. He was in danger, he may already have felt, of being mixed up in some treasonous plottings, but he willingly saw her privately "in a little chapel there." His own account of his interview is worth quotation.

" In the beginning thereof I showed that my coming to her was not of any curious mind to hear of such things as folk talked that it pleased God to reveal and show unto her, but for the great virtue that I had heard so many years every day more and more spoken and reported of her. I therefore had a great mind to see her and be acquainted with her, that she might have somewhat the more occasion to remember me to God in her devotion and prayers." To this she gave a very good and virtuous answer, that as God did far better by her than such a poor wretch was worthy, she feared that many people spoke more favourably of her than was the truth, and that she had already prayed for him. He spoke then of how she had told a certain Ellen of Tottenham, who professed also to have visions, that they were but illusions of the devil, whereon the maid had been less visited by them. So the Nun of Kent said to him that folk who are visited with such visions have great need to prove of what spirit they come, and that lately the devil in the form of a bird had been flickering about her chamber, and suffered himself to be caught and then suddenly changed into such a strange ugly-fashioned bird that they were all afraid and threw it out of the window. This was very midsummer madness indeed, but More seems to have been so impressed with the woman's sincerity that he was content merely to ask her prayers and warn her not to speak of politics, and that by a special letter. The Fathers of the Charterhouse and of Sion still tried to entangle him in talk about her, but he would not speak; and when at length she made her open confession of hypocrisy at Paul's Cross, he sent his servant "to tell the proctor of the Charterhouse that she was undoubtedly proved a false deceiving hypocrite." The "good man had so good an opinion of her that he could scarcely believe it."

The letter was indeed a full vindication; and no repudiation of any connexion with the nun could be more complete.[1] More told Cromwell that he had done a very meritorious deed in bringing forth to light such detestable hypocrisy.

More's candid explanation did not satisfy Cromwell or the King. Inquiries were made on all sides, and information of all kinds was greedily sought for, even as to More's "mumbling" in his son-in-law's parlour at Shacklewell about the King's immoral Court.[2]

When the bill of attainder against the Nun and her adherents was introduced into the House of

---

[1] F*r*. Bridgett prints the letter *in extenso* in his *Life of More*, pp. 323 *sqq.* I have been content to abridge it, with the help of Mr. Gairdner's abstract in the *Letters and Papers of Henry VIII.* Burnet, *History of the Reformation*, v. 431, accused Rastell of suppressing the letter in his edition of 1557, but the charge was satisfactorily disproved by Mr. Bruce (*Archaeologia*, xxx. 149). For further references to the case in the *State Papers*, see vol. vi. 1468.

[2] *Letters and Papers*, vi. 290.

Lords it was found that the name of the late
Chancellor was inserted,—a proceeding so entirely
without even colour of justice that Roper may be
supposed to be right in ascribing it solely to the
King's anger.[1] More at once wrote to Cromwell,[2]
expressing his surprise, and asking for a copy of
the bill that he might point out its errors in a
petition to the King; for he had, as we have seen,
previously written a full account of his knowledge
of the Nun.

In addition to this letter to the minister, More
wrote also to the King,[3] reminding him of his
promise on his resignation of the Chancellorship.
He begged that he might lose all, even life, if
Henry thought that he could be so monstrously
ungrateful as for a moment to digress from his
allegiance; but that if, on the other hand, his
master perceived his faithfulness, his name might
be put out of the bill. On the same day, March 5,
he wrote again to Cromwell,[4] this time a full
and clear defence of his whole conduct. He
reiterated his assertions of the perfect harmlessness
of his intercourse with the Nun. He then described
his behaviour throughout the history of the Divorce
question. He recalled the King's constant solicita-
tions, and his own ready willingness to study that
he might come to be reconciled to the Divorce,
wherein he "would have been more glad than of
any worldly commodities to have served his grace."

[1] Roper, p. 36.   [2] *English Works*, p. 1423.
[3] *Letters and Papers*, vii. 288.
[4] *English Works*, p. 1424.

The King had seemed to take his conduct in good part, and had used only those in the business " whose conscience his grace perceived well and truly persuaded." "So I am he," added More—and surely no more could have been desired—" that among other his grace's faithful subjects, his highness being in possession of his marriage and this noble woman really anointed queen, neither murmur at it nor dispute upon it, nor never did nor will, but without any other manner meddling of the matter among his other faithful subjects, faithfully pray to God for his grace and hers both long to live and well, and their noble issue too, in such wise as may be to the pleasure of God, honour and surety to themselves, rest, peace, wealth and profit unto this noble realm."[1] Thirdly, as to the primacy of the Pope, he gave the account of the King's conversation with him ten years before, which has been mentioned above.[2] He declared his own opinion now to be that there was a primacy instituted of the " corps of Christendom " for a thousand years past. " I cannot perceive," he added, " how any member thereof without the common assent of the body depart from the common head." Thus it did not matter whether the primacy was instituted directly by God or by a general council. Since the King had appealed to a general council, he wished him all success, for he had never considered the Pope to be above a general council. His

---

[1] This passage is omitted by Rastell—who dedicated his edition to Queen Mary—though found in the original letter, but see *Archaeologia*, xxx. p. 155. Rastell did not print from the originals.

[2] Pages 196, 197.

own writings that seemed to exalt the Papacy he
had utterly suppressed—a proof that he never meant
to "meddle in the matter against the king's gracious
pleasure whatsoever his own opinion might be."
Finally, he asked Cromwell to explain all this to the
King—"that in the matter of that wicked woman[1] or
in anything else, there was not on his part any other
will than good." The last words are most characteristic of the tender yet conscientious mind of the
writer. "Nor yet in anything else never was there
nor never shall there be any further fault found
in me than that I cannot in everything think the
same way that other men of more wisdom and
deeper learning do; nor can find in mine own heart
otherwise to say than as mine own conscience giveth
me; which condition hath never grown in anything
that ever might touch his gracious pleasure of any
obstinate mind or misaffectionate appetite, but of
a timorous conscience rising haply for lack of better
perceiving and yet not without tender respect unto
my most bounden duty towards his noble grace,
whose only favour I so much esteem that I nothing
have of mine own in all this world except only
my soul, but that I will with better will forego than
abide of his highness one heavy displeasant look."[2]

The day after these letters were written[3] the
Lords addressed the King praying him to declare
whether Sir Thomas More and others should not be
heard in their defence " before the Lords in the royal

---

[1] The printed text simply reads "of the nonne."
[2] *English Works*, p. 1428.
[3] *Lords' Journals*, March 6.

senate called the Star Chamber." The King had already found out that he would not be able to proceed severely against his late Chancellor, and had contented himself with taking away his salary or pension. He was not willing that More should have an opportunity of speaking before so large an audience as the Lords, and accordingly ordered the Archbishop of Canterbury, the Lord Chancellor, the Duke of Norfolk, and Cromwell to examine him privately. Roper entreated his father-in-law "earnestly to labour unto these lords for the help of his discharge out of the parliament bill," and More promised to do so. The examination was conducted at first in a friendly manner, but the questions were not confined to his connexion with the Nun. Promises were soon succeeded by threats, and he was accused of inducing the King to maintain the Pope's authority in his book against Luther. Nothing could be clearer than his denial of this, or more evidently truthful than his account of his interview with the King.

Henry's relations with the Papacy ten years before had been on a very different footing—"We are so much bounden," the King had said, "to the See of Rome that we cannot do too much honour unto it." When More reminded him of the Statute of Praemunire, Henry had replied, "Whatsoever impediment be to the contrary, we will set forth that authority to the uttermost: for we received from that see our crown imperial"—to which More with some shrewdness added, "till his grace with his own mouth told me it, I never heard of it before." So the examination ended. More indeed hoped always that a change of Pope might set all things right again. "In the next general council it may well happen that this Pope may be deposed and another substituted in his place, with whom the king's highness may be very well content." He had never thought the Pope above the general council. But this was not all Henry wished.

"Then[1] took Sir Thomas More his boat towards Chelsea, wherein the way he was very merry, and for that I was nothing sorry, hoping that he had gotten himself discharged out of the parliament bill. When he was come home then walked we two alone into his garden together, where I, desirous to know how he had sped, said, 'Sir, I trust all is well, because you are so merry.' 'It is so indeed, son Roper, I thank God,' quoth he. 'Are you put out of the parliament bill, then?' said I. 'By my troth, son Roper,' quoth he, 'I never remembered it.' 'Never remembered it, sir?' quoth I; 'a case that touched yourself so near and us all, for your sake. I am sorry to hear it, for I verily trusted when I saw you so merry, that all had been well.' 'In good faith, I rejoice, son,' quoth he, 'that I had given the devil so foul a fall, and that with these lords I had gone so far as without great shame I could never go back again.' At which words waxed I very sad."

Thus More met whatever temptation to insincerity may but too naturally have beset him. There had been a struggle. "As[2] he lay by his wife's side many

---

[1] Roper, p. 38.   [2] Cres. More, p. 204.

nights he slept not forethinking the worst that could happen unto him; and by his prayers and tears he overcame the frailties of his flesh, which, as he confessed of himself, could not endure a fillip." The victory was won. More now tried to prepare his family for what he knew would happen before long. "He hired a pursuivant to come suddenly to his house, when he was one time at dinner, and knocking hastily at his door, to warn him to appear the next day before the Commissioners."[1]

Henry was very reluctant to spare More; but the urgent entreaty of the Chancellor, who declared that the Lords would never pass the bill at all if his name were in it, induced him at last to yield; and Cromwell meeting Roper at Westminster was able to tell him that his father-in-law was "put out of the bill." He at once sent a message to his wife, who told her father. "I faith, Meg," said More when he heard it, "quod differtur non aufertur." On March 28, John Granfyld, who held office in the Chancery, was able to write to the deputy of Calais, "My old master, Sir Thomas More, is clearly discharged of his trouble."[2] Yet More well knew that his fate could not be long avoided. When the Duke of Norfolk, trying to win him to approve of the King's acts, said, "Indignatio principis mors est": "Is that all, my lord?" More answered. "Is there no more difference between your grace and me but that I shall die to-day and you to-morrow?"

Before a month had passed a new trouble had

[1] Cres. More, p. 205.
[2] *Letters and Papers, Henry VIII.*, vol. vii. 384.

arisen, and this the last. In the spring the Act of
Succession had been passed. It was to be fortified
by an oath which all persons might be called upon
to take, or on refusal be considered guilty of misprision of treason. The oath itself was not fixed by
the statute, but was submitted to the House of
Lords, just as the prorogation was taking place.
Its form, thus agreed upon without any close examination, was extremely strict. Allegiance was to be
sworn to the King and to the heirs of his body, "of
his most dear and entirely lawful wife Queen Anne
begotten and to be begotten." Oaths made to
another (that is to the succession of Mary) were to
be vain and annihilate; and all men were to defend
to the uttermost "the said Act of Succession and
all other acts and statutes made in confirmation or
for execution of the same, or for anything herein
contained,"—and this "against all manner of persons
of what state, dignity, degree, or condition soever
they be,"[1] and repudiating oaths to "any foreign
authority, prince or potentate." Cranmer, the secretary, Cromwell, the abbat of Westminster, and the
Lord Chancellor Audley were appointed Commissioners to administer the oath. On April 13, they
summoned More before them. He rose early, then
confessed and received the Blessed Sacrament in
Chelsea Church. His children used always, when
he went to London, to come down with him to the
boat, where he would kiss and bid them farewell;

---

[1] The actual oath is recited in 26 Henry VIII. c. 2, the Act
passed to confirm it, but the form in the *Lords' Journals*,
vol. i. p. 82, is incomplete.

but on that morning he would not suffer them, but parted from them at the wicket-gate of his garden, and with a sad heart took boat with Roper. He sat silent for a while; then said, "Son Roper, I thank our Lord the field is won." And his biographer adds[1] one of those touches of nature which are so pathetic in their simple truth. "What he meant thereby, then, I wist not. Yet loth to seem ignorant I answered, 'Sir, I am thereof very glad.' But as I conjectured afterwards, it was for that the love he had to God wrought in him so effectually that it conquered in him all his casual affections utterly." When he arrived at Lambeth he found many there before him, but he was at once admitted to the Commissioners. More, having read over the oath and the statute, at once declared that it was not in his purpose to point out any fault in the Act or in those that swore to it, or to condemn the conscience of any other man; but that his conscience would not suffer him to take that oath, though he would swear to the succession. Then they all said that the King would have great indignation against him, for he was the first that had refused the oath; and they showed him the roll of those who had sworn. As he still refused, they bade him leave them for a while. So he went into "the old burned chamber that looketh into the garden, and would not go down because of the heat." As he sat there patiently waiting, and unmoved in mind, he saw the London clergy joyfully going to take the oath and passing out again with great mirth; Latimer, as though he had "waxed wanton," and the

[1] Roper, p. 40.

Vicar of Croydon calling loudly for wine, "either for gladness or dryness, or else that it might be seen *quod ille notus erat pontifici.*" And he saw Dr. Wilson, one of the King's chaplains, who refused it, led off to the Tower. When the Commissioners had decided upon their further course, they called him back. Again they reminded him of the members who had sworn : again he replied that he blamed no man, but could not go against his conscience. They asked him to declare what part of the oath he objected to. He answered that he feared by doing so still further to exasperate the King. Yet when they reproached him with stubbornness he said that he would state his objections in writing, as well as promise to take the oath if any man would satisfy his conscience, if he received license to do so freely from the King. The Commissioners answered that a license from the King would be no defence against the laws—thus declaring a constitutional doctrine which was not regarded as fixed until a century and a half later. More said that he would trust to the King's honour : " so if he might not declare his objections without peril, to leave them undeclared was no obstinacy." Then Cranmer tried to find an escape for him, and said that if he condemned not those who swore he was not certain, evidently, that it was wrong to take the oath ; on the other hand, his duty to the King was certain. More paused, struck by the subtlety of the suggestion ; but after a moment he answered that in conscience the truth seemed not to be on the King's side. The abbat of Westminster reminded him of the whole Parliament that was against him. More

replied by a reference to the general opinion of
Christendom; an incautious saying which would be
sure to incense the King when he heard it. On
hearing this last refusal Cromwell swore that he had
rather his only son had lost his head than that this
should have happened, and declared that Henry
would now think that the matter of the Nun was all
More's contrivance. Sir Thomas answered that the
truth was well known, and that whatever should be-
fall him it lay not in his power to help it without
the peril of his soul.[1] And so, the Chancellor repeating what More had said to Cromwell, who was to
convey it to the King, the examination ended, and
Sir Thomas was committed to the custody of the
abbat of Westminster.

During the following days there was great discussion in the council as to what should be done
with him. Fisher, who, according to the graphic
phrase of the Bishop of Lichfield, was so worn with
age that his body could not bear the clothes on his
back, had given a similar answer. It may be inferred
that it was to the preamble of the Act of Succession
that they especially objected, for it contained a
denunciation of the Pope; and the oath committed
them to all the statements of the Act. Cranmer
wrote to Cromwell asking that they might be sworn
to the Act alone, without the preamble; but the
King would not suffer it.[2] Nor was another suggested compromise—that they should swear not to

---

[1] The account of this examination is taken from More's
letter to Margaret Roper, *Eng. Works*, pp. 1428, 1430.
[2] *Letters and Papers, Henry VIII.*, vii. 499, 500

divulge whether they had taken the oath or not—accepted.   Having again refused the oath, on Friday, April 17, More was committed to the Tower.   He had at first his own servant, John Wood, to attend on him, who was sworn to reveal anything that he might say against the King, the realm, or the council.

When he had been in prison a few days he wrote, with a coal, one of his most beautiful letters to his dearest daughter—

"My own good daughter, our Lord be thanked I am in good health of body and in good quiet of mind: and of worldly things I no more despair than I have.   I beseech Him make you all merry in the hope of Heaven.   And such things as I somewhat longed to talk with you all our Lord put them into your minds, and better too, by His Holy Spirit, Who bless you and preserve you all.   Written with a coal by your tender loving father, who in his prayers forgetteth none of you all, nor your babes, nor your nurses, nor your good husbands, nor your good husband's shrewd wives, nor your father's shrewd wife neither, nor our other friends.   And thus fare ye heartily ever, for lack of paper."[1]

Margaret Roper longed to see him, and knowing that all his letters were intercepted, wrote to him seeming to advise him to take the oath, hoping that Cromwell might then allow her to visit him.   More replied sadly—"I hear many terrible things towards me; but they all never touched me never so near, nor were they so grievous unto me, as to see you, my well-beloved child, in such vehement piteous manner

---

[1] *English Works*, p. 1430.

labour to persuade unto me the thing wherein I have of pure necessity, for respect unto mine own soul, so often given you so precise answer before."[1] Her answer to this showed that she had never meant to advise him against his conscience. "Father," she wrote, "what think you hath been our comfort since your departing from us? Surely, the experience we have had of your life past, and godly conversation, and wholesome counsel, and virtuous example, and a surety not only of the continuance of that same, but also a great increase by the goodness of our Lord to the great rest and gladness of your heart."[2] Before long, however, she was allowed to visit him: a little more than a month after his incarceration. First, before they talked of any worldly matter, they said the Seven Penitential Psalms and the Litany, and then they spoke freely. More said, "I believe, Meg, that they that have put me here ween they have done me a high displeasure. But I assure you on my faith, mine own dear daughter, if it had not been for my wife and you that be my children whom I account the chief part of my charge, I would not have failed long ere this to have closed myself in as strait a room, and straiter too"— thus showing that his longing for the monastic life had never left him.[3] After this his daughter was allowed to visit him constantly. He wrote a letter to be shown to all his friends asking them to regard all her requests as his own.[4] Once when she was with him he inquired how Queen Anne did.

---

[1] *English Works*, p. 1431.   [2] *Ibid.* p. 1432.
[3] Roper, pp. 41, 42.   [4] *English Works*, p. 1432.

"In good **faith, father**," said Margaret, "never **better.**
There is nothing in the court but dancing and sport-
ing." "Never better," said **More, "alas, it pitieth
me to** remember **unto what misery, poor soul, she**
will shortly come. **These dances of** hers will **prove**
such dances that she will **spurn** our heads off like
footballs. But it will not be long ere her head will
dance the like **dance."** [1] He had no scruple in speak-
ing of the illegality of his own imprisonment. "I
may tell thee, Meg," said he one day, "they that
have committed me hither for refusing of **the oath**
not agreeable to the statute **are not** able **by their**
own law to justify **my imprisonment. And surely it**
is a great pity **that a Christian** prince should by **a**
flexible council ready to **follow his** affections, **and by**
a weak clergy lacking **grace** constantly to stand by
their learning, with flattery so shameful be abused." [2]
Indeed the **oath** was not strictly legal until the
Second Act of Succession passed in the autumn
session of 1534, which declared that the oath that
had before been taken by so many should **be** *reputed*
to be the very oath intended by the former **Act.** [3]

During the first few months of his imprisonment
More had his own servant and his books, and besides
his daughter, his wife was **once allowed** to visit him.
Of their interview Roper **gives a** quaint account. [4]
Dame **Alice** reproached him for **his** scruples, and
asked how he could prefer a prison to his happy
household at Chelsea. After he **had a** while quietly
heard her, with a cheerful countenance he said **unto**

---

[1] **Cres.** More, p. 231.　　　　　　　　[2] Roper, p. 43.
[3] **25 Henry** VIII. **cap. xxii. sect. 9.**　　[4] Roper, p. **45.**

her—"'I pray thee tell me one thing: is not this house as nigh heaven as mine own?' To whom she after her accustomed fashion, not liking such talk, answered, 'Tillyvally, tillyvally.' 'How say you, Mistress Alice, is it not so?' quoth he. 'Bone Deus, Bone Deus, man, will this gear never be left?' quoth she. 'Well, then, if it be so, it is very well,' said More. 'Why should I joy in my gay house, when, if I should rise from my grave seven years hence, I should not fail to find some one there would bid me get out of the doors? What cause have I then to like such an house as would so soon forget its master?'"

In August, More's step-daughter Alice happened to see the Lord Chancellor, and wrote to tell Margaret Roper of what had passed between them.[1] Sir Thomas Audley had expressed his surprise that More was so obstinate, and declared that he was glad that he himself had no learning save in a few of Æsop's fables, of which he would tell her one. So he told a tale of a country where the rain that fell made all whom it wetted fools. The wise men kept underground till it was over, thinking then to come forth and rule. But the fools would have none of them, so the wise men wished they had been in the rain too. And he told her another fable " of a lion, an ass, and a wolf, and of their confession," in which the ass appeared over-scrupulous, and thus got the most severe penance. Thus the Chancellor told

[1] *English Works*, pp. 1434—1443. The letter seems to be the composition of Margaret, though Rastell says it is not known whether she or More wrote it.

fables to Mistress Alington, and she knew not how to answer him, but wrote to tell her "own good sister."

Then Margaret Roper at her next going to the Tower, told her father of the letter, and wrote [1] of the interview to Alice Alington. She found him in health not much worse. "His diseases, both of his breast of old, and his reins now by reason of gravel and stone, and of the cramp also that divers nights grippeth him in his legs," she found were not much increased; and after they had said the psalms and litany, he was ready to sit and talk and be merry. Then she told him of the good comfort of his wife and children disposing themselves every day more and more to set little by the world, and draw more and more to God, and that his household and his friends diligently remembered him in their prayers. Then she touched upon her sister's letter, and told him that "if he changed not his mind, he was like to lose all his friends," and so she hoped that he might find some way to satisfy his own conscience and please the King. More smiled upon her and said—"What, Mistress Eve (as I called you when you came first), hath my daughter Alington played the serpent with you, and with a letter set you awork to come tempt your father again, and for the favour that you bear him, labour to make him swear against his conscience, and so send him to the devil?" After that he looked sadly, and said, "Daughter Margaret, oftener than twice or thrice I have answered you that in this matter if it were possible for me to do the thing that might

----

[1] *English Works*, p. 1433.

content the king's grace, and God therewith not offended, there hath no man taken this oath already more gladly than I would do. But since I cannot take it, I have no remedy. And albeit I know mine own frailty full well, yet if I had not trusted that God would give me strength rather to endure all things than offend Him by swearing ungodly against mine own conscience, you may be very sure I would not have come here." Still Margaret urged the same arguments, and showed him her sister's letter. When he had read it carefully, he thanked God for so good a daughter, and declared how often he prayed for her and all hers. He thought that both the Chancellor and Cromwell were his friends. "But in this matter, Meg, to tell the truth between thee and me," he said, "my lord's Æsop's fables do not greatly move me." He had often before, he continued, heard the first fable, of the rain that washed away all their wits, that stood abroad : it had been a tale so often told among the King's Council by the Lord Cardinal, when his grace was Chancellor, that he could not lightly forget it. . . . That fable had in his days helped the King and the realm to spend many a fair penny. He thought the fable obscure, and he could not well tell who were the fools and who wise. "I cannot well read such riddles, for, as Davus saith in Terence, 'Non sum Œdipus,' I may say, you wot well, 'Non sum Œdipus, sed Morus': which name of mine what it signifieth in Greek, I need not tell you." So he was glad to be counted a fool, but his life proved that he had never desired power.

Of the second fable, for which he did not envy
Æsop the credit, though confession was not introduced
into Greece until after Christ—it was too subtle for
him. He supposed that the Chancellor and many
others accounted him the over-scrupulous ass; yet he
did not believe that all who said so thought so.
However that might be, even if Fisher took the
oath, with whom no man in the world could be compared for learning, wisdom, and virtue, yet he himself
could not. "Verily, daughter," he said, "I never
intend to pin my soul to another man's back, not
even the best man I know at this day living, for I
know not whither he may haply carry it." So they
argued together, till at last Margaret, seeing her
father fixed in his determination, became very sad.
He perceived it, and said, "How now, Mother Eve,
where is your mind now? Sit not musing with some
serpent in your breast, upon some new persuasion to
offer father Adam the apple once again." "In good
faith, father," said she, "I can no further go, but am,
as I trow Cresede saith in Chaucer, come to Dul-
camon, even at my wit's end. For sith the example
of so many wise men cannot in this matter move
you, I see not what to say more, but if I should look
to persuade you in the reason Master Harry Pattison
made. For he met one day one of our men, and
when he had asked where you were, and heard you
were in the Tower, he waxed even angry with you,
and said, 'Why, what aileth him, that he will not
swear? Wherefore should he stick to swear? I
have sworn the oath myself.' And so I can in good
faith go no further neither, but if I should like

Master Harry say, why should you refuse to swear, father, for I have sworn myself?"[1] More laughed and answered—"That word was like Eve, too; for she offered Adam no worse fruit than she had eaten herself." She could say nothing to move him, and so at last desisted. Then he sent messages to all his friends, and prayed his children to "be comfortable and serviceable to their good mother," and at last said—"If anything hap me that you would be loath, pray to God for me, but trouble not yourself; as I shall full heartily pray for us all, that we may meet together in heaven, where we shall make merry for ever, and never have trouble after."

This was the last attempt that any of his family made to change his resolution. As his imprisonment dragged on, though he remained firm in his own opinion, he was ever ready to excuse others. Two letters of his to Dr. Wilson, who had been imprisoned on the same day as himself, show how tender was his regard for the welfare of others.[2]

Meanwhile, though his imprisonment was lenient and he was attended by his own servant, the Government was proceeding against him in Parliament. He was attainted of misprision of treason, and the grants made to him in 1523 and 1525 were rescinded; even the small corrody which the Abbey of Glastonbury had bestowed on him was taken away, and Abbot Whiting, eager to flatter the powers that

---

[1] She had taken the oath with the addition "as far as will stand with the law of God"—a relaxation which would not be offered to her father.

[2] *English Works*, pp. 1431—1446.

were, conferred it on Cromwell with regret that it was of no greater value.[1] Save for a pension from the Order of S. John of Jerusalem,[2] he was utterly penniless—and the whole of his lands and goods and the inheritance of his children was taken away. Only the kind assistance of friends preserved his family from actual want.[3]

In the State Papers is a pathetic document, the 'Petition of the wife and children of Sir Thomas More,' for the pardon and release of the said Sir Thomas, who has remained more than eight months in the Tower of London, "in great continual sickness of body and heaviness of heart." [4]

They besought that his wife might be allowed to retain his goods and the revenue of his lands so that some provision such as the King might think fit "in the way of mercy and pity to grant to him," might be made for the poor prisoner. Lady More also wrote to Cromwell as to a private friend, whose "manifold goodness" was her husband's and her own "greatest comfort." She had been compelled to sell her very clothes to provide the fifteen shillings a week charged for her husband and his servant in the Tower. She begged to be admitted to the King himself.[5]

---

[1] Father Gasquet, from whom better things might have been expected, in his very special pleading life of *The Last Abbot of Glastonbury* (pp. 70, 71), makes no reference to the wretched time-serving tone of the letter Whiting wrote to Cromwell on the matter.   [2] *Letters and Papers*, vii. 1675.

[3] See the very beautiful letter of More to his "old and dear friend," Antonio Bonvisi. *Works*, 1455—1457.

[4] *Letters and Papers*, vii. 1591.   *Archaeologia*, xxvii. 361 *sqq.*   [5] *Letters and Papers*, vii. 300.

No notice was taken of these requests, and More's position was daily becoming more dangerous. Parliament had now conferred on the King the title of 'Supreme Head of the Church of England,' and made it high treason to 'imagine' anything against his titles. 'Malicious' silence was accepted as evidence of evil imaginings. Thus More's life was at last brought by law within the King's power.

The Government, however, had not yet abandoned all hope of overcoming his scruples. One day Cromwell visited him, and with great friendliness assured him that the King would henceforth trouble his conscience no more. When he was gone, the prisoner, " to express what comfort he conceived of his words, wrote with a coal (for ink he had none) these verses following—

> Fye, flattering fortune, look thou ne'er so fair,
> Or ne'er so pleasantly begin to smile ;
> As though thou would'st my ruin all repair :
> During my life thou shalt not me beguile.
> Trust shall I God, to enter in a while
> His haven of Heaven sure and uniform :
> Ever after thy calm, look I for a storm.[1] "

He was far from idle in his solitude ; but turned with more zeal than ever to writing devotional treatises : a Dialogue of comfort against Tribulations ;[2] a Devotional preparation for the Holy Communion ;[3] a treatise on the Passion,[4] which he was not able to complete, for all his books and writing materials were taken away, and several prayers and medita-

---

[1] *English Works,* p. 1432. Roper's version (p. 44) is slightly different.   [2] *Ibid.* pp. 1139—1264.
[3] *Ibid.* pp. 1264—1269.   [4] *Ibid.* pp. 1270—1404.

tions.[1] Of these writings it may be said that, tedious as the style may appear to modern readers, there are no more deeply devotional works in the English language. He managed also to correspond with Fisher, but this was no sooner discovered than he was subjected to much more rigorous treatment. After this he was not allowed to attend any religious services, and his wife and children were no longer admitted to see him. He gave himself to meditation, and kept his windows fast shut. Still he kept his quaint humour. When the Lieutenant of the Tower asked his reason for this, he answered, " When all the wares are gone, the shop-windows are put up."[2]

He was now able to write but very rarely, and with great caution,[3] and had begun to see clearly that his life would probably be taken. In the only two letters which he was able to write during the rest of the year, there are signs that he foresaw the end approaching. In this spirit he wrote,[4] " Thus, mine own good daughter, putting you finally in remembrance that albeit if the necessity so should require I thank our Lord in this comfort in mine heart at this day, and I trust in God's goodness so shall have grace to continue, yet I verily trust that God shall so inspire and govern the king's heart that he shall not suffer his noble heart and

---

[1] *Ibid.* pp. 1404—1418.   [2] Stapleton, cap. xiii. p. 286.

[3] " Yet still by stealth he could get a little piece of paper in which he would write down letters with a coal : of which my father left me one, which was to his wife, which I account as a peculiar jewel." Cres. More, p. 240.

[4] *English Works*, pp. 1446—1451.

courage to requite my true faithful service with such extreme uncharitable and unlawful dealings, only for the displeasure that I cannot think so as others do. But his true subject will I die, and truly pray for him will I, both here and in the other world. And then, my good daughter, have me commended to my good bedfellow and all my children, men, women and all, with all your babes and your nurses, and all the maids and all the servants, and all our kin and all our other friends abroad. And I beseech our Lord to save them all, and keep them, and I pray you all to pray for me, and I will pray for you all. And take no thought for me, whatsoever you shall hap to hear, but be merry in God."

The new year found More still firm in his opinion.[1] After a long silence, he found means again to write to his daughter, on May the 2nd or 3rd, 1534, to tell her of his last examination. The Charterhouse monks had been condemned, and on every side there were signs that the King's indignation was at its height. On April 30, More was called before Cromwell and others of less note. Cromwell asked if he had heard of the statutes lately passed in Parliament. More replied that he had, but had not thought it needful to peruse them carefully. Cromwell then reminded him of the Act giving the title of Supreme Head of the Church, under Christ, to the King, and asked his opinion on it. "Whereunto," says More in his letter to his daughter, "I answered 'that I had well trusted that the king's

---

[1] See his letter to a priest named Lever. *English Works,* p. 1450.

highness would never have commanded any such question to be demanded of me, considering that I ever from the beginning well and truly from time to time, declared my mind unto his highness, and since that time' I said ' unto your mastership, master Secretary, also, both by mouth and by writing.' And now I have in good faith discharged my mind of all such matters, and neither will dispute king's titles or pope's. But the king's true subject I am and will be, and daily I pray for him and all his, and for you all that are of his honourable council, and for all the realm. And otherwise than this I never intend to meddle." To this Cromwell replied that he feared that would not satisfy the King. Several more questions were put him. More simply said, " I am the king's faithful subject and daily bedesman. I say no harm, I think no harm, but I wish everybody good. And if this be not enough to keep a man alive, in good faith I long not to live." [1] It seems that now his relations were less strictly excluded; for on May 4,[2] when the monks of the Charterhouse were led to execution, Margaret Roper was with her father as he looked out on them from his window.[3] " Look, dost thou see, Meg ? " said More sadly, " that these blessed fathers be now as cheerful going to their deaths as bridegrooms to their marriages. For God, considering their long-continued life in most sore and grievous penance will no longer suffer them to remain here in this vale of misery

---

[1] *English Works*, pp. 1451, 1452.   [2] Roper, p. 54.
[3] The second band of the monks were executed on June 19. This is referred to by Mr. S. L. Lee, *Dict. National Biography*.

and iniquity, but speedily hence take them to the
fruition of His Everlasting Deity. Whereas thy
silly father, Meg, that like a most wicked caitiff hath
passed forth the whole course of his miserable life
most pitifully, God, thinking him not worthy so
soon to come to that eternal felicity, leaveth him
here yet, still in the world further to be plunged
and turmoiled with misery." But it was not for
much longer. Three days afterwards Cromwell
came to him, with the Archbishop of Canterbury,
the Lord Chancellor, the Duke of Suffolk, and
the Earl of Wiltshire. Cromwell declared that the
King was not satisfied with his previous answers,
and commanded him on his allegiance either to confess it to be lawful that he should be the Supreme
Head of the Church of England, "or else utter
plainly his malignity." More answered that he had
no malignity and therefore could utter none; that
he could say no more than he had said; and, remembering the King's charge to him when he entered
his service, he would take comfort from knowing
that the time would come when God would declare
his truth before the King and the whole world.
Then the Chancellor and Cromwell said the King
could force him to answer; to which he replied that
it would be hard to make him choose between the
loss of his soul and the destruction of his body—a
saying on which much stress was laid at his trial.
Then Cromwell reminded him of his duty as
Chancellor to examine heretics, and said that "men
were as well beheaded now for denying the King's
supremacy as they were then burned for denying the

Pope's." To this More replied that there was a difference between a national law and a law of all Christendom. Then they asked him to swear to answer their questions concerning the King. He refused, saying that he had not so little foresight as not to conjecture what the questions might be. Then they told him that the questions were whether he had seen the statute and whether he believed it to be lawful. He declared that he had before admitted the first, but would not answer the second question. The full brutality of his persecutors appeared in their last taunt. They said, " Why, then, did he not speak out against the statute if he cared not for life ? it appeared well that he was not content to die." More answered with noble simplicity : " I have not been a man of such holy living that I might be bold to offer myself to death, lest God for my presumption might suffer me to fall." So the examination ended, Cromwell declaring that he thought worse of More and believed him not to mean well.[1]

He was again examined more than once,[2] the object being to obtain sufficient evidence from his own lips, to make a case against him. He was examined twice by the Commissioners, and afterwards the Solicitor-General, Rich, Sir Richard Southwell, and Mr. Palmer were sent to take away his books. While the two last were packing them up Rich began to talk to More, asking, " If there were an Act of Parliament that all the realm should

---

[1] *English Works*, pp. 1452—1454.
[2] *E. g.* June 3. *Letters and Papers*, viii. 814, where his answers are given.

take me for the King, would not you, Master More,
take me for the King?" "Yes, sir," replied More,
"that would I." "I put the case farther," said Rich,
"that there were an Act of Parliament that all the
realm should take me for Pope, would not you take
me for the Pope?" "For answer," said Sir Thomas,
"to your first case, the Parliament may well meddle
with the state of temporal princes : but to make
answer to your second case, I will put you this case.
Suppose the Parliament should make a law that God
should not be God, would you then, Master Rich, say
God were not God?" "No, sir," said Rich, "I would
not, sith no Parliament may make any such law."
When More was brought to trial Rich swore that
he had replied to this, "No more could the Parliament make the King Supreme Head of the
Church."[1]

On June 14, minute interrogations were put to
him as to his correspondence with Fisher.[2] He
admitted writing "divers scrolls" to the Bishop.
In them, beside "comforting words," he had merely
stated on his first imprisonment that he had refused
the oath, and that in his last examination he had
declared that he would meddle with nothing henceforth, but give his mind to God. Fisher had questioned him on the meaning of the word "maliciously"
in the recent statute,—whether a man speaking nothing of malice did offend against it ; to which he had
answered that he took that to be its meaning, but

---

[1] Roper, p. 46 ; cf. Lord Herbert's *Henry VIII.* pp. 421, 422.
[2] His servants were also examined ; and interesting details
may be found in *Letters and Papers*, vol. viii. 856.

that "the interpretation of the statute would not
be taken after their mind; and therefore it was
not good for any man to trust to any such thing."
Further, he had advised the Bishop " to make his
answer according to his own mind and to meddle
with no such thing as he had written unto him,
lest he should give the Council occasion to ween
that there was some confederacy between them
both." Finally he had warned him that Rich had
told him that it was all one not to answer and
to say against the statute what a man would, and
had begged his prayers. Further he had written to
his daughter of his last examinations, fearing lest
she should suffer from hearing of them suddenly.
Then for the last time the following questions were
put to him—"whether he would obey the King's
highness as Supreme Head on earth immediately
under Christ, of the Church of England, and him so
repute, take, accept, and recognize, according unto
the statute in that behalf made ?" To this he said
that he could make no answer. Secondly—" whether
he would consent and approve the King's highness'
marriage with the most noble Queen Anne that now
is to be good and lawful; and affirm that the marriage between the King's said highness and the Lady
Katherine, Princess Dowager, was and is unjust and
unlawful." He answered " that he never did speak or
meddle against the same; nor thereunto could make
answer." Thirdly, it was declared that he being one
of the King's subjects was bound to answer both the
questions, and recognize the King as Supreme Head
of the Church as all are bound to do by statute.

He replied that he could make no answer.[1] His answers were taken down at length and are preserved in the State Papers. It was found impossible to extract from him evidence incriminating either Fisher or himself. He steadfastly denied all collusion and any discussion with others upon political matters.

But it was not evidence of Fisher's guilt that the Government desired to draw from More. The Bishop was executed on June 22.[2] Four days later a Special Commission of Oyer and Terminer for Middlesex was issued to the Lord Chancellor Audley, the Dukes of Norfolk and Suffolk, other lords, including Anne Boleyn's father and brother— his bitter enemies—Cromwell, and nine judges. The grand jury of Westminster returned a true bill; and the petty jury was summoned to meet on July 1.[3]

On that day More was brought to the bar by Sir Edward Walsingham, Lieutenant of the Tower. He was very weak from his long imprisonment, and as he leant upon his staff, his hair now gray and his beard long, his face still cheerful and content, many must have thought of the strong man who five years before, as Lord High Chancellor of England, in that same Court of King's Bench, had knelt down every morning to ask his father's blessing.

---

[1] *State Papers, Henry VIII.* vol. i. p. **432**.

[2] Mr. S. L. Lee, *Dictionary of National Biography*, says he was executed "six days later" than the Carthusians, who died on June 19.

[3] Details of the trial are to be found in *Letters and Papers*, vol. viii. 974, 996, 997, in *Spanish Papers*, v. 180, *Archaeologia*, xxvii. 361 *sqq.* etc.

The indictment was long. It charged him first with traitorously attempting to deprive the King of his title of Supreme Head of the Church of England, inasmuch as he had refused to answer on May 7 to the questions of the Councillors whether he would accept the King as Supreme Head pursuant to the statute, saying, " I will not meddle with any such matters, for I am fully determined to serve God and to think upon His Passion and my passage out of this world "; further that he agreed with Fisher in his treason, and wrote to him the words which he afterwards used to the Council— " The Act of Parliament is like a sword with two edges, for if a man answer one way it will confound his soul, and if he answer the other way it will confound his body "; further that he, on June 3, falsely, maliciously, and traitorously persevered in " refusing to give a direct answer, but imagining to deprive the king of the dignity, title, or name of his royal estate and to sow and generate sedition and malignity in the hearts of his true subjects, spoke openly " the same words as Fisher had used; that he and Fisher had burnt all the letters that passed between them, in order to conceal their most false and wicked treason; and lastly, that in conversation with the Solicitor-General Rich he had denied the right of Parliament to confer on the King the title of Supreme Head—"as to the primacy, a subject cannot be bound because he cannot give his consent to that in Parliament; and although the king is so accepted in England, yet many foreign countries do not affirm the same." When the indictment was read, the Lord Chancellor Audley, and the Duke of Norfolk, turned to him and said, "You see, Master More, that you have grievously offended his royal Majesty; yet if you will repent and change that opinion in which you have hitherto most obstinately persevered, we trust so much in his majesty's clemency and kind heart, that pardon and mercy will, we have no doubt, be obtained for you."

More answered—"My lords, I thank you very much for your good will, but yet I pray God Almighty to keep me firm in this opinion of mine that I may continue in it till the hour of my death. Respecting the charges brought against me, I doubt whether my understanding, my memory or my tongue will be sufficient to compass them all, grave and manifest as they are, especially considering my present imprisonment and great infirmity."

Thereupon a chair was brought him: when he was seated, he resumed. He pleaded "not guilty," declaring that if the terms "maliciously, traitorously and diabolically" were withdrawn, he saw no treason with which he could be charged. Concerning the King's second marriage, he asserted that it was his duty as a good subject to answer when the King asked him according to his conscience; and that when he had done so years before, it could have been no offence, or, if it had been, an imprisonment of fifteen months with forfeiture was sufficient punishment. With regard to the examinations, he saw no harm in his answers. "I wish no harm to any," he said, repeating words he had formerly used, " and if this will not keep me alive, then I desire not to live. By all which I know that I could not transgress any statute, or incur any crime of treason. For neither this statute nor any law in the world can punish any man for holding his peace. For they only can punish words or deeds, God only being Judge of our secret thoughts." Fearing lest these words, if repeated, might influence even the packed jury,[1] the Attorney-General hastily interrupted him, declaring that malicious silence to such a question, which all dutiful subjects would answer, was proof of treason. "Nay," said More, "my silence is no sign of any malicious mind, which the king himself may know by many of my dealings : neither doth it convince any man of breach of your laws, for it is a maxim among the Civilians and Canonists, 'Qui tacet, consentire videtur.' You say that all good subjects are bound to reply; but I say that the faithful subject is more bound to his conscience and his soul than to anything else in the world, provided his conscience, like mine, does not raise scandal or sedition, and I assure you that I have never discovered what is in my conscience to any person living. As to the second article, that I have conspired against the statute by writing eight letters to the Bishop of Rochester, advising him to disobey it, I could wish these letters had been read in public, but as you say the Bishop has burnt them, I will tell you the substance of them. Some were about private matters connected with our

---

[1] One at least of the jury, Parnell, was a personal enemy of More.

old friendship.   Another was a reply to one of his asking how I had answered in the Tower to the first examination about the statute.   I said that I had informed my conscience, and so he ought also to do the same.   I swear that this was the tenor of the letters, for which I cannot be condemned by your statute."

He thus repeated the assertion of the innocence of his correspondence with Fisher, which he had made at his last examination.   With regard to the saying that the law was a two-edged sword, he urged that his answer was but conditional.   "If there be danger in both either to allow or to disallow this statute, and, therefore, like a two-edged sword, it seemeth a hard thing that it should be offered to me, that never have hitherto contradicted it either in word or deed."   Those had been his words: what the Bishop answered, he knew not; "if his answer was like mine, he said, it proceeded not from any conspiracy of ours, but from the likeness of our wits and learning.   To conclude: I unfeignedly avouch that I never spake such against this law to any living man: although, perhaps, the king's majesty hath been told the contrary."   Then the jury of twelve men was summoned, and the charges proceeded with.

The Solicitor-General, Rich, was then called to give evidence of his interview with Sir Thomas in the Tower: which he did in the manner that has been already noticed.[1]   Then said More: "If I were a man, my Lords, that did not regard an oath, I need not, as it is well known, in this place at this time

1 Above, pp. 260, 261.

or in this case, stand as an accused person. And if this oath of yours, Mr. Rich, be true, then I pray that I may never see God in the face: which I would not say were it otherwise, to gain the whole world." He then reluctantly spoke of the badness of Rich's character, and asked if it were likely that he would trust to such a man an opinion on the Supremacy, which he had carefully concealed from the King and all his Council. Again, even if he had thus spoken, which he denied, any statement in 'familiar secret talk' could not be construed into 'malicious' speaking. Sir Richard Southwell and Mr. Palmer, who were called in support of Rich, admitted that they had heard nothing of the conversation. In spite of this, the jury, staying out of Court "scarce one quarter of an hour, for they knew," says Cresacre More, "what the King would have done in that case," returned a verdict of guilty. It must be admitted indeed that as the law stood the trial itself was not unjust. If the evidence were to be believed and the law to be obeyed, the jury had no choice but to find More guilty.

The Chancellor was about to pass sentence immediately, when More demanded the usual license to show cause why judgment should not be passed upon him. He spoke simply and directly in solemn protest against the injustice of the law by which he was condemned. He declared that Parliament could not give the King a spiritual pre-eminence, or supreme government of the Church; or make a law for the Church against the consent of Christendom, and contrary to Magna Charta. The Chancellor demanded how he could stand against the bishops, and the Universities of the land. More replied—" If the number of bishops and universities be so material as your lordship seemeth to take it, I see little cause why that thing in my conscience should make any change. For I doubt not, but of the learned and virtuous men that be yet alive, not only of this realm, but of all Christendom, there are ten to one that are of my mind in this matter : but if I should speak of those learned and virtuous doctors that be already dead, of whom many are now saints in heaven, I am very sure that they are far more who, while they lived, thought in this case as I think now. And therefore am I not bound, my Lords, to conform my conscience to the counsel of one realm, against the general counsel of Christendom : for one bishop of your opinion I have a hundred saints of mine ; and for one parliament of yours, and God knows of what kind, I have all the General Councils for one thousand years ; and for one kingdom I have France and all the kingdoms of Christendom." Norfolk told him that now his malice was clear. He forgot how readily such weapons as Henry now used might be turned against himself. More replied— " What I say is necessary for the discharge of my conscience and satisfaction of my soul, and to do this I call God to witness, the sole Searcher of human hearts. I say further, that your statute is ill made, because you have sworn never to do anything against the Church, which through all Christendom is one and undivided, and you have no authority, without the common **consent of** all Christians, to make **a law or** Act **of** Parliament or Council against **the union of** Christendom." **The** Chancellor then asked the opinion of the Lord **Chief** Justice **on the sufficiency** of the indictment. **The** reply was cautious: " **My** Lords **all,** by **S. Julian, I** must needs confess that, if the Act of Parliament be not unlawful, then is not the indictment in my conscience insufficient." The Chancellor then passed sentence "according to the form of the new law." More, now throwing **away all** disguise, declared that **he had studied** the matter for seven years, and " could find **no colour for holding** that a layman could be head **of the Church." Once** more the judges **asked if he had anything to say.** He replied—" More have I not to say, **my** Lords; **but like** as **the blessed** Apostle **S. Paul,** as we read in **the** Acts of the Apostles, was present and consenting to the death of S. Stephen, and held their clothes, that stoned **him** to death; and yet be they now both holy **saints in** heaven, and shall continue there friends for **ever, so I** verily **trust and therefore** right **heartily** pray, that, **though your Lordships have now in earth** been judges to my **condemnation, we may yet,** hereafter in heaven, merrily **all meet together to our** everlasting salvation."

The trial ended, More was **led** back by **his old** friend, Sir William Kingston, the Constable of the **Tower, who** could **not** restrain his tears. **On the way, his son threw himself** at his feet, **and** implored his blessing; **yet even at this** parting More remained **calm. When** the sad procession reached the Old Swan by London **Bridge, there was a short pause.**

There More was in a familiar place, very near to
S. Anthony's School. The scene must have recalled
strange thoughts and memories at such a moment.

> "Life all past
> Is like the sky, when the sun sets in it,
> Clearest when farthest off."

There he parted with Sir William Kingston, whom
he comforted with the thought of a happy meeting
in heaven. "In faith," said Kingston, when he spoke
of it afterwards to Roper, " I was ashamed of myself,
that at my departure from your father, I found my
heart so feeble, and his so strong, that he was fain
to comfort me, which should rather have comforted
him." [1]

There was still the last and saddest parting
of all.[2]　As he came to Tower-wharf, his dearest
daughter, Margaret, pushed her way through the
sympathetic crowd and past the guard which surrounded him, and flung herself into his arms, "not
able to say any word but 'Oh, my father ! Oh, my
father !' " [3]　He was still calm enough to give her
his blessing, "and many goodly words of comfort."
"Take patience, Margaret," he said, "and do not
grieve ; God has willed it so. For many years didst
thou know the secret of my heart." They had already
parted once, when she ran back and threw her arms
around him. "Whereat he spoke not a word, but
carrying still his gravity, tears fell from his eyes :
yea, there were very few in all the group who could
refrain thereat from weeping, no, not the guard

<hr>

[1] Roper, p. 52.　　[2] *Ibid*. p. 53.　　[3] Cres. More, p. 264.

MARGARET GIGGS

(MARRIED JOHN CLEMENT).

From the drawing by Holbein.

To face page 271.

themselves." So, too, Margaret Clement[1] embraced him, and Dorothy Colley, one of Margaret Roper's maids, and so they parted.

The few days of life that were still left him, More spent in severe mortification, and wore his shroud constantly. He had no intimation of when his sentence was to be carried out; but on the 5th he seemed to feel that death was at hand. He sent to his daughter Margaret his hair shirt, which he had worn secretly for many years, with the last of his tender letters, so beautiful in its pathetic simplicity. "Our Lord bless you, good daughter, and your good husband, and your little boy, and all yours, and all my children, and all my god-children, and all our friends. Recommend me, when you may, to my good daughter Cicely, whom I beseech our Lord to comfort : and I send her my blessing, and to all my children, and pray her to pray for me. I send her an handkercher. And God comfort my good son her husband. My good daughter Daunce hath the picture in parchment that you delivered me from my lady Conyers. Her name is on the back side. Shew her that I heartily pray her that you may send it in my name to her again, for a token from me to pray for me. I like special well Dorothy Colley. I pray you be good unto her. I would not whether this be she you wrote me of. If not yet I pray you be good to the other, as you may, in her affliction, and to my good daughter[2] Joan Aleyn too. Give her, I pray

---

[1] Margaret Giggs, his adopted daughter, now married to Dr. Clement.

[2] *Note by Rastell* to edit. 1557. "This was not one of his

you, some kind answer, for she sued hither to me
this day to pray you be good to her. I cumber you,
good Margaret, much : but I would be sorry if it
should be any longer than to-morrow. For it is
Saint Thomas even, and the utas of Saint Peter :
therefore to-morrow long I to go to God : it were a
day very meet and convenient for me. I never liked
your manner toward me better than when you kissed
me last : for I love when daughterly love and dear
charity hath no leisure to look to worldly courtesy.
Farewell, my dear child, and pray for me and I shall
for you and all your friends that we may merrily
meet in Heaven. I thank you for your great cost.
I send now to my good daughter Clement her
algorism stone, and I send her and my godson and
all others, God's blessing and mine. I pray you at
good time convenient recommend me to my good
son, John More; I liked well his natural fashion.[1]
Our Lord bless him and his good wife, my loving
daughter: to whom I pray him be good as he hath
good cause : and that if the land of mine come into
his hand he break not my will concerning his sister
Daunce. And our Lord bless Thomas, and Austin,[2]
and all that they shall have." [3]

Even in his last hours he was exposed to inter-
ruption and vexation : yet he still maintained his
playful humour. He had thought of shaving off his

daughters, nor no kin to him, but one of Mistress Roper's
maids."

[1] At his last meeting when he came from judgment : John
More was now in prison.

[2] John More's children.   [3] *Eng. Works*, pp. 1457, 1458.

beard, and coming forth to his execution that all might see him as he had been, his clear pale features as we know them in Holbein's drawing. A courtier came troubling him with exhortations to change his mind. "Well," said More at last, "I have changed it." This was at once reported to the King, by whom a message was sent to the prisoner to know what was the change. "Then Sir Thomas rebuked the courtier for his lightness that he would tell the king every word that he spoke in jest: for he had meant merely that he would not be shaven."[1]

When it was communicated to him that, by the King's merciful pardon, the horrible sentence of the law would be commuted into beheading, he exclaimed, "God forbid that the king should use any more such mercy unto any of my friends; and God bless all my posterity from such pardons."[2]

Very early in the morning of July 6, Sir Thomas Pope, "his singular dear friend," came from the King and Council, to say that his execution would take place that day before nine o'clock. "Master Pope," said More, "for your good tidings I most heartily thank you. I have always been bounden much to the king's highness for the benefits and honours which he hath from time to time heaped on me. Yet more bounden am I to his grace for putting me into this place where I have had convenient time and space to have remembrance of my end; and most of all that it pleased him so shortly to rid me of the miseries of this wretched world. And therefore will I not fail to pray for his grace, both here

<hr>

[1] Stapleton, cap. xvi. p. 322.   [2] Cres. More, p. 268.

and in another world."   Pope then told him that the
King wished him not to use many words at his execution.   "You do well to give me warning of his
grace's pleasure," he replied, "for otherwise I had
purposed somewhat to have spoken, but of no matter
wherewith his grace or any other should have cause
to be offended.   Nevertheless I am ready to obey
his command."   Then they spoke of his burial, at
which the King gave leave for his wife and children
to be present.   So they bade farewell, and, as Pope
could not refrain from tears, More comforted him—
"Quiet yourself, good Master Pope, and be not dis-
comforted; for I trust that we shall once in Heaven
see each other full merrily, where we shall be sure to
live and love together in eternal bliss."

When his friend had left him, More dressed himself
in his best apparel, ' and put on his silk camlet gown
which his entire friend Mr. Antonio Bonvisi gave him.'
The Lieutenant of the Tower begged him to change
it, 'for the executioner, who should have it, was but
a javill.'   "What," said More, "shall I account him
a javill that will do me this day so singular a benefit ?
Nay, I assure you, were it cloth of gold, I would
think it well bestowed on him, as S. Cyprian did,
who gave his executioner thirty pieces of gold."   He
was persuaded, however, to change it for a 'gown of
friese,' but he sent an angel to the executioner.

"He[1] was therefore brought by Master Lieu-

<hr>

[1] Mr. Froude professes to quote throughout his account of
More's last days from Cres. More : he does so however very
loosely, and Roper is in many places much more simple and
beautiful.   The following short passage is Cres. More's own
words, not Mr. Froude's version.

tenant out **of** the Tower, his beard being long, **which** fashion **he** had never before used, carrying **in his** hands **a red cross,** casting his eyes often towards heaven." **A woman** on the way to **Tyburn offered** him wine, **which he** refused. Another called after him that he had done her wrong when he was Chancellor, to whom he gave answer, " that he remembered her cause very well, and that if he were now **to** give sentence thereof, he would not alter what he had already done." [1] A man whom his counsel had often restrained from religious despair, cried to him with great earnestness that **he** was **again** in **terrible** temptation. "**Go** and pray for **me,**" said More, "**and** I will pray for **you.**"

When **he came** to the scaffold, he **was too weak to mount it, and** nearly fell. "**I pray you, Master Lieutenant,**" he exclaimed, "**see me** safe up, **and for my coming down** let me shift for myself." Then **he** asked the prayers of all the people, **and** said to them simply that he died **in and** for the faith **of** the Holy Catholic Church. **Then** kneeling down he said the *Miserere*. **When the** executioner asked **his** forgiveness he **kissed** him. "Thou wilt do me this **day a** greater benefit than ever any mortal man can be able **to** do me. Pluck up thy spirit, man, and be not **afraid to** do **thine** office. My neck is very short : **take heed** therefore that thou strike not awry, for saving **of** thine **honesty.**" **When they** would have **covered** his eyes, **he said,** "I will cover them myself," and **wrapped them with a cloth** he had brought with

<hr>

[1] Cres. More, p. **273.**

him.   As he laid his head on the block, he put aside his beard, saying, 'that that had never committed any treason.' [1]

" Thus," as Addison beautifully says, "the innocent mirth which had been so conspicuous in his life did not forsake him to the last.   His death was of a piece with his life : there was nothing in it new, forced, or affected.   He did not look upon the severing of his head from his body as a circumstance which ought to produce any change in the disposition of his mind : and as he died in a fixed and settled hope of immortality, he thought any unusual degree of sorrow and concern improper." [2]

Of all the brave deaths upon English scaffolds [3] which that sad century and the next produced, there was none more calm and bright than his.   Of one who a hundred and ten years later died also for his conscience, it was said that "never did man put off mortality with better courage."   Of More at least it may be declared that no man was ever more willing to die.   And not only death was welcome, but happy was the path of affliction that led to it.   More had learnt to tread in the road of the Passion of his Master, and it seemed to him to be strewn with flowers.   With Mason he might cry—

> "I sing to think this is the way
> Unto my Saviour's Face."

Whatever may be thought by theologians or

---

[1] Cres. More, p. 275.   [2] *Spectator*, No. 349.
[3] I do not understand the statement, *Dict. Nat. Biog.* xxxviii. 439, that " his composure on the scaffold is probably without parallel."   Strafford, Laud, Charles I. do not seem to have shown anything but composure.

historians of the speculative opinion for which More shed his blood, there can be no doubt that he died a martyr.

A candid examination of the Act of Supremacy, in the light of legal interpretation and constitutional precedent, must show that it was not necessarily contradictory to the opinions which Roman theologians held dear. It was accepted by many who are still revered on the Continent as pillars of the orthodox faith.[1] But no man can deny that More was a witness to the absolute supremacy of conscience. He was also, in the words of Pope Paul III., excellent in sacred learning and bold in the defence of truth. He laid down his life rather than surrender for fear of death what he again and again admitted to be but an opinion. He would lay no burden on the souls of other men: he would not speak against the new laws, the divorce, the King's marriage, the measures by which the Church was freed from foreign subjection. These were matters upon which his own views had changed, and upon which he could not feel that his judgment need be final or binding for other men. He condemned no man; but he would not yield an inch himself. To him almost alone among his contemporaries the conclusions of the intellect seemed no less sacred than the chastity of the body. He died rather than tarnish the whiteness of his soul.

His position was the more noble because some of his dearest friends were not of his mind. Colet had spoken

---

[1] *E. g.* Abbats Whiting and others; cf. Gasquet's *The Last Abbot of Glastonbury*, p. 47.

too freely for us to doubt that he would not thus have
interpreted the historic claim of Rome. On Erasmus
the critic the Papal authority sat but lightly.
Tunstal declared clearly that "the Church of Rome
had never of old such a monarchy as of late it hath
usurped."[1] But the foreign scholars to whom he had
appealed were, from the first, in almost every case in
his favour.[2] Lutherans condemned him as an enemy
of the Gospel,[3] but Italians saw in him a martyr and
a saint.[4] Gregory XIII. in 1572 did honour to his
memory, but it was not till December 29, 1886, that
a decree of Beatification was issued from Rome.

More's fame did not wait for such tardy honours.
He had been for many years renowned among the
writers of Europe. It may be doubted indeed if any
event in English history since the murder of S. Thomas

---

[1] I venture to quote the passage from Fr. Bridgett's valuable
Life of More, p. 347, who has taken the extract from British
Museum MS. Cleopatra, E. vi. f. **389**. Tunstal states that
the meaning of the Royal Supremacy was "to reduce **the**
Church of England **out** of all captivity of foreign powers,
heretofore usurped therein, into the pristine estate that all
Churches of all realms were in at the beginning, and to
abolish **and** clearly put away such usurpation as theretofore
the Bishops of Rome have, to their great advantage and im-
poverishing of the realm and the king's subjects, of the **same.**
. . . Would to God you had been exercised in reading the
ancient councils, that you might have known from the beginning, **from** age to age, the continuance and progress of the
Catholic Church, by which you should have perceived that the
Church of Rome had **never** of old such a monarchy as of late
it hath usurped."

[2] Cf. **Letter** of Cochlaeus to Henry **VIII.**, Leipzig, 1536.
Letters and Papers, x. 34.

[3] Cf. *Letters and Papers*, x. 587.

[4] Cf. Poem of Zenobio Ceffino (see *Letters and Papers*, x.
844).

of Canterbury had excited such universal interest abroad. Letter after letter published throughout the Continent proclaimed his merits and deplored the barbarity of his death. An " expositio fidelis de morte Thomae Mori," appeared before the year was out. Almost every foreign nation issued its own record of his pathetic fate. Erasmus called heaven and earth to witness against the monstrous cruelty of the King, and Pole in his bitter remonstrance on the Unity of the Church cried out, "You have slain, you have slain, the best Englishman alive."

The excitement aroused by his execution was felt to be a real political danger. The King caused a formal defence of his action to be put forth. For years after the State Papers show how minute was the investigation into any circumstances which seemed to show personal association with the murdered man.[1] From the first his memory was regarded in England with extraordinary reverence. But strange to say, no certain record of his burial is preserved, and it is not even clear whether the story of Margaret Roper's devotion which Tennyson has made immortal is more than a pathetic fiction.[2]

A number of relics of him were preserved, many of which are now at Stonyhurst.[3] His descendants were careful to claim kinship to the martyr. It is a common thing to see on the tombs of even remote kindred in different parts of England some reference

---

[1] E. g. *Letters and Papers*, vol. xiii. pt. i. Feb. 30, 1538; pt. ii. 695, 702, 828, 854.

[2] The whole question is exhaustively discussed by Fr. Bridgett, pp. 435 *sqq*.

[3] See Fr. Bridgett's *Life of More*, Appendix A,

to the stock of the great man from which they came.[1] In the male line the family became extinct with the death of Father Thomas More, sometime English provincial of the Jesuits, in 1795. His sister, Bridget More, by her marriage with Peter Metcalfe, left a daughter who is represented by the Eyston family of East Hendred. There are probably many descendants of More in the female line. The male line of the Ropers died out, but females of their families became ancestresses of the Winns, Constables and others.[2]

The multiplication of portraits is a prominent proof of the permanent interest taken in the great man's memory. The fame of such a man was indeed what neither England nor the world would willingly let die.

"The web of our life is of a mingled yarn, good and ill together : our virtues would be proud if our faults whipped them not." More's character was not faultless. In his youth indeed he wrote not a little that his religion in later life must have deplored. He was beset by keen temptations of the flesh. But certainly the spirit triumphed. His life was not without its mistakes; but no man ever redeemed his errors more nobly. A great historian has said that there are no famous men of the six-

---

[1] A curious instance of this is afforded by a slab in Brize-Norton Church, Oxfordshire, in memory of "Thomas Greenwood, e Thoma Moro olim Angl. Cancell. Oriundus," who died in 1678.

[2] See Fr. Bridgett's *Life*, Appendix E, and Hunter's edition of Cresacre More's *Life*, Preface, part iv.; and Auction Catalogue of Books of Baron von Druffel (Munster, 1894).

teenth century whom it is possible wholly to admire; [1]
but it is difficult not to claim that More forms an
exception to this stern judgment. The fascination
which won the hearts of his contemporaries affects
even the least emotional of his biographers. Admiration is no sufficient tribute: we love him as if he
were our own friend.

Of such a character it is difficult to speak critic-
ally. His was not a mind of the subtlety which is
the fit subject for psychological analysis. The leading
lines stand clearly out. He was a man of very
single-minded purpose, laboriously studious and conscientious in public as in private life. Deeply
reverent and truly pious, he had yet a keen sense of
the follies of his fellow-men; but his mirth was that
of the humorist, not the cynic. He was sensitive
and therefore observant; affectionate and of a beautiful patience. Few men have had more power of
inspiring love. His wide tastes—learned, musical,
scientific—no doubt helped to win him so wide a
fame; but the deepest cause was the beauty of his
life. His character, perfect as it is, is delightful
chiefly because it is so natural. There was never
in him anything strained or affected, weak imitation

---

[1] Bishop Creighton, in the *Laud Commemoration Volume*,
p. 14—"It is well to abandon all illusions about the sixteenth
century. There were strong men, there were powerful minds,
but there was a dearth of beautiful characters. A time of
revolt and upheaval is a time of one-sided energy, and of
moral uncertainty, of hardness, of unsound argument, of imperfect self-control, of vacillation, of self-seeking. It is
difficult in such a time to find heroes, to discover a man whom
we can unreservedly admire." In delivering his lecture the
Bishop added emphatically, " I know none."

of others, or striving after what he could never be. Its beautiful calmness, its even tenor, the peace that seems always to hang over it, make it easy to forget the troublous scenes in which his life was passed. It was an age of fightings and fears. More passed through the thick of them; and no man, it may be said truly, passed through so unscathed. Well may his reverent descendant proclaim that " his soul was carried by angels into everlasting glory, where a crown of martyrdom was put on him which can never fade nor decay."

No estimate of More's life would be satisfactory which did not consider his position and his influence in relation to the great movements of his age. Posterity will here rank him at least as highly as did his contemporaries. No one who reverences the heritage of faith bequeathed to the Christian Church will remember him without gratitude. He was placed suddenly in face of a critical question. He answered it as his successors in the English Church would not now answer. But it would be difficult to find in his writings any formal statement of doctrine which the English Church since his day has ever formally abandoned. It would be idle indeed to dispute with Roman hagiologists their right to revere him as a martyr of their own; but no true theological estimate would deny that he belongs to the historic and continuous Church of England. A close study of his religious writings, as of his life, shows that More was a saint of whom England may still be proud.

As a man of letters he has claims as great upon

the reverence of literary men. It would not be a mistake to regard him as the founder of modern English literature. His fresh and vigorous use of a vocabulary hardly any part of which is yet obsolete, his power of narration, of declamation, and of criticism, make him to stand out among the earliest masters of English prose. As a scholar he linked the learning of the Renaissance to the faith of the medieval Church, and he brought classical interests within the range of ordinary English men of affairs. He was one of the first of our fathers to whom rightly belonged the titles of a scholar and a gentleman.

Most of all, perhaps, he will be remembered as the years go on for his passionate ideal of social progress. So long as men suffer and thinkers search for remedies for human misery and human sin, the author of the *Utopia* is immortal. And it should never be forgotten that the social ideal which he gave to the world came from a heart and a mind stored with practical statesmanship and Christian theology.

INDEX